W9-AQX-116

THE LARK'S LAMENT

Also by Alan Gordon

THE FOOLS' GUILD MYSTERIES

Thirteenth Night

Jester Leaps In

A Death in the Venetian Quarter

The Widow of Jerusalem

An Antic Disposition

THE LARK'S LAMENT

A FOOLS' GUILD MYSTERY

Alan Gordon

ST. MARTIN'S MINOTAUR NEW YORK

This is a work of fiction. All of the characters, organizations, and events portrayed in this novel are either products of the author's imagination or are used fictitiously.

THE LARK'S LAMENT. Copyright © 2007 by Alan Gordon. All rights reserved. Printed in the United States of America. No part of this book may be used or reproduced in any manner whatsoever without written permission except in the case of brief quotations embodied in critical articles or reviews. For information, address St. Martin's Press, 175 Fifth Avenue, New York, N.Y. 10010.

www.minotaurbooks.com

Translations of songs by Folquet de Marseille are from *Where Troubadours Were Bishops: The Occitania of Folc of Marseille (1150–1231)* Copyright © 2001 by N. M. Schulman. Reproduced by permission of Routledge/Taylor & Francis Group, LLC.

Design by Dylan Greif

Library of Congress Cataloging-in-Publication Data

Gordon, Alan (Alan R.)
The lark's lament / Alan Gordon.
p. cm.
ISBN-13: 978-0-312-38202-5
ISBN-10: 0-312-38202-2
1. Feste (Fictitious character)—Fiction. 2. Fools and jesters—Fiction.
3. Monks—Crimes against—Fiction. 4. Murder investigation—Fiction. I. Title.

PS3557.O649 L37 2007
813'.54—dc22

2006053302

First St. Martin's Minotaur Paperback Edition: May 2008

10 9 8 7 6 5 4 3 2 1

To my own Fools' Guild,
my fellow members of the Legal Aid Society of New York.
Friends, scholars, warriors.

I'm sure you know that picture well,
A monk, all else unheeding,
Within a bare and gloomy cell
A musty volume reading;
While through the window you can see
In sunny glade entrancing,
With cap and bells beneath a tree
A jester dancing, dancing.

—ROBERT WILLIAM SERVICE,
"ROOM 5: THE CONCERT SINGER"

THE LARK'S
LAMENT

ONE

Here come the jesters, one, two, three.

—BAD COMPANY, "ROCK AND ROLL FANTASY"

"Hag!" I screamed at my wife as she ran from me. "Foul harridan!"

"Bastard!" she screamed back, dashing to the far side of the fire. "Ill-smelling cur!"

"I will teach you manners, woman," I growled, holding up an iron saucepan. "I will teach you to obey your husband."

"You wouldn't dare," she snapped.

"Wouldn't I?"

I whirled it around my head three times and whipped it across the fire at her head. At the last possible moment, she stepped to the side and caught it by the handle, the force of the throw spinning her around completely.

A second spin added just enough speed to the pan to send it flying back at my chest. I caught it clumsily with both hands, but the impact sent me reeling back. I tripped, fell backwards into a somersault that left me sitting, dazed, with the saucepan now perched on my head.

My wife laughed uproariously as I regained my feet.

"So, woman," I began, pointing at her; then there was a loud clang as something hit the pan from behind me. I stumbled around, clutching my head, then turned to see Helga standing at the edge of the firelight, a broom raised in both hands. It was the stick end that had rung my pan so resoundingly.

"You leave my mother alone!" she barked, and I had to restrain myself from smiling because it was a perfect impression of my wife.

"So, little girl, you think you are too old for a spanking?" I sneered.

"If I'm a little girl, how could I be too old for anything?" she asked.

"Well, because . . ." Then I stopped, confused by the question. "Never mind. Put down that broom, or there will be hell to pay."

"You want this broom? Then take it from me," she cried. She ran toward me and suddenly planted the broom handle into the dirt, using it to vault into the air. She landed with both feet on my shoulders. I grabbed her ankles to steady them; then her skirts settled over my face, blocking my view of the world.

"Am I too old to do this?" she shouted, and she started pummeling me with the business end of the broom.

I staggered around as she kept hitting me, veering perilously close to the fire as the children in the audience screamed in terrified delight. Helga rode my shoulders like a Minoan acrobat, then leapt into the air, flipping over the broom and landing easily on her feet as the crowd applauded.

"Finally, I can see you, brat," I said.

"But you can't see behind you," she retorted, and I turned just in time to take an oversized club on the noggin, courtesy of my good wife. I toppled like a tree, and the two females planted their right feet on my back.

"And that, ladies, is how you teach obedience to your husband," concluded Claudia, and the men roared and the women cheered. Claudia and Helga hauled me to my feet, and we held hands and bowed together, the saucepan falling to the ground before me.

Helga grabbed a tambourine and darted around the crowd, begging for their hard-earned pennies while I dashed over to our wain to fetch our lutes. Portia looked at me nervously, sitting on the lap of the girl we had hired to watch her for the evening.

"Everything is fine, poppet," I assured her. "Papa was just pretending. Papa's not hurt at all."

She seemed dubious. I leaned forward and kissed her on the tip of her nose, and she suddenly smiled, that six-toothed grin that stopped my heart every time.

"Kiss Papa on the nose," I said, and she planted a wet smack on my nose that probably did nothing good for the whiteface coating it. "All better."

I ran back to the fire and tossed Claudia her lute.

"And now, good people of Le Cannet," I shouted. "We will close with a song written by one of the greatest troubadours I have ever come across, a man who was born in a great city south of here: Folquet of Marseille."

I raised my hand and brought it down on the lutestrings, singing:

O give me leave, fair lady mine,
For I have worshipped at your shrine.
I saw your face, your lips divine,
And Cupid's swift arrows are stinging.

Then Claudia sang:

Now, get you gone, O suitor mine,
I know full well that men are swine
Who only want their maids supine,
Sweet pillows on which to be springing.

Then I sang:

Return my love, fair lady mine,
A married life will suit me fine.

Just say you'll let our loves combine,
Then Heavenward I will be winging.

Then she sang:

Let other lovers wait in line.
Just yesterday, I turned down nine.
But since our fates you'd intertwine,
Then at your side I will be clinging.

Then we both sang:

So let us welcome God's design,
So long as sun and moon both shine,
And long as there are joy and wine,
Then we'll have a reason for singing.

The crowd applauded madly, and a few more coins flickered into view like shooting stars out of the darkness.

"I am Tan Pierre," I shouted, catching them. "This is my wife, Domna Gile, and our daughter, Helga. We are the Fool Family, and we thank you!"

We bowed again, then began to collect our gear and store it on the wain, chatting with those who came to see us up close and sweaty. The fire had been built in the center of the little square of the town, a small collection of stone buildings on top of a hill with a wall running around it. A church looked out at us from one end, and a square, fortified stone *maison* with three levels loomed over the other, the wall circling around it like the prow of a ship, ready to take on all comers.

Bertrand, the local seigneur, came up clapping his hands as the villagers drifted off to their houses or down the hill to their farms. "Marvelous, Fools, just marvelous," he chortled. "I have not laughed like that in an age of ages."

"Then we have fulfilled our purpose," I said, bowing. "And we thank you for graciously permitting us to entertain your village."

"Oh, that was the best part of it all," he said. "To have something like this, and not even a feast day! Why, they will think me the very soul of benevolence."

"And so you are," said Claudia. "So many lords would not deign to waste their peasants' time with the likes of us."

"As their lord, I consider them my children," he said grandly. "Does not every parent wish to keep their children happy?"

"We certainly do," said Claudia, taking Portia and giving her evening's guardian a penny, which the girl accepted with awe.

"Two daughters," said Bertrand, looking from Portia to Helga with delight. "I myself have six boys."

"I bow to your superior efforts," I said as Claudia and Helga squealed in outrage.

"A daughter would have been a welcome change," he said. "Someone to outsmart me and keep me on my toes."

"They certainly do that," agreed Claudia as I threw the last prop on the wain.

I helped Claudia and Helga up, then took Zeus's reins quickly before he had a chance to bite me.

"Lead on, milord," I said.

He fell into step by me and we walked around his *maison* down the slope to the stables. "The hay in the loft is fresh and dry," he said. "It should be comfortable enough."

"More than enough, milord."

"You know, that troubadour friend of yours lives not far from here," he remarked.

"Folquet? Here?" I exclaimed in surprise. "I didn't know he still lived. I've heard nothing about him in ten years. Does he still sing as magnificently as he once did?"

"I have never heard him sing," he replied. "He's at the abbey at Le Thoronet."

"He joined the Cistercians?"

"Not only joined," he said. "He's the abbot there."

My jaw must have been hanging below my neck. He started laughing at my expression; then I joined him.

"Truly a marvelous world," I said when I was able to catch breath. "The Folquet I knew was hardly a candidate for holy orders."

"It strikes suddenly with some men," he said. "I would not have guessed a family of fools to be so religious, yet here you are, returning from pilgrimage."

"We wanted to have the baby blessed in Rome," I said as I unhitched Zeus and carefully put him in an empty stall.

"Did the Pope bless her himself?" asked Bertrand with reverence.

"Hardly," said Claudia. "All we could afford was a bishop. But well worth it."

"We wanted her to start her life right, just like we did with Helga," I said, mussing the girl's hair affectionately. "You were too young to remember your first pilgrimage."

"Yes," she said, yawning, "but you tell the story so often, I think I do remember it."

Claudia and I beamed at Helga, as proud of her as if she had been our own.

"Inspiring," said Bertrand. "Perhaps I shall go there. I would like to see Rome once before I meet my maker. Fools, you have blessed my humble abode. I shall see you in the morning."

We bowed low as he left, humming Folquet's melody.

"We've only blessed his stables," muttered Claudia. "It would have been nice to bless his *maison*. From the inside."

"I'd like to bless a real bed sometime," added Helga. "It's been a while."

"I guess we merit his praise, but not his full protection," I said. "But once we get to Toulouse, I promise we will all have beds."

"A mighty promise. Should we trust it?" Claudia asked Helga.

"He does lie an awful lot," said Helga.

"That's because he's good at it," said Claudia.

"Yes, he is," agreed Helga. "Will you teach me? And why did you pretend you didn't know Folquet was nearby?"

"Just trying to make our little visit to him seem natural," I said. "In case anyone asks questions. Nothing unusual about a family returning from a pilgrimage, even if it's a family of fools. Speaking of which: Apprentice, front and center!"

Helga scampered through the hay and stood at attention before us. She was a spry young girl of twelve, although small enough to pass for younger if the need arose. I had thought she was ten when we first met. When her hair was washed, it was blond. Or so we believed.

"You followed my story about Rome with an excellent bit of improvisation," I began. "Full marks."

"Thank you, Master," she said.

"Your command of langue d'oc is excellent, and any slips in the accent we can attribute to your constant travel," I continued. "Your performance tonight was generally good. However, in the part where you were hitting me in the face with the broom, you actually hit me in the face with the broom."

"You can't fault her for that," objected Claudia. "She's standing on top of your shoulders while you're lurching about the fire."

"But she knows which way I'm lurching," I said. "Or she should know. Anything that could throw me off balance could end up sending one of us into that fire, and I know which one I will choose if that happens. Roast Apprentice is an excellent dish for early autumn."

"Maybe the routine is too hard for her," said Claudia.

"No, it isn't," said Helga. "I made the mistake. When I'm on his shoulders, it's step left, back, whack, back, right, whack, left, right, whack, forward, whack, back, whack, and jump. I was early on the third whack."

"Exactly," I said.

"I'll rehearse it in the morning," she said. "After exercises."

"Yes, you will," I said. "Now, get some sleep, little one."

I tossed her her bedroll, and she spread it out. Then she went over to Portia.

"Hug for Helga?" she whispered, and the baby opened her arms wide. Helga embraced her, then lay down on her bedroll and pulled a blanket over her body.

"Good night, Princess," said Claudia to Helga, kissing her on the cheek.

"Good night, Apprentice," I said.

Claudia nursed Portia until the babe was full, then handed her to me to burp. The resulting belch was loud enough to wake the horses, and Portia looked around in astonishment, then giggled.

"Good night, little Fool," I whispered, kissing her. I put her in her cradle and tucked her blanket around her. Claudia kissed her, then rocked her for a few minutes until her eyes closed.

We lay on our blankets, holding each other for warmth.

"You were hard on her," whispered Claudia.

"Because she's good," I said. "Did you notice her imitating you?"

"I sound nothing like that!" she protested.

"No, it must have been someone else," I said. "Someone else with the exact same voice as you."

"Hmph. How far is Le Thoronet?" she asked sleepily.

"One day's journey north," I said.

"Do you think he'll agree?"

"We'll see."

We woke to the sounds of the stable boys whistling as they mucked out the stalls. Portia was still asleep, so I picked the cradle up gently and carried her outside. Claudia and Helga joined me, and we began our stretches, then moved on to some quick tumbling routines. After that, Claudia began her juggling warm-ups, while Helga picked up her broom and faced me.

"Put down that broom, or there will be hell to pay," I said.

"You want this broom? Then take it from me," she cried.

She ran toward me and vaulted onto my shoulders.

"Left, back, whack, back, right, whack, left, right, whack, forward, whack, back, whack," she chanted as I did the steps, the broom whistling harmlessly past my face. "And jump!"

She landed neatly on her feet as the stable boys cheered. She curtsied to them impishly.

"Again?" she said.

"It's not necessary," I said.

"Again," she insisted.

"Very well," I said, pleased, and we repeated it. This time, it was even better. I bowed to her, then tossed her her juggling clubs. She sent them into the air in a pattern that accidentally carried her closer to the stable boys.

"Behave, daughter," I called.

"Of course, Papa," she replied innocently.

"Oh, to be twelve again," I said to Claudia. "Our little apprentice is growing up."

My wife stopped to watch the girl, a sad look in her eyes.

"What is it?" I asked softly.

"It's Celia's birthday today," she said. "She's eleven. If she still lives."

"I am certain that she does," I said.

"I wonder what she looks like now," said Claudia. "She resembled her father so. I wonder if she thinks of me at all."

"Of course she does."

"She must hate me," said Claudia.

"I doubt that," I said. "Her last letter sounded quite cheerful."

"That was months ago. She's at such a crucial stage in her life, and I'm not there to guide her."

"And if you were there, you would not be allowed to guide her," I said. "That was the agreement you made. They might even lock you up as a madwoman if you return."

She was silent.

"Do you want to go back?" I asked.

"Would you come with me?"

"I have a mission to accomplish," I said.

"I left my world for yours," she said.

"By choice," I pointed out.

"By choice," she agreed. "Would you ever choose mine?"

"I lived that life once," I reminded her. "It ended badly. And how would I reenter it? In Orsino, they know me as the jester who ran off with their lady. How could I be anything else but that? Once you choose this foolish world, it is hard to go back to your old one."

She looked at Helga, who had four clubs in the air and three boys enraptured.

"Look, Mark will be of age in two more years," I said. "Once your sister-in-law no longer has the regency in her fat greedy hands, we can go back safely. For a visit, at least."

"Promise?"

"Promise."

She walked over to Helga, snatched the clubs from above her, and hugged her suddenly.

"Mama, stop," said Helga in muffled protest.

Claudia held her tightly for a long moment, then released her, smiling gently, and tossed her clubs high overhead. Helga scrambled to make all the catches.

Portia woke up, and Claudia went to attend to her. Helga came over to me, still juggling.

"Why does she always do that?" she complained.

"She's playing a mother," I said. "Go pack our gear. I'm going to take Zeus for a run."

"Can't I?" she pleaded.

"When your legs can reach the stirrups."

"I could shorten them."

"What good would shorter legs do you?"

She pouted. I pulled a carrot out of my bag and walked into the stable. Zeus looked at me suspiciously.

"Want to stretch your legs for a bit?" I asked, taking his saddle from the wain. "It would do you some good before we hitch you up."

I opened the door and stepped carefully inside the stall, holding the carrot at arm's length. I let him snatch it out of my hand, then threw the saddle on his back and cinched it quickly before he had time to finish eating. I jumped on and grabbed the reins, then leaned over to untether him.

It was the leaning that nearly undid me. He bucked from the rear, throwing me half off the saddle, then burst through the stable, the other horses watching in envy. The stable boys and Helga scattered in all directions as we galloped through them toward a stone wall some five feet in height. It occurred to me that this might be a good time to try riding him from on top, rather than clinging precariously to his side with my legs as my head dipped toward the swiftly moving ground. I grabbed the pommel, hauled myself back up, then flung myself onto his neck as he jumped the wall.

Much to my relief, there was level ground on the other side. I looked around his neck to see a pasture zipping by us, with another wall coming up all too soon. Zeus gathered himself on the run and jumped, and I had several quick and pessimistic thoughts about my mortality.

Enough was enough. I hauled on the reins until he was at a sedate trot, huffing mightily.

"Back to the wain for you, steed of Satan," I growled. "And, if you don't mind, we'll go through the gates this time, not over them."

The stable boys, who had had more amusement in this one morning than in their entire lives before it, cheered as I approached, and scrambled forward eagerly to help harness Zeus to the wain. He glared at me.

"I understand entirely, old friend," I said, patting him on the rump. "Responsibilities are burdensome things."

I limped over to Claudia.

"Good ride?" she asked as she dressed Portia.

"A little bumpy," I said. "Good thing I got it out of his system."

"His? Or yours?" she laughed. "Maybe you should become a trick rider."

"The trick is not dying," I said. "Helga!"

"Yes, Papa?"

"You may exercise him tomorrow."

"Thank you, Papa."

The cook ran out with a basket of food for us, an unexpected gift for which we thanked her profusely. She tickled the baby under the chin, kissed Helga and my wife, and winked at me before going back to her kitchen.

Bertrand himself came to see us off.

"Which is the road to Le Thoronet?" I asked him.

"Come, you can see it from the hill," he said.

We walked past the *maison* to the top of the hill. The valley spread out before us, a patchwork of farms ringed by mountains. He pointed to a road going northwest, disappearing into a forest that clung to the lower slopes.

"The abbey is about eleven miles, as I recall," he said. "A day's journey. I am giving you a few sacks of wheat to take them. Tell them to throw in a prayer or two for us."

"I will, milord, and much thanks," I said.

We climbed onto the wain, and were off to Le Thoronet.

It was only half a day's journey northwest. It might have been shorter, but there was not much in the way of an actual village to find. It was more like a series of tiny hamlets and isolated farms. We saw few people, and the few that we saw stared at us in astonishment as we asked for directions.

"I don't think our pretense for traveling will work so well out here," commented Claudia with amusement.

"On the other hand, who would they tell?" I replied. "Helga?"

"Yes, Papa?"

"Take a seat at the rear, and keep your bow within reach."

"Yes, Papa," she said, clambering over the piles of props and costumes.

"Is this a dangerous place?" asked Claudia, eyeing the forest ahead of us with trepidation.

"Any forest is a dangerous place," I said. "I would hope that there is so little traffic on this road that banditry would be a bootless profession, but I haven't lived this long by ignoring simple precautions."

Claudia said nothing, but reached back, patted the baby, and felt underneath the cradle for her own bow.

The trees closed over us, and I slowed Zeus down to a walk, watching the sides of the road. But we came through without attack. The road climbed once the forest cleared, and the trees took on a regular spacing.

"Olives and chestnuts," I pointed out. "We must be near the abbey."

"Can I come with you?" called Helga.

"No, sorry," I said. "They don't allow women inside."

"Why not?"

"It's the Cistercian Rule," answered Claudia. "You wouldn't like them, anyway. They only bathe once a year, and they wear the same robe and cowl all the time."

"She's exaggerating," I said. "They bathe twice a year, not once. But she's right about the robes."

"They stink to high heaven," continued Claudia. "Which may be how they reach God."

"Eww," said Helga.

We passed by fields that were being worked by monks in white robes and lay brothers in brown copes, many wearing mittens to protect their hands. A small group of dairy cattle grazed under the watchful eye of one wizened fellow. The road rose ahead of us, and we saw the steeple of the church against the sky.

We passed a lay brother balancing two wicker baskets filled with olives on a pole across his shoulders.

"Greetings, Brother," I said. "Could you tell me where visitors may set up camp?"

He pointed to a clearing nearby. I guided the wain to it and reined Zeus to a halt. Portia woke and began to cry.

"Right on cue," I said to Claudia. "You nurse; we'll set up the tent."

Once Helga and I had finished that task, I sent her to the stream running in front of the abbey to fetch water. Claudia walked with me while I picked up kindling.

"Will it be safe for us here?" she asked.

"We're in the middle of nowhere," I said. "I would think so."

"What about them?" she asked, nodding toward the abbey.

"Not a violent group, in my experience," I said. "But we can trade watches, if it will make you feel better."

"It would," she said. "I don't know why, but I have an odd feeling about this place."

I glanced at the sky. It was just past noon.

"We'll eat, then I'll go pay my respects," I said.

I don't like cathedrals, but I have nothing against churches when they are built for worship and not for display. Nothing could have been simpler than this abbey, yet it was beautiful in its simplicity. The construction was without mortar, each stone carved to fit its neighbors perfectly. There were no statues, neither gold nor gilt to catch the eye, and the irregular slope of the ground had forced whatever master builder they had to adjust and innovate rather than force Nature to accommodate his wishes. The building was very much of a piece with the land, and many of the monks and lay brothers seemed old enough to have become of a piece with both.

The entrance was to the right of the church, past a two-story building that I guessed was the chapter house. I rapped on the door. It was opened by a massive man crammed into his robe, looking down at me impassively. He was clean-shaven, as was the custom of the Cistercians, and had an old scar running up his left cheek to his ear. No, to part of an ear. He saw me glancing at it and shrugged slightly.

"What do you seek?" he asked.

"An audience with your abbot," I said.

"Wrong answer," he said, shaking his head. "What do you seek?"

"Sorry," I said. "God's mercy."

"May you find it," he said. "Please come in."

Everyone has their passwords, I thought. I wondered what it would take for me to get by Saint Peter when my time came.

It occurred to me, not for the first time, that that was not likely to be a problem given my moral state.

"My name is Antime," said the monk. "I am the cellarer here. Normally, our hosteler would be greeting you, but we have just finished our noon meal and it is permitted to have a short nap afterwards."

"I begrudge no man his nap," I said. "Forgive me if I have interrupted yours."

"I never nap," he said. "Our parlor is here."

He led me to a small room off to the right, containing a pair of roughhewn benches. Gardening and farm implements were stacked against the wall. A small table held some cups and a ewer of water. He poured some for me.

"Thank you," I said.

"Have you come a long way?" he asked.

"We were in Le Cannet this morning," I said. "I heard by chance that an old friend had settled here and is now the Abbot. I thought that I would take the opportunity to pay my respects."

"The Abbot will be happy to see you, I am sure," said Brother Antime. "What name shall I give him?"

I searched my memory for a moment. Too many names.

"Droignon," I said, hoping the hesitation did not show. "Droignon, the Fool."

"I will bring him." He bowed his head and left, walking with his hands crossed on his chest.

Some time later, I heard footsteps approaching the parlor. Lighter ones than those made by the massive Brother Antime. I stood with my hands down at my sides, a gesture of respect in the Fools' Guild because it puts them at a distance from any concealed weapons. A man in a white robe came through the door, glanced at my motley, then down to my hands, and smiled.

"Ah, my old friend, Droignon," he said loudly. "It has been years. How gracious of you to come visit."

"To see the legendary Folquet of Marseille?" I laughed. "No distance is too great."

He glanced behind to make sure that no one was within close range, then pointed to the bench. "Sit," he commanded me quietly.

I sat, and he took the other bench and leaned toward me, pulling back his cowl so that I could see him more clearly. I knew that he was about fifty, but he looked older, a more gaunt and weathered man than the troubadour I remembered.

"I am sorry to keep you waiting," he said. "Brother Calvet caught Brother Pelfort dipping into our wine supply, and we needed to find both the appropriate punishment and a better way of securing the wine. We have met, haven't we?"

"Once," I said. "In Marseille. I was returning from Outremer late in '92—"

"With your petty king," he interrupted. "I remember now. You were in Marseille for a week. We invited you for dinner. You drank too much wine and told some highly inappropriate stories to my sons. They were delighted to hear them, as I recall."

"That does sound like me," I admitted. "Forgive me. You can do that now, can't you?"

"I can. I must say, I am surprised that Monsieur Droignon would dare come back to this part of the world, if what I heard was true."

"That depends on what you heard," I said. "And, in any case, that was three days north. Not here."

"Password," he said suddenly.

"God's mercy?"

"Don't waste my time," he snapped. "Give me the Guild password or I'll call for Brother Antime. He was a soldier for thirty years before he came here. I've seen him throw a sack of flour forty feet."

"Then let him throw a sack of flour," I said. "Guild passwords are for Guildmembers. You quit."

He was silent, clasping and unclasping his hands repeatedly. "How do I know you're still with the Guild?" he asked.

For a reply, I pulled a small scroll out of my sleeve and handed it to him. He studied the seal carefully.

"So Father Gerald is still running things," he said. "How is he?"

"Old," I said. "Blind now. One might say not long for this world, but that was first said twenty years ago."

He broke the seal, read the letter, then handed it back to me. "Theophilos," he said. "That is your Guild name."

"Yes," I said. "Yours was Marcello, Abbot Folquet."

"Fine, your credentials are accepted," he said. "By the way, it's Folc, now. Abbot Folc. Folquet was a diminutive, a frivolous name for a frivolous time long since passed."

"Very well, Abbot Folc," I said. "Curious how the diminutive is longer than the true name."

"Why are you here?" he asked. "What does the Guild want from me?"

"Your help."

"My help," he said, laughing bitterly. "The great and powerful Fools' Guild seeks aid from a retired troubadour?"

"From a former member who is now an abbot," I said. "When is the last time you heard anything about the Guild?"

"I heard that our Holy Father was considering an interdict against you, but settled for routing the Guildhall," he said. "Where did you end up fleeing to?"

I shook my head. "Again, you're not a Guild member," I said.

"No, I'm not," he said. "And I have no interest in resuming a troubadour's life."

"No one is asking you to," I said.

"Then why are you here?"

"Because we need an abbot."

"For absolution?" he laughed. "You have Father Gerald for that."

"We need an abbot to help save the Guild."

"To help save the Guild," he said flatly. "How could I possibly do that?"

"By being who you are—an abbot who once was a Guildmember. By bringing your influence to bear on Rome."

"We are not in Rome. We are in Le Thoronet, a place of retreat from the world. A place of quiet worship."

"But you've been to Rome," I said. "When Innocent assumed the Holy See, you were there. You met the Pope; the Pope met you. You liked him; he liked you. We think he'll listen to you."

"Listen to me say what, exactly?"

"We have enemies within the Church," I began.

"Hardly surprising," he said. "The Guild has always campaigned against the Church."

"Not the Church, just the hypocrisy and corruption that take hold there," I said.

"Which is most of it, nowadays."

"Maybe," I said. "Certainly, the Guild has rubbed more than a few powerful people the wrong way. That's our goal, after all. But the consequences lately have been severe."

"Hence, your pilgrimage to see me," he said.

"Yes."

"I don't travel to Rome on a regular basis," he said. "I've been there twice in nine years. I send my monthly reports to Marseille, I go over our accounts, lead my flock in prayer, supervise the building of the new quarters for the lay brothers, and help press the olives when an extra hand is needed. Of what use to the Guild is an abbot in Le Thoronet?"

"Very little," I agreed. "But we think you are due for a promotion."

"What?" he exclaimed.

"Of all the fools and troubadours who have taken vows, only you have risen as far as becoming an abbot. And a Cistercian abbot, at that. We like the Cistercians. We think that we can live with them, especially compared to some of the other orders. You value simplicity and piety over ostentation."

"We also despise flattery," he said.

I bowed my head in acknowledgment. "Anyhow, we thought a man of your worth should become a bishop," I continued.

"A bishop," he said. "You think that you can arrange that?"

"That is the second part of my mission," I said. "You being the first."

"And where am I to be elevated to this lofty stature?"

"Toulouse."

He shook his head. "Ridiculous," he said.

"Why?"

"First, they already have a bishop in Toulouse."

"His name is Raimon de Rabastens," I said. "He is a weak man, corrupt and vulnerable, according to our reports. The town deserves better, and it needs it soon. Toulouse occupies a precarious position in the world."

"The more reason for me to shun it," said Folc. "I am not too popular there."

"You aren't? I was under the impression that you had never been to Toulouse before."

"No, but my songs have," he said. "Don't you know who my patrons were when I was composing? Guilhem of Montpellier, Barral of Marseille, both enemies of the Count of Toulouse. How do you propose to place me in the bishopric when the Count controls the selection?"

"That's my problem," I said. "Father Gerald didn't choose me because he thought this was going to be easy."

"What was the plan if I refused?"

"If I cannot persuade you, then there is no plan," I said. "But hear this—the very life of the Guild is at stake. You know what we stand for. You were part of it once. I know that you believed in it then. There are still friends of yours carrying on the Guild's mission, and hundreds more you've never met who risk their lives on a daily basis. All we ask is that you intercede for us."

"All you ask is that I leave everything that I have built here and become bishop in a town that is half corruption and half heresy," he replied.

"Sounds like a worthy target for a man of your holiness," I said.

"Do not mock me," he said furiously. "I am not meat for your japing."

"I am sorry," I said. "I was speaking to Folquet. But you are not Folquet."

"Not anymore," he said.

"When is the last time that you sang your songs?" I asked.

"The Cistercian Order forbade the composition of nonreligious songs five years ago," he said.

"You must miss it," I said.

"No," he replied. "I gave up my old life with a willing heart when I came here. The world is a wicked place, Theophilos, but here one finds respite. Here one finds God."

"Here one finds a tomb," I said. "I prefer to participate in the world. Among the living."

"You made your choice," he said. "I made mine. And there's an end to it."

He stood and offered his hand. I took it.

"You have a family now, I see," he said as he walked me to the entrance. "I must confess my surprise. You never struck me as a fool who would settle down."

"My family is quite unsettling," I said. "They suit me fine. And what became of your sons when you joined the Order?"

"My sons are in the abbey at Grandselves," he replied. "My wife is with a community of women in Gémenos who serve the Bishop of Marseille. I do not hear from any of them much."

I walked outside, then turned. "We may not win this fight," I said.

"Then I will pray for your souls," he replied, and he closed the door in my face.

I walked across the low bridge over the stream and back to our camp. Claudia had a fire going and beans cooking in a pot. Helga was playing with Portia, who was crawling around the clearing at a rapid pace, giggling.

"How did it go?" asked Claudia.

"He refused," I said.

"You thought that he would," she said.

"Yes, at first."

"But you believe that he will come around?"

"Maybe tomorrow. Maybe in a week."

"Why?"

"Because I appealed to his ambition," I said. "Something he keeps trying to push down. But it's still there."

"Do ambitious people become monks?"

"They must. Because it takes an ambitious monk to become an abbot."

She stirred the pot, then tasted it. "Done," she said. "Tell me, husband. What do ambitious fools become?"

"There are none," I said. "Being a fool means that you have achieved your highest ambitions already."

After our dinner, Claudia tutored Helga in Arabic while I played with Portia. She could not quite walk yet, but had mastered sitting on my soles as I lay on my back with my feet in the air. I bounced her up and down gently, then brought my knees past my head until they touched the ground behind me. Slowly, I curled my way through the somersault while my daughter sat unperturbed on her perch.

"Must you do that where I can see you?" complained Claudia. "You know how it unnerves me."

"I haven't dropped her yet," I pointed out.

"It is the 'yet' that's discomforting," she said. "All right, Helga. Music time."

"Let me teach you one of Folquet's," I said as we picked up our lutes. "It's called, 'Singing will reveal my faithful heart.' "

"How lovely," said Helga.

We strummed away as the sun began to set. I wondered if Folc could hear us. I turned so that my voice would carry toward the abbey.

"I'll take first watch," said Helga after we were done.

"Two hours," I said. "Watch the stars to know when to wake me."

We crawled into our tent and went to sleep.

A sleepy apprentice shook me awake on time, and I sat outside, listening to an owl hoot somewhere in the distance, wondering if my words had reached Folc. Or, better, if they had reached Folquet.

Roosters at the abbey sounded the coming of the dawn. And with the dawn came trouble. Helga spotted it first, and came flying into the tent to shake me awake.

"Master," she whispered urgently. "Monks are coming from the abbey. Many of them. And they have staves."

I came outside in a trice. Sure enough, ten monks were filing into the clearing, surrounding us. Brother Antime approached me, carrying a club larger than Helga.

"Come with us, Fool," he said.

"Time for morning prayers?" I asked.

"Now," he said.

"Husband, is everything all right?" came Claudia's voice from inside the tent, and I knew from the tone of it that she had an arrow nocked.

"Everything is fine," I reassured her. "I will be back soon. Get the wain loaded."

"Fine," she replied.

I bowed to Brother Antime. "Lead on, my friend."

To my surprise, instead of taking me to the entrance again, they led me around to the west entrance to the church. There were two doors on either side leading in, a pair of long, narrow windows with semicircular tops between them, and a large round window above everything.

Brother Antime suddenly shoved me against the wall and searched me quite thoroughly, removing my knife from my boot.

"I can have that back when I leave, right?" I asked.

"Inside," said Brother Antime, indicating the door at the left.

Folc was standing at the foot of the steps inside the door, his face distorted with rage. "How dare you come to this house of God and defile it!" he shouted.

"What on earth are you talking about?" I asked.

Brother Antime came up behind me and knocked me to the floor. Folc squatted in front of me. "There will be judgment for this, Fool," he hissed.

"For what?" I said; then I rolled to one side as Brother Antime's foot thudded into the floor where I had just been. I kicked his legs out from under him, and as he toppled, I snatched the club out of his hands. The rest of the monks edged forward, nervously clutching their staves.

"Tell them to stop," I said to Folc.

"Hold, my brothers," he barked.

They held.

"Now, I don't have a clue as to what I am supposed to have done," I said. "But, in good faith, I am surrendering. Here."

I held the club out to Brother Antime, then offered a hand to help him up.

"Sorry about that," I said. "But you are really not supposed to hurt people inside the church. I saved you from committing some kind of sin."

"Arrogance," muttered Folc. "Come with me, and we will see what sins have been committed here."

The church was without decoration inside. The nave was maybe sixty feet high, with galleries on both sides, the right one raised a few steps. The chevet and apses were semicircular, which was unusual. The Cistercian churches I had been in before were flat and rectangular, but whatever builder had come here had some beauty in his heart.

Folc turned left just before reaching the transept and led me down a flight of steps. He opened a door and stepped out into the corner of a gallery that enclosed an irregularly shaped cloister. Off to the right, a low doorway split by a column revealed a small room, maybe ten feet square. He went inside. I had to duck to avoid cracking my head on the lintel, and found myself in a librarium.

"There." He pointed.

On the floor on the other side of a wooden bench lay the crumpled form of a monk, his white robe soaked in dark crimson. His head rested near an oaken bucket.

Someone had splashed his blood over the books and scrolls on the shelves that lined one wall. On the stones above it, the killer had painted the words, FOLQUET: COLD IS THE HAND THAT CRUSHES THE LARK.

"What do you have to say about that, Fool?" demanded Folc.

"Looks like the world wants you to know it's still there," I said.

TWO

You are the jester of this courtyard.

—SUZANNE VEGA, "GYPSY"

"Husband, is everything all right?" I called from inside the tent, kneeling with my bowstring back at my right ear. Helga knelt to my left and back a step, her bow steady in her hands. For now.

"Everything is fine," he called as the giant monk with the giant club beckoned. "I will be back soon. Get the wain loaded."

"Fine," I shouted back.

Portia whimpered behind me.

"Hush, little fool," I whispered to her. "Everything is fine."

We held position until we counted all the monks leaving, my man in motley at the van.

"Stay here," I whispered. I put my bow down at the edge of the tent and stepped cautiously outside. I saw no one.

"Fine," I said, and Helga emerged. She was trembling now that it was over. I gave her a quick hug of encouragement. "You did well, Apprentice," I said. "Which one were you aiming at?"

"The one to the left of the leader," she said.

"Good," I said. "I had the one on the right. If anything happened,

Theo would have taken on the giant, but the two closest were likely to be the most proficient in battle. And the signal?"

"If he said, 'all right' instead of 'fine,' then we attack," she said.

"And how do we attack?"

"I stay in the tent shooting for as long as I can while you come out with your sword, screaming like a deranged harpy."

I looked at her sternly. "I would prefer avenging angel, Apprentice."

"Yes, Mama," she said, grinning.

Portia started crying at being left alone. I fetched her from the tent, and she settled in to suck. I sat on a tree stump.

"Where were you aiming?" I asked as Helga began to break down the tent.

"At the body," she said. "That's the nice thing about shooting at monks. No armor."

"You can't assume that," I said. "They might have been rogues, or bandits dressed as monks, but armored underneath. Go for the throat if he's standing still. Otherwise, aim for the thigh. It's a big target on a man, and it will take him out of battle right away."

"Yes, Domna," she said. She looked out at the abbey. "Will he be all right?"

"Don't worry, he'll wriggle out of it. He can talk the very Devil into selling his soul."

"What if he has to fight his way out?" she asked.

"Theo against eleven monks?" I laughed. "No contest. You've never seen him fight, and I hope that you never do, but he's quite deadly when need be."

"Have you ever killed anyone?" she asked me.

"Yes," I said, shifting Portia to the other breast.

"More than one?"

"Yes. But I don't like to talk about it."

"Why not?"

"Because then it becomes a story," I said. "Then I become some-one in a story named Claudia, and that makes it less of me. And I don't want to ever become complacent about it. Does that make sense to you?"

"A little," she said. "It will make more sense when you tell me what 'complacent' means."

We loaded the wain, keeping our bows handy, then waited. It seemed like an eternity, but then we saw my husband walking cheerfully toward us, the giant monk with a firm grip at his elbow.

"Hello, family," he called. "Did you miss me?"

"For a little while," I said. "But then I thought, here I am, the only adult woman for miles, and dozens of bachelors at hand. My fortune is made!"

"I could leave," he offered. "Or join. It's very quiet and peaceful in there. I think it's the absence of women that causes that."

The giant may have cracked a smile for a second, but it vanished. Maybe I imagined it.

"Oh, this is my new friend, Brother Antime," Theo said. "Cellarer, and former sergeant with the army of Philippe Auguste. Turns out we had some friends in common in Acre back in our younger days."

"Pleased to meet you, Brother Antime," I said, doing him courtesy. He nodded. "Will you be requiring my husband's elbow any further?"

The giant released him, then leaned over him menacingly. "That little trick of yours won't work the next time," he growled.

"Then I'll use a different one," said Theo pleasantly. "Peace be with you, my friend."

Brother Antime glared, then walked back to the monastery.

Theo waited until he was out of sight, then started rubbing his elbow. "Ow," he sighed. "Quite a grip for a holy man."

Portia looked at him, her lip quivering.

He smiled at her. "Papa's fine, see?" he said, whirling his arm around. He kissed her on the nose. "Kiss Papa on the nose?"

She did.

He looked at me impishly. "Kiss husband on the nose?" he said, leaning toward me.

I kissed him hard on the mouth. "Damn, missed again," I said.

"All better," he said. "Although that always makes me a little wobbly."

"Will you teach me how to kiss?" Helga whispered to me.

"If I teach you how to lie, and she teaches you how to kiss, then you'll be the most dangerous woman alive," said Theo sternly. "Everything ready? Good."

"Are we leaving?" I asked.

"I'm afraid so, and quickly, before Folquet changes his mind," he said. "There's been . . ."

He stopped. A monk was approaching us.

"Yes, Abbot? Is there something we can do for you?" asked Theo.

I stared at the man. By this time, I had met hundreds of jesters and troubadours, thanks to our sojourn at the Guildhall in exile. I had even met several who had taken vows, and every one of them was filled with life and good humor. But this stick figure in robes had had his vitality sucked out of him. He was a very wraith, and part of me wanted to invoke some ancient spell to ward him off.

"This is your family?" asked the abbot.

"My wife, Guildname of Claudia," Theo said. "Helga, our apprentice. And our daughter, Portia."

The abbot looked at us, then nodded abruptly. "It seems unlikely that you would travel with your family all this way just to commit this despicable act," he said.

"But you haven't even seen our act," I protested. "Really, the storyline is quite entertaining, and once we bring out the cooking utensils—"

"Enough," he said wearily. "I had all too much of the Guild when I was in it."

"Well?" said Theo.

"I know that you are capable of killing," said the abbot. "But you've never stooped to murder. Not to make a point like this, anyway."

"Murder?" I exclaimed.

"It's not my way," agreed Theo. "And I shouldn't think that the threat of violence would have any effect on you whatsoever."

"Excuse my simple feminine curiosity," I interjected. "Was someone murdered? I would like to know more about it, if you don't mind."

"A monk," said Theo. "What was his name again?"

"Brother Pelfort," said the abbot.

"Had a habit of sneaking into the wine supply when nobody was looking," explained Theo. "This time, somebody was looking. His throat was slit and his blood drained into a bucket."

"A bucket?" squeaked Helga. "Why?"

"He used the blood to paint a message for our former colleague here," said Theo. He turned back to the abbot. "Are you satisfied that it wasn't me?"

"Satisfaction is hardly the word for the occasion," said the abbot.

"The librarium faces the cloister from under a covered gallery," said Theo. "And the dormitorium is directly above it?"

"Yes."

"And does everyone in the abbey share the dormitorium?"

"The lay brothers sleep in the barn and the workshops."

"Which are also out of view of the cloister?"

"Yes," said the abbot.

"So, a lit candle in the librarium in the middle of the night would not be visible to anyone," mused Theo. "Do you maintain a regular watch at night?"

"We never felt it necessary," said the abbot. "It would have been easy enough for you to slip in unseen."

"Me, or anyone else," said Theo. "Why would I do something to annoy you when I want you to do something for me?"

"That's an excellent point," I said to Helga, who nodded furiously.

"When have you and logic ever shared company?" asked the abbot.

"Also an excellent point," I said to Helga, who nodded even more furiously.

The two men looked at us, and the abbot smiled slightly. "Unsettling, I believe you said," he remarked.

"Very," replied Theo. "But I have grown attached to them in my dotage. Look, if it wasn't me, and it wasn't, then there are two other possibilities. Either it came from an enemy from without—"

"Or one from within," finished the abbot. "Do you really expect me to believe one of my own did this?"

"There are dozens of men living in close quarters here," said Theo. "Brother Pelfort may have had some enemy among them unbeknownst to you. Much more likely than me showing up out of the blue after so many years just to kill him."

"Unless you were leaving that message, and he stumbled in on you," said the abbot.

"And you think that I would find it necessary to kill under those circumstances?" protested Theo. "I'm more resourceful than that."

The abbot looked at him, then sighed wearily. "My heart, if not my reason, says that it wasn't you," he said. "But reason must prevail if the Guild wants any help from me. Prove to me that you didn't do this."

"How could I possibly do that?" asked Theo.

"Father Gerald didn't choose you because he thought this was going to be easy," said the abbot. "Find whoever is responsible, and I will consider Father Gerald's request. If you do not, then the Guild can burn in Hell for all I care. I might even send a letter to my good friend, the Pope, to expedite the process."

He turned to leave. Theo suddenly swung his fist at him. The wraith moved more quickly than I would have thought possible and managed to block it. The two stood frozen, glaring at each other.

"If the killer is inside the abbey, then I would do better to stay here," said Theo. "You're in danger. All of you."

"No," said the abbot. "I can take care of things here. Seek elsewhere for your prey."

"You might want to consider resuming your Guild exercises," said Theo. "You've slowed down."

"I blocked you, didn't I?"

"Yes, but I've slowed down, too," retorted Theo. "I recommend, my holy shepherd, that you start watching your flocks by night."

"Go with God," said the abbot. "Go with God now." He walked back to the abbey without a single glance back.

"You're not that slow, normally," said Helga.

"I didn't want to hit him, child," said Theo in exasperation. "I just wanted to put the fear of God back in him. Let's go."

"Where?" I asked.

"To the past," he said, putting Portia's cradle in the wain.

"Which way is that?"

"South."

We rode on until we were out of sight of the abbey.

"So that was Folquet of Marseille," I said.

"Please, it's Folc now," he said in perfect imitation of the man. He grimaced.

"What was the message?" I asked.

" 'Folquet: Cold is the hand that crushes the lark.' "

"The lark is a songbird," I observed.

"Yes, it is."

"As was Folquet . . ."

"Folc."

"As was Folc, once upon a time."

"Yes, he was."

"That certainly sounds like he's being threatened," I said. "Yet here we are, running away."

"We can't exactly sneak into a Cistercian abbey," he said.

"We have sneaked into better places," I pointed out.

"They know everyone there," he said. "And they know me."

"Then let me do it," I said. "I could disguise myself as a man, get hold of one of those hideous robes—"

"Wash it thoroughly," added Helga helpfully.

"And join. They wouldn't know I was a woman until it came time to bathe. That would give me months to investigate."

"Terrible idea," he said.

"Why?"

"Because it would take you away from me," he said simply, and he put his free arm around me and drew me to him.

"Why are we going south?" asked Helga.

"Because we are seeking someone from his past," answered Theo.

"How do you know?"

"Because the message was for Folquet, not Folc," said Theo. "He hasn't been Folquet in years. So, we look to his past to find where the threat comes from."

"Marseille," I said.

"Exactly," he replied. "Damn!"

"What?"

"Brother Antime still has my knife."

"We can't go back for it."

"No, I suppose we can't," he said, suddenly moody. "That's my favorite knife, too."

And we continued our journey with at least one jester in a bad temper.

"What do you know of Folc?" I asked that evening. Helga had volunteered to cook dinner, and Portia was asleep in her cradle, bless her, so we had a rare moment alone inside the tent.

"Not much more than what Father Gerald told us," he said. "He grew up in Marseille, son of a Genoese merchant. Talent for singing showed up early, then for composing songs and poems. The Guild recruited him when he was about thirteen. We persuaded his father to send him to the University in Bologna, and from there, it was easy enough to sneak him off to the Guildhall for training during the breaks."

"But what was he like? When you knew him?"

"I knew him for a week," he said. "I knew of him, knew people that knew him, but I only spent a week in his company, and just parts of that week at that."

"Was he this dour a man?"

"Not at all," he said. "Quite a cheerful, lively fellow. He had a nice wife and two young boys, a thriving business that he inherited from his father, and a voice that could make angels laugh and devils weep."

"Did he have enemies in Marseille?"

"Couldn't say. I didn't get around the city that much."

"Although no doubt you could find every tavern there in the dark, blindfolded."

"It's a gift," he agreed happily.

"What kind of merchant was he?"

"Whatever could be shipped out of Marseille, he shipped, and whatever could be shipped in from anywhere else, he also shipped. He rode the troubadour circuit from Marseille to Montpellier, which was his main function for the Guild."

"Could his Guild activities have stirred anything up?"

"That's one thing we'll have to find out," he said.

"The beans are ready!" called Helga. "Are you done?"

"Done doing what?" I called out.

"Done doing what I spent all this time cooking dinner for so you could do it," she called back.

Theo and I looked at each other ruefully.

"So that's why she volunteered," he said. "A missed opportunity."

"Next time, we'll know," I said. "Let's look like we actually did so she won't be disappointed."

We emerged hastily adjusting our clothing as Helga arched an eyebrow in perfect imitation of my husband.

"She's doing your look," I said.

"I don't look like that," he objected.

"Yes, you do," I said. "And I'm the only one who can see both of your faces, so that makes me the expert."

Helga ladled out the beans, and we dug in.

"What's the plan when we get to Marseille?" I asked when we were done.

"Look up the local fool and find out what he knows," said Theo.

"You mean gossip, rumors, old stories distorted by constant retelling, passed on by one drunken jester to another?"

"Something like that, yes," he said. "You make it sound so unreliable."

"What about Folc's family?" I asked. "Where are they?"

"He told me his boys are at the abbey in Grandselves," he said.

"But his wife is still in Marseille, isn't she?" I asked.

"Outside the city," he said. "With a community of women who serve the Bishop."

"She's a nun?"

"I don't know if it's quite that formal. It's not a convent."

"Where is this group of non-nuns?"

"In Gémenos. They watch the cattle for the Church."

"They serve the Church by watching cattle?"

"They watch them religiously."

"I see," I said. "I think we should talk to her first. She'll know more than a fool would."

"If something happened while he was a Guildmember, then the other Guildmembers would be more likely to know about it."

"But if it happened while he was married, then she would be our best bet," I insisted.

"Not necessarily. Wives know only what their husbands choose to tell them," he said haughtily, his eyebrow arched.

"Husbands only think their wives know only what they choose to tell them," I replied. "But wives in truth know much more than their husbands think they do."

"I assure you that there are vast expanses of my life of which you are ignorant," he said. "And you should thank God that you are, considering the depths of depravity to which I sank before I met you."

"I have secrets in my past as well," I said, fluttering my eyelashes mysteriously.

"I have more."

"Only because you are so much older than me," I said.

"Ouch."

"I was but an innocent flower, barely in bloom, when I was plucked from my maiden bed by this reprobate," I explained to Helga who had been following the conversation wide-eyed.

"Actually, she had been plucked quite a few times by the time I got to her," commented Theo. "I am her second husband, after all. And when I say, 'after all,' I mean after all of the other—"

"Sir, you are no gentleman!" I interrupted.

"Which is why you married me, I believe."

"Is she your first wife?" asked Helga.

That caught him up short for an instant. Then he recovered and played the fool again. "Why, I have a veritable harem of them scattered about," he said, grinning lewdly. "Most are recovering, still in bed."

"And some took vows, and some have fled, and some do live, and some are dead," I chanted derisively. "I care not who came before. I am his last wife, because I will hunt him down and kill him if he ever betrays me."

"And thus does fear keep our marriage intact, and that's a conclusion," he said. "All right."

"All right what?"

"All right, we'll go visit his wife first."

I hate traveling in a wain. I had a very nice mare named Hera who had carried me from Orsino to Constantinople, then back and across the Alps to the Black Forest where the Guild was hiding out—half that journey with Portia when a newborn—and nothing contented me more than to be astride that gentle, intelligent creature, moving to her rhythm. But riding on anything with wheels being pulled by Zeus meant that you felt every bump at the base of your spine. He bitterly resented being in harness, and took it out on us by single-mindedly seeking out the worst ruts and rocks to pull us over. I think the Guild made us use him because none of them wanted him.

We traveled by a route through the mountains that must have been first made by either a madman or pilgrim, not that there is much difference. It snaked through the massif, coiling and doubling back upon itself so that we would frequently find ourselves after an hour's ride back at the same place, only a few hundred feet higher. The clouds bumped against the upper slopes just enough to make the whole business dangerously slick.

After three days of this, we came through a pass. On either side, the mountains were capped with white ridges, the limestone forming strange and wild shapes, like shrines for some pagan mountain gods. A small stone chapel had been set up by the road for pilgrims, whether to give thanks for safely arriving at this point or to pray that they would make it down this last descent unharmed, I don't know. It was deserted. Below us stretched a green valley, a tiny village at the base of the mountain we had just skirted.

"If our directions are correct, then we've just come through the Eagle's Pass," said Theo. "And that makes this the Valley of the Eagle below us."

"That village is Gémenos?" I asked.

"Barely big enough to be called a village," he said. "Now, all we have to do is find a large number of cows with a small number of women minding them."

"And then what?"

"And then you will go talk to his wife."

"I will?"

"I can't go into a community of religious women," he said, looking slightly shocked. "Think of the scandal, not to mention the temptation. On both sides."

"Can't have that," I agreed. "All right. Sounds like a job for me."

"Her name is—"

"Hélène, I know," I said.

The trip down from the pass took longer than I thought. At many points Theo jumped down from the wain and guided Zeus through the turns, gripping his bridle while I held the reins so tightly, my knuckles were whiter than my face. Portia slept blissfully throughout.

We passed through the forest clinging to the massif, enormous oaks and slender beeches giving way to dogwood, hazel, and linden as we neared the valley floor, their scent permeating everything. We emerged near sunset, so we pulled the wain over by a stream that had joined us after first cascading over a stone outcropping to our left. The water was cold and delicious.

"Nothing like being the first to taste of a stream," I said. "It's so much better than city water. You never know what has polluted it by the time it gets to you."

"That's why I prefer wine and ale," said Theophilos. "There's a farm up ahead. Let's see if they'll let us spend the night."

The astonished faces of farmers seeing fools emerge from the forest is one I always enjoy. We have been mistaken for fairies, or worse, devils, but it didn't take long for us to win their friendship, especially when they saw Portia. We soon were sitting at their table, trading songs for soup.

I woke in the morning to hear a *chardonneret* singing, a good little jester bird with a motley of red, white, and black on its face. I walked out of the stables where we were sleeping and spotted it trilling at the top of a yoke elm. We looked at each other curiously; then it shot into the air. Before I could figure out why, a sparrowhawk swooped out of the sky and sank its talons into the little bird's neck.

I must have cried out, because Theo was at my side in an instant, dagger in hand, looking everywhere. "Are you all right?" he asked.

"It was just a bird," I said. "A pretty little thing. A hawk killed it."

"Oh," he said, slipping the dagger back into its scabbard. He glanced behind him and nodded approvingly. "Everything's fine, Apprentice."

I looked to see Helga lowering her bow.

"Being a fool means that you are jumpy everywhere," I observed.

"If you want to live to be an old fool, yes," he said.

Our hostess was out, feeding the chickens. She smiled as I walked up with Portia, who was looking everywhere.

"She looks like a mischief," said the woman.

"She comes by it honestly," I replied. "Do you know of a community of women who serve the Bishop of Marseille here?"

"Certainly," she said. "Over that end of the valley, about two miles. They'll be bringing the cattle up to pasture about now. You're not joining them, are you?"

"Hardly," I laughed. "I know one from earlier times. I want to see her since I'm in the area. Hélène of Marseille."

"Oc, I know her," said the woman. "One of the older ones, but she does a full day's work."

"Don't we all?" I said, patting the baby, who burped and caused a minor panic among the chickens.

We gathered our gear, thanked our hosts, and rode south. Eventually, we saw a herd of cattle in the distance, grazing on the lower slopes of the mountain, a group of women tending to them with a pack of small dark dogs dashing about.

"You're on," said Theo. "Do you want to ride Zeus? It would be quicker."

"Not if my life depended on it," I said, jumping down from the wain and stretching my legs. "No offense," I said to the beast, patting him on the neck as I walked by. He craned his head around and snapped at my hand.

The walk was pleasant but uphill, and despite the cool air, I was sweating heavily by the time I reached the women, who were resting in the shade of a solitary oak. They had seen me approaching for some time, of course, and their expressions were curious but not unfriendly.

"Greetings, good ladies," I said. "I am Domna Gile, a jester. I seek Hélène of Marseille."

One of the women rose. "I am Hélène," she said.

She was brown from so much time in the sun, and the skin around her eyes was cracked and slightly spotted. The eyes themselves were sharp, focusing intently on mine. She wore a simple gray woolen robe, much like those of the lay brothers at Le Thoronet. The hair peeking out from under her scarf was gray as well. I knew that she had to be close to Folc's age, but she looked twenty years older.

"May I have a private word with you, Domna?" I asked.

She looked at another woman there who nodded.

"Very well," said Hélène. "Come with me."

As she walked, a pair of dogs bounded up to her sides. They came over and sniffed me, then went back to their mistress.

"Is my husband dead?" she asked softly as I joined her.

"He lives and is well," I replied. "How did you know this concerned him?"

"He was a troubadour of the Fools' Guild," she said. "And here come a flock of jesters, something rarely seen here. I could see your motley for miles. I thought it must be bad news."

"I apologize," I said. "We did not mean to cause you unwarranted distress."

"What about warranted distress?" she asked, smiling ruefully.

"You are too quick for this poor fool, Domna," I said. "We have come in his behalf. He may be in danger from some old enemy. We seek any information about his former life that might help us."

"Tell me," she said, sitting on a large rock and beckoning to me to join her.

I quickly recounted the details of the murder and the message left on the walls of the library.

She gasped in horror during the telling, and looked faint when I had done. "Tell me what I can do to help you," she said immediately.

"We thought the 'lark' might have been your husband," I said. "Was that ever his nickname?"

"Not that I knew of," she said. "Folquet was the name he used when performing. His real name is Folc."

She stopped to give a brief command to the two dogs, who promptly darted off to retrieve a cow that had wandered off from the herd. The beast lumbered back, looking mildly perturbed, then lowered its head and grazed again. The dogs bounded back to us, and she patted them on the head.

"They mind you well," I said.

"Yes, they do," she said fondly. "They are named after my boys. Something to remind me of them."

"They have become monks, too, I understand. Your sons, I mean, not the dogs."

"They have," she said with pride. "I hear from them once in a while."

"When did you last see them?" I asked.

"In 1195, when my husband decided to devote our lives to Christ," she said. "Eight—no, nine years ago. They would be eighteen and twenty, now. I miss them. You never stop being their mother."

I felt a sharp pang of sympathy.

"Tell me, what enemies did your husband have before he joined the order?"

"Enemies," she mused, frowning slightly.

"Either from his commercial dealings, or his Guild activities," I added. "Someone who might carry a grudge to the present day."

"The merchants of Marseille were ever a fickle lot," she said. "Forming alliances only to betray them, undercutting their own families at every turn. But to pursue my husband after he left all that after all this time—no, I can't imagine any of them would spend a bent penny to do that."

"From his Guild activities, then?"

"He never told me much about them," she said. "You know how it is—you're married to one. Although it must be different, being a jester yourself."

"I am a Guildmember," I said. "But we are a married couple just like any other. We each have our secrets."

"Of course," she said. "Still, you're lucky. It's much easier being in the Guild than being married to it. The disappearances for months at a time, never knowing what dangers he might be in."

"That actually describes life with my first husband," I said. "He went off on Crusade, and I spent two years praying for his safe return."

"Did he return safely?"

"He did."

"Then he had your prayers to thank for his well-being."

"It is good of you to say so."

"But this jester is your second husband?"

"Yes. I married him after my first husband died, and then became a jester myself. He was my teacher."

"How strange life is," she said. "I could never have become a troubadour. I sing like a crow."

"I like crows," I said. "They're mischievous and smart. What was it like being married to a troubadour? I always thought that would be wonderfully romantic."

"He wooed me with song," she said, suddenly a dreamy young girl again. "And after we wed, there were oft times when he would sing only to me, even if there was a crowd of people around."

"That must have been lovely," I said.

"For a long time, it was," she said. "But one day, he stopped singing."

"To you?"

"To all," she said. "He came home from his travels on some business with a cloud over his face. He went into our room and stayed there for three days without saying a word. Then he came out and announced that he was becoming a monk."

"Just like that? Had he never shown any signs of this religious fervor before?"

"Never before," she said. "He sold all of our possessions, and bundled us off into holy orders."

"Why, that's—" I was about to say something sharp, but she looked at me serenely. Very well, it was not my life. "That must have been a . . . difficult adjustment."

"It was, at first," she admitted. "But there's something to be said for having regular order to your life. The Cistercian rules, and the cows' rules. We know what we are going to be doing every day of our lives."

"Who's stricter, the Cistercians or the cows?"

"Oh, the cows," she laughed. "If they don't get milked or fed on time, they can become quite surly. God is willing to wait for His prayers."

"Ah, but His wrath is more powerful than a cow's."

"You'd be surprised," she said. "If they stampede—One of our order was trampled to death a month ago."

"How horrible! Were you close?"

"She had just joined us," she said. "No one knew her well. She was a city woman who came to us from a convent, and knew nothing about the real world. She didn't see the warning signs. It was a stormy day, and the herd was agitated. Then something startled them, and she didn't know where to take cover."

"Never underestimate the wrath of females," I said, and we sat and watched the herd for a while. They looked peaceful enough.

"See that bull down there?" she said, pointing to a large black beast in a fenced-off enclosure.

"Is he the only one?" I asked.

"Yes," she said. "We call him the Bishop."

"That doesn't bode well for breeding," I said.

"He does just fine," she said. "We call him that for luck. We're hoping that Marseille will recognize us as an official order and build us our own abbey."

"This would be a lovely spot for it," I said, getting to my feet. "I wish you luck."

"Where will you go next?"

"To Marseille," I said. "Maybe the answer lies there."

"My brother, Julien Guiraud, is a merchant there," she said. "Tell him that you spoke to me, and he will give you any assistance you require."

"Thank you, that is most gracious," I said.

"Will you be seeing my husband again?" she asked.

"God willing, yes," I said.

She looked across at the bull, grazing quietly in his little enclosure. "Tell him that he is in my prayers," she said softly.

"I will, Domna," I promised.

By the time I had walked back down the hill, it was noon. I heard Portia squealing happily, which aroused my suspicions. Sure enough, I came upon my husband tossing her into the air and catching her.

"I should have had triplets so you could juggle three," I said as I came up.

"But how do you nurse triplets?" he asked. "Speaking of which, take her. She's starving."

"So am I," I grumbled. He helped me up onto the wain, handed me Portia, and tossed me a piece of bread.

"Any luck?" he asked as he flicked the reins.

"Not really," I said. I recounted my conversation.

"The merchant angle seems unlikely," he mused. "I can't think of a purely monetary reason to hold a grudge that long. But we can look up the brother when we get there."

"How long to Marseille from here?"

"Hopefully, we'll arrive before sunset tomorrow. This valley sends milk and cheese there, so it can't be too long a journey."

He glanced back at the holy women and their charges. "Pretty spot," he said. "Quiet, peaceful. I think I'd go mad."

"Would you ever join a holy order?" I asked.

His laughter subsided about eight minutes later. "What on earth possessed you to say such a thing?" he asked, wiping the tears streaking his whiteface with his kerchief. "You know me better than that."

"What possessed Folc to join? There he was, prosperous merchant, celebrated singer, wife and two boys—then overnight, he is a servant of Christ. Why couldn't that happen to you?"

"Because I am me, not Folc," he said. "Besides, no respectable order would take me."

"All I am saying is that it could happen," I persisted. "And then what would become of Portia and me?"

"Ah, so that's what this is about," he said. "I vow by all that is sacred that if I suddenly turn monk, I will not condemn the two of you to the cloister. Satisfied?"

"Could I have it in writing? Sworn and sealed by a reputable notary?"

"Are you serious?"

"I have never been more serious," I said.

"Well, stop it at once; it's bad for the act," he said.

Something in my look caused him to wince. I made a mental note to teach Helga that look. And Portia, when she was older.

"Fine, one sealed and notarized release if I turn monk," he said. "Shall I draw up my will while I'm at it?"

"Maybe," I said.

"What will you do if I die?" he asked.

"Hélène said they want their own abbey here. Maybe I'll join them."

"Become a milkmaid?"

"It would be a welcome change from living with a fool," I

snapped. "Peace and quiet at last. I think it's the absence of men that causes that."

He guffawed and held out his hand. "Truce?" he asked.

"Truce," I said, taking it.

Behind us, I heard Helga sigh with relief.

THREE

Where is my clown? I need him now, to take my troubles away.

—BLACKMORE'S NIGHT, "FOOL'S GOLD"

"Ever been to Marseille?" I asked as we were ferried across the river that flowed into the city's harbor.

"Once, as a child," said Claudia. "When Father took my brother and me to Paris, we sailed first from Sicily into Marseille. I remember seeing Lazarus's Grotto and having nightmares that he was going to rise again and come looking for me."

"You actually believed that story?" I asked. "My most skeptical wife, I am astounded."

"I was eight years old," she said defensively. "The priests at the abbey said it was where Saint Lazarus heard confession after he became Bishop, and who was I to contradict all of those priests?"

"The abbey does very well with that legend," I said. "I think they also say Mary Magdalene ended up here. Along with all of the others whose story didn't finish in the Gospels."

"I thought she ended up in that cave in the mountains," she said. "Wasn't there some abbey we passed claiming her?"

"At least three, I think."

"Why would she come all the way to Languedoc just to live in a cave?" asked Helga. "Didn't they have caves in the Holy Land?"

"They did," I said. "But they became very popular and overpriced after Our Lord and Savior made his appearance. All those hermits competing for space. It's no wonder she left."

"And how did people here know who she was?" persisted Helga. "She would have gotten here before the Book was written. Nobody would have known she was of importance, and it's not as if she could tell them, yes, that was me, I was the girl in the story. She wasn't anyone yet."

"Everyone who isn't anyone comes to Marseille," Claudia said as the ferry bumped into the wharf. "And now, we are here."

The ferrymen secured the boat and lowered a plank ramp. I guided Zeus and the wain carefully onto the wharf.

"Do you know Pantalan, the Fool?" I asked one of the ferrymen.

"Sure," he said, grinning. "He spilled a pint of ale on my head once. Funniest thing you ever saw."

"It certainly sounds it," I said. "Do you know where he lives?"

"Somewhere in the Ville-Haute, near the church of Saint-Martin," he said. "Ask around. Try—"

"The taverns?" guessed my wife, smiling sweetly.

"Oc, Domna," he said. "I expect a looker like you will be welcome there."

"How gallant!" sighed Claudia, doing that fluttering business that so often swayed lesser men. Helga watched her studiously.

"Come, wife," I said. "The sun is plummeting, and we must find our friend before the nightwatch comes out."

I guided Zeus past the competing hostels of the Templars and the Hospitalers and stopped. In front of us was the mad profusion of wharves, inns, brothels, warehouses, and shops that made up the Ville-Basse. Through them swarmed hundreds of pilgrims seeking supplies to keep them alive during the forty-day journey to the Holy Land, and twice as many Marseillese seeking to overcharge them for those supplies. On the other side of the harbor, a safe distance away, the walls of the Abbey of Saint-Victor stood in solitary rebuke to the manifestation of greed facing it. Where Lazarus died a second time, and no one there to raise him. I looked at the abbey shutting out the world, then back at the Ville-Basse, which made one appreciate why they would want to.

"What's wrong?" asked Claudia.

"I barely recognize this place," I said. "It's doubled in size since I was last here."

"This Pantalan will help us," she said. "Do you know him well?"

"I knew him for the same week that I knew Folc, and that was a long time ago," I said. "I wasn't expecting to come here. I thought that we would go to Le Thoronet to convince Folc, then go straight to Toulouse. I didn't bother bringing myself up to date on Marseille."

"Well, Pantalan's in the Guild; so there's our start," she said. "And we now have Hélène's brother, so that's twice as much help. We came into Constantinople with less."

"And almost got ourselves killed several times over," I reminded her.

"But if Constantinople couldn't kill us, I doubt that Marseille can," she said confidently.

"Your logic is impeccable," I said. "I feel much better now."

"But just in case, let's find that notary in the morning," she added.

The Ville-Haute was the section of the city ceded to the Church during the great partition some forty years before. The Church promptly built walls around the district, and we found them easily enough. From there, it was just a short ride to the gate.

"Why do they want to wall themselves off from the rest of the city?" asked Helga.

"Because as great and noble Christians, they do not wish to sully themselves with common pilgrims," I replied.

"Why then would a fool live here?" she wondered.

"Ask him when you see him," I said. "In fact, that will be your next assignment, Apprentice."

We spotted the church of Saint-Martin by its bell tower and made our way toward it, passing rows of carpentry shops. The Ville-Haute had an unusual but not unpleasant assortment of smells, the fresh-cut wood and sawdust mingling with the aroma of cured leather from two streets down, both giving way to flower and herb gardens near the church.

Queries to a series of locals brought us to a courtyard with a cistern in its center. One of the two-storied houses facing it had a grinning white face surmounted by cap and bells painted on its door. We pulled up in front of it.

"A serenade?" I suggested, and we stood on the wain, Claudia with Portia in her arms, and sang:

Lord of emptiness, King without subjects,
Ruler with no rules.

A short, stout man stuck his head out of the second-story window, his whiteface, cap, and bells the mirror to the image painted on his door.

All hail Pantalan, a jester's jester,
Emperor of Fools!

"Passable!" he cried. "Now, once more, sing from the gut, especially that poor excuse for a scarecrow on the tenor voice, and above all, give me sincerity!"

We repeated the song as the women of the other houses leaned out their windows and their children poured through the doorways to see what was causing the commotion. Pantalan conducted us from above, waving his arms grandly, then led the applause when we finished.

"Excellent, and welcome to Marseille, my peripatetic, peregrinate pelerins," he called. "I'll be down in a trice."

We waited, watching the door for his entrance. We should have known better. He came hurtling out the window, arms outstretched, and before anyone could scream, he reached the end of the rope tied around his waist. He swung down to the ground, landing lightly just before the front wall of the house. Everyone cheered, and he bowed, then slid the rope down and stepped out of it.

"Nicely done," I said, jumping down from the wain and helping the ladies. "A fool's welcome if ever there was one."

"Welcome again, my friends," he said, then added under his breath, "and who the hell are you?"

I whistled a few notes softly, and his eyes narrowed for a moment. Then he whistled the countermelody back.

"I know you," he said quietly. "You came back from Outremer with some silly minor king. End of '92 or thereabouts. I don't know the woman, though."

"I'm Tan Pierre, Guildname of Theophilos," I said. "My wife, Domna Gile, Guildname of Claudia."

"Pantalan, Guildname of Artal," he replied. "And the brats?"

"Our apprentice, Helga, and our daughter, Portia," I said, waiting. Sure enough, he walked over to Helga and looked her up and down.

"Scrawny little thing like this thinks she can be a jester?" he sneered. "I've seen more meat on a diseased chicken. After it's been plucked."

"And I've seen better manners from a hog," she replied. "After it's been slopped."

"Insult given, insult received," he said, nodding. "Not bad, child. Well, a passel of fools to put up and provision. Just a quick visit, I hope?"

"We may be a few days here," I said. "Something came up. You can keep us?"

"Two adults, a squalling infant, and a diseased chicken," he sighed. "My love life is over, not to mention any hope of sleep. I'll take your horse around to the stables."

As he reached for the reins, all three of us shouted, "Look out!"

He snatched his hand back just in time, the sound of Zeus's colliding teeth echoing through the courtyard.

"Don't tell me," said Pantalan. "The legendary Zeus. I've heard some stories about the two of you, but even more about this vicious beast. I'm surprised he wasn't eaten years ago."

"He's too tough and ornery to eat," I said. "Like me. We get along."

"Let's take your things inside and you can bring him to the stables yourself," said Pantalan.

The bottom room was filled with props and costumes, but there was a stack of pallets in one corner. We sent Helga with a brace of buckets to the cistern; then I took Zeus and the wain to the stables and paid for a week's accommodation.

When I returned, Pantalan was sitting on a low stool with Portia bouncing happily on his lap.

"Looks like her mother, at least as far as I can tell under your whiteface," he said. "Lucky for her."

"It is," I agreed as Claudia smiled at me. "Did you have that rope trick ready and waiting for us?"

"Oh, it's there all the time," he said. "You never know if a jealous husband or a spurned lover is going to barge in suddenly."

"Does that happen a lot?" asked Helga.

"Well, I live in hope," he said, grinning at her. "Come back for a visit when you're older."

"Looks like you could use a stronger rope," I said, leaning forward and patting his ample belly. "Have we been neglecting our exercises?"

"The fool must reflect his environment," he said serenely. "Marseille has grown fat and happy under my reign, and so have I. Now, am I to gather from your choice of password that you've come straight from Father Gerald?"

"With a few stops along the way," I said. "I am to be the new Chief Fool in Toulouse."

"My blessings upon you. It's that way," he said, jerking his thumb toward the west. "Leave in the morning, and you'll be there in a week or two."

"Yes, well, we have one little task to take care of first," I said. "Remember Folquet?"

"Of course," he said. "We worked together for years, from when I came to when he left."

"He may be in trouble," I said, and I told him what we knew.

He whistled softly when I got to the murder. "Who was this Brother Pelfort?" he asked.

"Someone who got in the way," I said. "The message was meant for Folquet. Any idea why someone would be looking for him?"

"A dozen years ago, I could give you a dozen reasons," he said. "He was the Guild chief here, and things were very active then. How much were you aware of?"

"Very little," I confessed. "I was just passing through."

"And that was after things had settled down," he said. "The real fun was when Barral died."

"Who was he?" asked Helga.

"The Viscount of Marseille. The man in charge, if anyone could be said to be in charge then. Lovely fellow, and quite fond of entertainers, lucky for us. He got along equally well with the decaying gentry, the mercenaries, the merchants, and the common folk, and he was smart enough to leave the Church to its own devices, so they didn't get in the way of anything. He had a wife, Adalaïs de Porcelet, who was considered the great beauty of the town."

"I remember hearing about her. Folquet wrote about her in a couple of songs."

"Yes, he called her Lady Pons. And Peire Vidal was another troubadour here back then—I'm sure you know his work. Absolutely besotted with the Viscountess, which got him in loads of trouble."

"I never heard that story."

"Oh, he was always mooning around, presenting her with one love song after another, sighing loudly whenever her name came up in conversation. God, it was embarrassing after a while. Anyhow, one day he waited for Barral to go off inspecting some vineyards somewhere, and slipped into her room while she was asleep. The word is, he started kissing and caressing her, and it was so dark that she mistook him for her husband."

"At least, that's what she told people after," guessed Claudia.

"No, apparently she was quite upset when she realized who it was," said Pantalan. "Screamed bloody murder, and went straight to her husband when he returned and demanded Vidal's head on a platter. Barral was too fond of Vidal to do that, but our heroic colleague was too frightened to believe it and caught the next boat to Genoa."

"Seems a prudent course to take."

"Well, things went downhill after that," continued Pantalan. "Adalaïs never forgave her husband for not smiting the troubadour, and he grew weary of her constant berating. So he divorces her and marries this younger woman, Marie de Montpellier."

"Of course," sighed Claudia.

"But he dies inside of a year, leaving her pregnant," said Pantalan.

"Natural death?" I asked.

"As far as we could tell, and we looked into it," said Pantalan. "Basically, he was no spring chicken, and he had a lusty new young wife, so we think that she just wore him out."

"Served him right," muttered Claudia.

"They say he died smiling," said Pantalan.

She glared at him, and he chuckled.

"What did this have to do with Folquet?" I asked.

"Well, needless to say, with Barral dead, the succession was very much in question. No one wanted the young widow from Montpellier or her spawn to be running things, but that left everything up in the air. Marseille was ripe for taking over. Toulouse was always claiming it,

Montpellier wanted to gain a toehold, and Aragon and Genoa were itching to send their navies in. The key to power was a cousin of Barral's named Adalacie, who was the heiress to the family fortunes. This cad, Hughes de Baux, came on the gallop from Orange to woo and win her. After the wedding, it turns out that he was in league with King Alfonse of Aragon, who promptly shows up with his navy and asks everyone to bow down and give homage."

He paused and looked at Portia, who had been listening to him raptly, straight in the eye.

"Only they didn't," he whispered to her, wagging his finger. "They wouldn't let the big bad king and his nasty navy into the harbor. They raised the chain and barred him from sea and land."

"And that was the Guild's doing?" I asked.

"Folquet brought his fellow merchants together, and I raised the rabble," he said proudly. "But Folquet realized that the town needed a leader to rally behind as they had with Barral. So, he came up with another Barral."

"How did he do that?" asked Claudia.

"Because there was another Barral—his little brother, Roncelin. Only problem was he had gone monk years before and joined the Abbey of Saint-Victor. Folquet convinced his fellow merchants that Roncelin was the man for the job, and they got the mercenaries to join them. Unfortunately, the monks liked Roncelin at the abbey, liked him so much that when they saw the crowds coming across the harbor to storm the walls, they tried to make Roncelin their abbot so it would be harder for him to leave. But the Marseillese dragged him out and carried him in triumph to the Hôtel de Barral and installed him as the new viscount, with a wife thrown into the bargain. Barral's widow was bought off, her pregnancy hushed up. Roncelin has been here ever since, and Aragon has stayed away."

"So he's now in charge?" I asked.

"Not in the least," said Pantalan. "He's a viscount who doesn't count. Marseille is run by a consulat made up of merchants and gentry, backed up by the mercenaries, all for the great purpose of running the city profitably with as little outside interference as possible. Roncelin mopes in luxury. The Pope excommunicated him, and periodically threatens to impose an interdict on the entire city, but nobody cares as long as they can keep fleecing the pilgrims, coming and going."

"Did this Roncelin know that Folquet was behind his being pulled out of his monastic life?" asked Claudia.

"Probably," said Pantalan.

"And do you know why Folquet became a monk himself?"

"He never told me," said Pantalan. "Just up and left without so much as a good-bye."

"What are you thinking?" I asked Claudia.

"Roncelin is forced by Folquet to leave an abbey, then Folquet joins one," she said. "It restores a balance, somehow."

"I don't see the connection," said Pantalan. "Folquet didn't join the Cistercians until three years after Roncelin was made Viscount."

"I am thinking about the impact of being forced away from God to serve Mammon," said Claudia. "To be deprived of His love and protection, to be excommunicated by the Pope himself, and to be held a prisoner in your own house. I could see Roncelin wishing to take revenge on the man who caused his sorrows."

"But after all these years?" objected Pantalan.

"Resentments can grow over time," said Claudia. "And revenges can take time to plan. God knows my husband and I have seen such in our own lives after years of quiet."

"It's a possibility," I said. "Certainly a place to start. You have access to the Hôtel de Barral?"

"Of course," he said huffily. "I have access to every house in Marseille."

"Then you and I shall go there tomorrow," I said.

"What about me?" exclaimed Claudia. "It was my idea."

"It was," I said. "But we have to split up. I need you to speak with Hélène's brother to see what he knows."

"Ah, the noble Julien," said Pantalan. "He's in the Ville-Basse near the Saint-Esprit hospital. He lives over his shop near the mercers' wharf."

"Why do you call him noble?" she asked.

"Because he's a good man for a merchant," replied Pantalan. "Visits his sister monthly ever since she was thrust into holy orders. There are plenty who abandon their relatives once that happens."

Portia suddenly nestled against the fool's chest, her eyes half-closed. He looked down at her in astonishment.

"I've become boring," he whispered. "My conversation usually doesn't have this effect until after the fourth cup."

"Looks like he's got your job, Helga," I said.

Pantalan rocked the baby expertly back and forth until her eyelids completed their downward journey; then he placed her gently in her cradle. He looked at her and sighed. "I enjoyed that," he said softly. "Never thought about having children."

"Why not?" I asked.

"Because then I would have to grow up," he said, smiling. "Good night, fellow fools. I will see you in the morning."

We were up and doing our stretches in the courtyard when our host emerged, yawning and blinking in the midmorning sun. He watched us for a while.

"I remember that one," he said as Helga stood on one leg and put her other foot behind her head.

"Could you ever do it?" she asked.

"When I was thirteen, after four years at the Guildhall," he said. "Two decades and many meals ago."

He bent over, scraped the tips of his fingers against his toes one time, straightened, and rolled his head from side to side. Then he shrugged his shoulders until they cracked. "Ready," he announced.

I collected my gear, planted kisses on various noses and lips, and joined him.

"The Hôtel de Barral is in the Ville Prévôtale," he said as we emerged from the courtyard and headed west. "That's the part of the city the nobles reserved for themselves in the partitioning. They have their own wharves and one fortified château after another. The Barrals have their place near the prison, appropriately enough."

"And they are free to receive visitors?"

"They are free to do what they want and go where they want," he said. "Just so long as guards from the Viguerie are with them at all times. If Roncelin takes one step toward his old abbey, they will gently escort him back to the château and remind him of his limitations."

"What's the wife like?"

"Her name's Eudiarde. She's from Aragon, related to the current king in some way. They threw her in as a sop to Alfonse, just so he thought he had some sway here, and they thought she was pretty enough to make a monk forswear his vows, as if that's ever a problem."

"So they make a happy couple?"

"About as far from it as I have ever seen," he said. "And I've seen plenty of unhappy marriages. Present company emphatically excluded, of course. How do you two do so well?"

"We get to throw dangerous objects at each other daily," I said. "It builds trust."

He snorted, and we walked along. This part of the city was up high, giving us a good view of the harbor, which was busy. Ahead was the sea, dotted with fishing boats returning with their catch. It was a pleasant sight, and Pantalan was humming, which might normally have fit in with the day, but it was a sad melody.

"What is that tune?" I asked. "I've never heard it."

"I'm not sure," he said. "It popped into my head this morning. I can't remember all of it, and I don't know the words, but I can't shake it. Does that ever happen to you?"

A sudden memory of a man lying on the ground, my dagger in his throat.

"All the time," I said, and I started humming something happier to clear my mind. Pantalan joined in with the counterpoint; then we started singing in earnest, bouncing the song off the walls, sending it around corners and up to Heaven, just in case God needed some cheering up.

The Hôtel de Barral was a three-story stone building, with an entrance gate set in a stone arch facing a large wharf. Beyond it, the Saint-Jean fort squatted at the entrance to the harbor, the great chain dangling from its windlass, its length resting peaceably at the harbor floor. The lowest level of the château doubled as a warehouse for whatever was coming in or going out, but there was no activity at the moment. There were large windows on the second story, smaller ones at the top, but all of them were shuttered tight. A pair of bored-looking guards stood in the shade of the entrance, their attentions directed toward the château rather than at the street.

"Greetings, Arnaut, Matieu," said Pantalan, startling them.

"What's going on?" said the guard nearer to us. "And who's the other one?"

"Entertainment is going on," replied Pantalan. "A colleague has come for a visit, so I thought I would introduce him to the Viscount, just so he could brag to his family about it. This is Tan Pierre."

"Not much to brag about," said the guard. "Welcome to Marseille, Fool, and good luck entertaining His Solemnity. It's like a tomb in there."

"Nothing like a pair of fools to rouse the dead," said Pantalan cheerfully. "May we pass?"

"Sure, why not?" said the guard. "Wish we could watch the show."

"We'll be at the Green Pilgrim tonight," said Pantalan. "It will be worth the visit just to see this fellow's wife. Prettiest thing in whiteface you've ever laid eyes on."

"But married," I said hastily.

"More's the pity," said Pantalan.

"Green Pilgrim it is," said the guard, and we went inside.

An underworked seneschal eyed us dubiously but nevertheless led us up a grand staircase to the second level, then through an immense set of oaken doors into a large empty room. Tapestries depicting various ancestors of the Viscount in chivalric settings hung around us, but the room was too dark for me to see them in detail.

"The parties this room would see when Barral was alive were something," murmured Pantalan. "There would be hundreds of guests and as many servants, dozens of musicians and entertainers. Now, this."

"Where is your lord?" I asked the seneschal, who was taking a cloth cover off an ancient pair of chairs carved from wood darker than the room.

"At prayer," he replied. "He has a private chapel. It gets more use than any room here."

"How long will he be?" asked Pantalan.

"Until his prayers are answered," said the seneschal.

"I don't know if we can wait that long," said Pantalan.

"I don't know if anyone can wait that long," I said. "Could you tell him that a pair of fools have come to visit?"

"Yes, let him cease his prayers for a while," said Pantalan. "God could probably use the break."

The seneschal grimaced and shuffled off.

"There's something missing here," said Pantalan. He walked over to the large windows at the far end of the hall and threw the shutters open, one by one. "Let there be light!"

And there was light, which illuminated the dust that had collected on every surface in the room. The tapestries' colors were dull and faded, and the wooden floor was pitted and stained.

"Servants' day off has lasted a good twelve years, I'd say," commented Pantalan.

"Which may have been the last time you set foot in this place," said a man standing in the doorway opposite.

"Viscount Barral, a pleasure to see you," said Pantalan as we both bowed.

"What brings you here?" said the Viscount, blinking rapidly as he stepped into the light.

"I would have come sooner, but I was waiting for you to throw a party," said Pantalan. "I sat by my door, listening for the footsteps of your messenger bearing my invitation. People would come by, urging me to give up, to entertain elsewhere, at the very least to partake of some meager sustenance, but I never lost hope. 'No, no!' I would cry. 'What if my lord sends for me and I am not here to rush to his side and lighten his heart with a song?' Finally, I decided to come myself and find out when I could expect it."

"When Hell freezes over," said the Viscount.

"But that happened just this morning," I said. "We put on our skates and came immediately."

He looked at me for the first time, and I looked back at him. I saw a man I would have taken for a monk, albeit a more affluent member of the order. His robes were white, but trimmed with ermine, and he was nervously fingering a large gold pendant that would have been out of place in an abbey. He was balding, which gave him the effect of being tonsured.

"Who is this?" he asked Pantalan.

"A fellow fool, come to visit Marseille," said Pantalan. "His name is Tan Pierre, and he is of abundant talent."

"Tell him to take it to someone who needs it," said the Viscount. "Tell him to—"

"Roncelin, my lord, is this any way to behave to your guests?" scolded a woman coming into the room.

"They aren't guests. They are fools," he replied ungraciously.

"Even better," she said, beaming at us. "Much more entertaining than your relatives."

"Domna Eudiarde, how delightful to see you," said Pantalan, winking at her as he bowed.

She simpered happily, then turned to me. "And who is this tall fellow?"

"Tan Pierre, at your service," I said, bowing deeply. "A visitor to your fair city."

She was a robust woman with black hair that was coiled into a pair of elaborate braids on either side of her head. She wore a gown of the vivid red cloth that was a specialty of this city. That, combined with her olive complexion, managed to make her husband look even more corpselike by comparison. She posed in a manner that was meant to be grand, but swayed like a boat in bad weather.

"Two fools, two of us," she said. "I have an excellent fancy, my lord husband. Allow me to show this visitor the splendor of your house while you and Pantalan catch up on old times."

"Take both of them and leave me in peace," suggested the Viscount.

"Nonsense," she scoffed. "He's just what you need right now. Well, you need to have a cup of wine more than anything, but start with the fool. I would like to see you smile once this year."

"But—"

"Husband, will you do me this small favor!" she shouted.

Her voice echoed faintly about the room, muffled quickly by the dust-ridden tapestries. He looked down at his feet and nodded.

"Thank you," she said. "Sieur Pierre, if you will?"

I offered her my arm, and she took it greedily. I caught a look of warning from Pantalan as I escorted her out of the room. She was tottering unsteadily despite her death grip on my arm, and when we reached the top of the stairs, she looked at them with trepidation.

"I must beg your indulgence, Fool," she said. "Will you put your arm around me as we descend? I am so fearful of falling."

"Of course, Domna," I said.

She leaned into me heavily as we negotiated the steps, and did not immediately relinquish my hold as we reached the bottom. I gently dislodged her, and she pouted for a moment. "I must apologize for my husband's behavior," she said. "He was the baby of his family, and has never truly grown up. Sometimes, one must treat him as the child that he is."

"There is no need for a noble lady such as yourself to apologize for anything," I said.

"That's true, isn't it?" she replied, brightening. "I often think that the world owes me an apology or two. Laurent! Fetch me wine, and bring it to the garden!"

"Yes, Domna," came a faint voice from somewhere in the château.

"The garden is lovely this time of year," she said. "Would you care to see it?"

"Of course," I said, and she latched on to my arm again and pulled me toward the interior courtyard.

The garden was not all that lovely. Whoever had planted it must have had a mind for the spring and summer only, but this late in the year, little was in bloom and much was dry and brown. An elderly gardener, also dry and brown, was trimming back some bushes, a pile of sackcloths by him to wrap them for the winter. The stoppered neck of a wineskin poked out from beneath the top cloth, no doubt having been shoved there just before our entrance.

"We'll walk about the perimeter, shall we?" she said. "It's my only exercise. It is precisely eighty-seven steps around if I go to the right, but only eighty-six if I go to the left. I've never understood why."

"You know your garden well," I said as we began walking.

"I know the exact dimensions of every place in this prison," she said. "Château, I mean. I know over which point the sun will emerge on every day of the year, and which stars will pass over each night. I should become an astronomer."

The seneschal emerged with two large cups of wine and a pitcher. She motioned to him impatiently, and he brought them to us. She snatched one from his hand, saluted us briefly, and downed it in one gulp. She held it out, and he refilled it, then placed the pitcher on a low table and left us. I sipped mine slowly.

"I know the life history of every servant here," she continued. "And of every soldier that keeps us inside."

"And that of your husband?"

"I know him, and I know him not," she said, glancing up at me slyly. "You're a tall fellow."

"Only from the feet up," I said, and she giggled girlishly.

"I like tall men," she said. "I once was courted by a tall man."

"What happened to him?"

"Oh, the family wanted to keep a foothold here," she said. "I am that foot."

"Of course, you're of the royal family of Aragon," I said. "That explains it."

"Explains what, Fool?"

"The source of your beauty. The women of Aragon are legendary for it."

Her mouth hung open for a second; then she quickly filled it with wine and swallowed.

"Now, that was wonderful!" she exclaimed. "That is how a compliment should be paid. Just try and find some courtly behavior in this giant market that passes for a city. None! And along comes a fool, and he's got more manners than anyone here."

I bowed.

"Have you ever been to Aragon?" she asked, her eyes misting.

"I'm afraid not, Domna," I said. "The closest I have come was Barcelona. But had I known that you were in Aragon, I would have made the pilgrimage."

"There, you see? That's how it's done!" she said, almost crying. "You must give my husband lessons. Do you speak Catalan?"

"I do, and I understand Aragonese. I know a few of your songs."

"Oh, would you sing one? I haven't heard my tongue sung in ages."

I unslung my lute and sang an alba by Giraut de Bornelh. It was a favorite at the Guildhall, and when I was done, she sighed and dabbed at her eyes with her kerchief.

"I cannot remember the last time I heard anyone sing in this house," she said.

"Your husband does not care for it?"

"He cares for nothing but God," she said.

"A very pious man," I said carefully.

"What good is a pious man to his wife?" she said, holding her cup out.

I refilled it, and some of it slopped over the lip onto a rosebush as she rushed it to her lips.

"A libation," she said. "Let its sacrifice be not in vain."

"To whom do you make sacrifice?"

"To the old gods," she said. "To anyone listening. Am I truly beautiful?"

"The most beautiful flower in this garden," I said.

She glanced about uncertainly, and I hoped that there was something nearby in bloom to which she could compare herself. Fortunately, some faded pansies lingered in a corner, and she nodded, satisfied.

"I was only beautiful enough to be bartered for this man," she said. "He is the viscount of a great city, they told me. He's been living in an abbey for years, they told me, and he'll be on you like a thirsty man diving into a desert oasis. To seduce a monk, what could be simpler, I thought? But he prefers the desert, and I am the one left parched."

She was thirsty, I observed as she spilled the dregs of the pitcher into her cup.

"What does he pray for?" I asked.

"Release," she said. "Release from care, release from responsibility, release from duty. Release from this house, and from me."

"He must be bitter indeed to wish to escape such a lovely warden."

"Bitter doesn't begin to describe him," she whispered. "He cries out for punishment and for vengeance. He lashes himself."

"My goodness!"

"I have offered to help him with that part," she said, giggling again. "For charity's sake."

"You are indeed a virtuous lady, Domna," I said. "You said that he prays for vengeance? Surely that is not a proper subject for prayer."

"But our God is a wrathful god," she argued. "If He has wreaked His vengeance on so many people so many times, then that must be something we can pray for, don't you think?"

"I think that God's vengeance is His alone," I said. "But I am merely a fool. These philosophical debates I leave to great ones such as yourself. Do you know who your husband wishes God's wrath to visit?"

"Just about everyone here," she said.

"Have his prayers ever been answered?"

"Oh, every now and then some merchant or nobleman dies, and Roncelin starts dancing with glee, claiming his plan is working. But it always seems to be a death from old age, or illness, things that happen in the natural course of events. And it's never someone I've heard him single out. I shouldn't be saying all of this, but I do so enjoy talking to you. I haven't had a good, old-fashioned gossip in such a long time."

"I enjoy listening, Domna," I said. "Did he ever mention a man named Folquet in his prayers?"

"Among others," she said. "I remember him. Handsome man, voice like an angel."

She yawned abruptly, her wine-stained teeth in full view back to the molars.

"I must have a little nap, I think," she said. "This exercise has done me much good. If you like, you may join me."

"Domna, I am flattered beyond comprehension," I said. "Alas, I have duties elsewhere."

"But you will come back," she said urgently, clutching my arm.

"I will visit you again," I promised, hoping that she had drunk enough that she would not remember my words enough to hold me to them.

"That's good," she mumbled, and she reached out for a stone bench that was in the middle of a tiny tiled square in the midst of some pear trees. There was a cushion that someone had thoughtfully left there, no doubt anticipating such spontaneous naps. I left her in her garden as she snored lustily away, and made my way back to the grand staircase to wait for my colleague.

After a while, I heard shouting from upstairs. Then a door opened, and Pantalan came running out at top speed. He grabbed the stair post and swung around it as a spear sailed through the doorway and struck the floor just behind him.

"Let's go!" he shouted as he leapt down the steps.

We flew out the door.

"Stop!" he commanded. "Breathe. Stroll until we are past the guards."

We ambled by them as if we hadn't a care in the world.

"How did it go?" asked one of them.

"Splendidly," said Pantalan. "Don't forget the Green Pilgrim tonight."

We walked quickly until we were out of sight of the château.

"Time for a drink," he said, pulling me into a tavern where he was greeted by the barmaids with smiles and wine. He poured two cups and raised his.

"The Guild," he said.

"The Guild," I echoed, and we knocked cups and drank. "What was that all about?"

"He's insane," he said. "I was using my best material, and not a single laugh. I swear I will make him smile if it's the last thing I ever do."

"It might have been if he was any good with that spear," I said. "What prompted that?"

"I was saying that maybe if he started taking an interest in the world outside his chapel, he might find that the city would welcome him with open arms. He starts screaming that he wanted no part of anyone or anything that belonged to Marseille, and grabs this spear that must have been mounted on the wall since the Phoenicians founded the place. I took that as my cue to exit."

"Pretty good throw for a man of the cloth."

"I've been neglectful," he said. "I should have looked in on him long before this. He may only be a figurehead, but he still has the potential to make trouble. And if he has this much anger—"

"Anything about Folquet?"

"No. And I couldn't really steer the conversation that way without being obvious. But I don't think it's him."

"Why not?"

"Because I don't know how he could have gotten a man to Le Thoronet. He has no access to anyone."

"Except the guards," I pointed out. "What if he's corrupted one of them?"

"But he has no money of his own," said Pantalan. "Oh, hell, maybe there's some stashed away in the château that nobody knew about. Well, if one of the Viguerie has gone on any long trips recently, I should be able to find out about it. How did you get on with the wife?"

"My virtue remained intact, but it was a near thing."

"Poor Eudiarde. Can't even have a decent affair in this house."

"I leave her to you."

"Oh, no," he protested. "Roncelin may despise being married, but I don't think he'll take kindly to being cuckolded for all that."

"Did Folquet ever throw a romantic song her way? Something to make Roncelin jealous?"

"Never. Folquet wasn't like that at all. Devoted to his wife. He just wrote the romantic songs for show."

"I give up," I said, getting to my feet. "Let's go back to your place and rehearse something for this performance you've roped me into at the Green Pilgrim."

"All right," he said.

As we walked back, he started humming that plaintive song again.

"There it is," he said, shaking his head. "Can't get rid of it. *Tum tum ti tum, tum tum, tum ti tum.*" He stopped, his eyes widening.

"What's wrong?" I asked.

"'Cold is the hand that crushes the lark,'" he sang to the tune; then he looked at me in triumph. "It's from a song."

FOUR

A mon amic Folco
Tramet lai ma chanso . . .
[To my friend Folc, send him my song . . .]

—PEIRE VIDAL, *"AJOSTAR E LASSAR"*

Salt.

That was what first met our eyes upon entering the shop of Julien Guiraud—barrel after barrel of gleaming white or yellowed salt, in fine and coarse powders, chunks, and large bricks stacked on thick wooden planks. Here we were next to the sea, and the most popular commodity was the flavoring of that vast soup. Sailors, pilgrims, and cooks thronged the store, buying it by the barrel to pack with dried fish and pork.

"Salt sales for salts who sail," I muttered to Helga, who gave me a tolerant nod.

I cannot taste salt without thinking of an old saltpanner I once knew named Hector. He lived at the foot of the cliffs in Orsino, the town I came to call my own after marrying my first husband. Old Hector, everyone called him, for no one could remember when he was young, except for him, and even he was forgetting toward the end. He lived in a tiny shack surrounded by large pans of beaten tin or copper that he would laboriously drag down to the water's edge, fill, and even more laboriously drag back out of the reach of the tide so that wind and sun could take away the water and leave him his living. He would walk up and down, staring at his pans, trying to will the process along, or just sit and mend fishnets that looked too widely spaced to catch small fish and too weak to hold large ones. Yet somehow he eked out his existence, earning enough to keep him in bread and wine while the cold, wet winds whipped through his world.

It was he who saw my husband plummet from those same cliffs, he who staggered drunkenly through waves and rocks to drag him back like one of his salt pans before the tides could take him from me forever, who covered him with his only good blanket so that the crabs and gulls wouldn't get at him, then ran screaming into the town for help.

Which would bring my eventual second husband back into my life.

Old Hector died that spring. It turned out that he had once been a sailor who drifted along for years with different ships until he was too old to pull his weight. He had no people of his own. I arranged for his burial at the beach, high enough and far enough from the water to keep him dry until Judgment Day, but near enough so that he could still hear the surf. At the burial were the gravedigger, a priest, myself, and Theo, or Feste as he was called them. Nobody else.

Beyond the salt were baskets of spices, zealously guarded by Guiraud's staff, who measured them scrupulously onto small scales. Peppercorns, gingerroots, cinnamon bark, all of which had traveled much farther in their short lives than I had in mine, come to Marseille to hook our nostrils and beg to be put into stews and puddings.

And there were tables of silks—plain, dyed, and patterned—drawing the appreciative gaze of my apprentice, who was in turn drawing the appreciative gazes of the young clerks in the shop. Or were they looking at me? Certainly, my whiteface alone causes its share of staring, but underneath it I am still capable of having an effect on men, I like to think. Older, less attractive men, to be sure, but an effect is an effect.

Not that this matters to me.

"Here," I said to Helga, passing Portia to her. "Don't let her eat anything. Especially things that aren't meant to be food."

A clerk directed me to the rear of the shop where there stood a pale doughy man stabbing his finger impatiently at a line in a large ledger book while an older man seated at a small desk slid his fingers back and forth on an abacus and took notes.

". . . he's shortchanged us by two barrels; don't you see that?" said the doughy man. "I expect some losses during transit; everyone has their fingers ducking under the lid, but two entire barrels? I won't have it!"

The abacist cleared his throat, and the other man looked up at me and jumped slightly. "Good day, Domna," he said, stammering slightly. "Forgive me, I was startled by your makeup."

"I do have that effect on men," I said, smiling. "It is one of the tools of my trade. I am to perform later."

"How may I help you, Domna Fool?" he said.

"I seek Sieur Julien," I said.

"You have found him," he said, bowing slightly.

He was pudgier than his sister, but the facial resemblance was strong, particularly around the eyes. If you had taken him, rolled him out and let him bake in the sun as she had all these years, you would have seen her clearly.

"Let me first convey the warm regard of your sister," I said.

"Hélène? You saw Hélène? Is she all right?"

"She is well, Sieur, and content in doing God's work. She bade me come to you for guidance in a peculiar matter of my own."

"Then I shall be right with you. Martin, have Étienne look into it. Ask him to have a quiet talk with the sailing master. Domna, be so kind as to step into my office."

He showed me into a small back room whose walls were covered with maps. Tiny, carved models of boats were pinned onto them at different locations.

"I carve them myself," he said as he saw me look at them. "It seems childish, but it's the easiest way for me to remember where everything is. When they don't show up after a certain point, I have to assume that they have either sunk or been taken by pirates."

"So much risk to bring us luxuries," I said.

"More and more what were once considered luxuries have become the birthright of us all," he said. "God gave us this great sea and the wit to cross it and uncover the treasures on the other side. We all benefit, so the risk is worth it. Where would fools like you be if no one had the money to throw at them?"

"We would still be fools," I said. "We would just be amateurs."

"How came you to visit my sister?" he asked.

"We actually were looking for information concerning her husband," I said. "We thought that she might be able to enlighten us."

"Folquet?" he exclaimed. "You know Folquet?"

"I have met him," I said. "My husband and he were once friends. The abbot asked us to look into this—"

"Abbot?"

"Your brother-in-law is the abbot of Le Thoronet."

He started to laugh. "They made that pious old fraud an abbot," he said, wiping his eyes. "I hadn't heard. Still a climber, no matter what the setting."

"Really?" I said. "He was like that here?"

"Well, he's my brother-in-law; I shouldn't be saying anything," he said. "Especially to a friend of his."

"I am not his friend," I said. "I'm just running this petty little errand for my husband, thank you very much." I leaned forward and looked into his eyes. "But there is one thing that I adore more than anything in the world, and that is gossip."

"Do you?" he replied, his eyes brightening.

"Yes, I suppose that makes me a typical woman," I said.

"You seem nothing like a typical woman," he said, winking. "Would you like a cup of wine?"

Private office, closed door, a wink and wine—a bad combination for a married lady. But I had my Guild training for emergencies. I decided to chance it.

"I would love some," I purred. He poured us each a cup, and I raised mine. "To your sister."

"To Hélène," he said, sipping it parsimoniously.

I tilted my head back for a good gulp, but let most of it trickle back into the cup. It was good wine, I must say.

"You must be the younger brother," I said.

"What makes you say that?"

"Your appearance, Sieur," I said. "I thought to myself when I saw you, how could such a young-looking man be in charge of such a vast enterprise?"

"I am older than I seem," he confided. "In truth, Hélène and I are twins."

"How remarkable!" I exclaimed. "I myself have a twin brother."

"No!"

"It is God's truth," I replied, my hand to my bosom. His glance lingered there, and I desperately hoped that I wasn't leaking any milk. That tends to spoil the effect. "Alas, it has been some time since we have seen each other."

"Did you and he have a private language?" asked Guiraud.

"When we were little," I said. "I still remember some of it."

"As do I," he said, leaning forward and patting my hand. "Well, fellow twin, what can I tell you about my brother-in-law?"

"Tell me everything," I said.

"He was this greasy, charming little man from Genoan parents. His father was the representative of some wealthier family back in Genoa who nobody trusted. Little Folquet used to be picked on mercilessly by all the local children."

"Including yourself?"

"Of course," he declared proudly. "You know how children gang up on each other. Marseille children will fight anyone anywhere, especially Genoan children."

"But wasn't Folquet born here?"

"His father wasn't, and that's all we cared about. We listened to what our fathers said about Genoans, and acted accordingly."

"He must have been miserable."

"Oh, for certain. But then everyone found out he could sing."

"Aha!"

"Well, a voice like that becomes much in demand. He starts in the taverns, the brothels, in the worst of places, making his pennies from drunken sailors. Then he crosses the street to the hostels, singing holy ballads and prying more coins from between pressed palms. He works his way up to private performances at merchants' dinners. He's growing up, dressing better, and giving him his due, turning into quite the handsome devil."

I tried to visualize the walking corpse I had met as this charmer. I couldn't see it.

"Didn't he work for his father?" I asked.

"Reluctantly," said Guiraud. "He would disappear for periods of time, come back with new songs and tales of adventures no one believed he had had, but everyone wanted to hear. Rumor was he went somewhere in Italy."

The Guildhall, no doubt. Guiraud suddenly looked gloomy.

"Your sister?" I prompted him.

"My sainted sister," he sighed. "She always took pity on people. When we picked on Folquet, she would comfort him, wipe his brow with her kerchief, and keep the damn silk after like it was a holy relic. She had been sent away to a convent for schooling for a few years. When she returned, my father invited Folquet to sing for our dinner. He was sixteen. We were sixteen. I sat at the table and snickered with my friends, and Hélène fell in love."

"Did Folquet love her?"

He paused. "I think that he thought he loved her," he said, measuring his words as carefully as he would a pennyweight of clove. "I think that he was convinced by the sound of his own romantic voice that he loved her. But I think that he truly loved what she was—the daughter of a well-connected merchant. My father thought he had promise, and the Genoan connection useful, so there was profit to be had on both sides."

"When merchants make matches, money must be made," I said. "But that is hardly unusual."

"No, it isn't," he said. "But not every marriage involves my sister."

"You objected," I said.

"I had neither the right nor the place," he said. "They were married, and every merchant in Marseille was at the wedding. Once Folquet entered the family, many doors opened for him. He charmed his way into one house after another."

"Including that of Viscount Barral."

"Oh, Barral loved a good singing voice. Folquet and that other one, what was his name? Vidal, that was it. They were in there half the evenings, strumming away. Barral thought he was a singer, too. Have you heard the story about Barral's wife and Vidal?"

"Yes," I said, and he looked disappointed for a moment. "Tell me, did you ever hear Folquet called 'the lark' by anyone? Or hear of anyone else so called?"

"The lark," he said, looking up at the ceiling to think. "No. He usually called my sister his turtledove."

"How sweet. So, life was good for Folquet and your sister?"

"As far as anyone could tell, it was perfect. She doted on him, he doted on her, they raised two fine sons, the business was good. And then, out of the blue, he decides to become a monk."

"You had no warning?"

"None. You could have knocked me over with a piece of silk when I heard. And to put his family in holy orders, well . . . Of course, he had the right to do it, and we should respect someone who gives up everything to devote his life to serving God. . . ."

"We should, shouldn't we? But it seemed out of character?"

"Completely," he said. "Blinded on the road to Damascus, I suppose, only . . ."

"Only what?"

"On the day he left for the abbey, he didn't seem particularly devout or fervent. He seemed . . ."

"What?"

"Frightened," said Guiraud. "I rode with them as far as Gémenos, trying to dissuade him, but he was resolute. But he kept looking back as if he expected Satan's hounds to be on his tail."

"Had he been under any kind of threat, as far as you knew? Were there any competitors who could have driven him away? Any political machinations?"

"Is that what you are seeking now?" he asked.

"Possibly," I said. "There seems to be some danger for him, but we don't know who would want to threaten him after all this time."

"I would have to think," he said. "It's been nearly ten years. I remember a merchant named Marin Itier who had become heavily indebted to him. He ended up turning over his business to Folquet, but he then went on a pilgrimage to the Holy Land, and that's the last we heard of him."

"Could you think of any reason why anyone would want to threaten Folquet now?"

"Well, there are some who still resent the role he played in abducting Roncelin from Saint-Victor, especially now that there's talk of a papal interdict against the city. There was a rumor going around last spring that a repentant Folquet might return on behalf of the Pope to bring Roncelin back to the fold. Or that he's a Genoan spy trying to do the same thing. That could cause some panic if anyone took it seriously."

"Really? Who would take over if Roncelin left?"

"That's a question," said Guiraud thoughtfully. "Whoever has the real power at the moment, I suppose. The Viguerie is the largest pack of armed men in the city, and they answer to the Anselme family, but the Anselmes have always stayed behind the scenes and cooperated with the rest of the merchants. I don't see anyone else in the consulat with the ambition and resources to take over unopposed."

"Well, you've certainly given me much to think about," I said, standing.

He stood, and started to come quickly around the desk. I stepped to the doorway, and he leaned against the door, his arm blocking my path. "Won't you stay a little longer?" he implored me. "I do so enjoy your company."

He began reaching for me. I contemplated which part of his body would be the most vulnerable when I heard Portia crying.

"Mama, the baby is hungry again," called Helga from just outside the door.

"Forgive me," I said. "There is one with a greater claim. Some other time, perhaps?"

"Yes, yes, of course," he said reluctantly. He reached around me to the door latch, bringing his body closer to mine. He paused for a moment; then the baby howled even louder. He sighed, and opened the door.

"My thanks, Sieur," I said, slipping out.

Helga handed me Portia, who settled down quickly as we left the store.

"You didn't pinch her, did you?" I asked Helga.

"A little," she confessed sheepishly. "It seemed like the right moment."

"Good decision, Apprentice," I murmured. "How much did you hear?"

"Most of it," she said. "I put on my little-girl-looking-for-her-mama face, and the man with the abacus let me sit by the door. He gave me some candy. Would you like a piece?"

"Very much," I said, and she handed me a piece of rock candy that was flavored with a little cinnamon.

"Maybe this Marin Itier came back from pilgrimage looking for revenge," she said.

"That's not the usual result of a pilgrimage," I said.

"Maybe he never went on pilgrimage," she said. "Or maybe he went, but was captured by pirates, sold into slavery, and blamed Folc for his horrible life in chains and spent every waking and dreaming minute planning his horrible retribution."

"Which was to splash some blood on some books?" I asked, smiling at her enthusiasm. "That hardly seems adequate for such a tale of woe."

"Maybe that was just a warning, and he . . ." She sighed. "Fine. No pirates, no slavery. But we could still . . . Look! There's a fleet!"

I looked toward the mouth of the harbor, where four ships were maneuvering past the jetty. There was a stir of activity at the wharves, but no alarm raised. I tapped on the shoulder of a sailor who was watching them with professional curiosity.

"Pardon, Sieur, but whose colors are those?" I asked.

"Looks to be Aragon," he said. "Guess they've come to visit."

"Is that a good thing or a bad thing?"

"If they're spending money, it's good. If they're wanting money, it's bad," he replied.

"Sounds like family," I said. "Come, daughter. Let us return home."

We walked up the hill and returned to the house of Pantalan.

I heard the sound of an argument as we entered the courtyard. Two angry male voices, muffled by walls, but I immediately recognized them as belonging to my husband and our host. Helga and I glanced at each other; then I cautiously pushed the door open.

"Come on, curse you, it's in that thick skull of yours somewhere," shouted Theo.

"I swear, that's all I can summon up," pleaded Pantalan.

"But you're a jester, damn it. You're supposed to remember songs."

"It's not a jester's song, is it?" retorted Pantalan. "It's a *planh*, a dirge of some kind. Not the sort of thing I'd bother learning. It's too lugubrious. I'm here to cheer people up, remember?"

"You've never played a wake?" asked Theo in disbelief. "Never sang at a gravesite to carry the soul to the hereafter on wings of music?"

"That's just not done in Marseille," said Pantalan. "They take death very seriously in these parts."

"What's going on?" I asked.

"This feeble excuse for a fool, after wasting a full precious day of my existence, has suddenly dredged up the remarkably useful information that our mysterious message in blood was from a song."

"A song!" I exclaimed. "Sing it, please."

" 'Cold is the hand that crushes the lark,' " Pantalan began. " 'Cold is despair unending. *Tum tum ti tum, tum tum, tum ti tum . . .*' And that's all I have."

"That is a sad tune," I said.

"I like the *'tum tum ti tum'* part," chirped Helga. "Did you write that yourself?"

"When did you hear it?" I asked.

"I can't remember when. I just heard it once sometime," he said, throwing his hands in the air. "Probably some troubadour passing through. There have been so many, and there's usually drinking. You more than anyone should appreciate how that goes, Theo."

"Which troubadour?" demanded Theo. "It had to have been someone coming to Marseille after Folc left, or he would have known the song when he saw it."

"Not at all," I said. "In fact, more likely before. Someone painted that message expecting him to get the reference. It's a threat to a troubadour."

"Maybe from another," said Theo. "Is there a troubadour based in Marseille?"

"No," said Pantalan quickly. A little too quickly, I thought.

"Well, who is riding the circuit?"

"It's not a regular circuit at the moment," said Pantalan. "Gui de Cavalhon pops up every now and then, but he mostly goes between Montpellier and Toulouse. He might be able to help you."

"Montpellier?"

"That way, about four days' journey," said Pantalan, jerking his thumb over his shoulder. "You'll have to cross five rivers, I think it is."

Theo sat on the pile of pallets, then stretched out lazily, resting his head on his hands. "That's a long journey just to see if he happens to be in town, and if he happens to know a song," he said, his eyes closed.

"Well, I don't know what else you can do here," said Pantalan.

"I could find out why you are trying to get rid of us," said Theo.

"What?" squeaked Pantalan. "You insult me. I have given you my hospitality, forgone my extensive love life for an entire day just to play hosteler—"

"Which is your job when Guildmembers come to town," I reminded him.

"There is a little mouse of information that is scurrying around in that tiny warren you call a brain," said Theo. "I can play hide and seek with it all day, or I can take a shovel and start excavating."

"Helga, be a dear and go borrow a shovel from somebody, will you?" I asked.

"Let me remind you again of the oath of loyalty that you swore to the Guild, my fat and prosperous colleague," said Theo, swinging his legs around and sitting up. "I want to know what you are concealing from me. If it is anything that will help me trace this song, then I have to know. I don't need to reveal anything to the Guild about the source."

Pantalan looked down at his feet, shamefaced. "Will you swear that?" he asked. "Will all of you swear that it will not get back to the Guild?"

Theo looked at us. We nodded.

"By the First Fool, Our Savior, I swear it," he said.

"By the First Fool," Helga and I echoed.

Pantalan started pacing back and forth, wringing his hands. "Very well," he said. "I heard it from Vidal."

"Peire Vidal? He wrote the song?"

"I don't know," said Pantalan unhappily. "I told you about him and the Viscountess."

"And he fled Marseille, yes," said Theo.

"But that wasn't an end," said Pantalan. "He came back. In secret."

"When?"

"End of '95? Maybe '96, I can't remember. Folquet was gone; I was the only Guildmember here. Vidal suddenly shows up at my door, drunk as a lord. He had come back for Adalaïs. He had been all over, Toulouse, Aragon, Montferrat, Hungary, trying to forget her. Then he heard, years too late, that Barral had divorced her and then died. So Peire Vidal came back. But he was too late again. Adalaïs, Lady Pons, had died a year before."

"Poor man," I said softly.

"He was insane with grief," said Pantalan. "He screamed, he cried, he spouted blasphemies like a whole herd of heretics. But most of all, he sang. I stayed up with him for three days without sleep as he drank and sang, one lament after another. My God, I've never seen a performance like it. That voice, those melodies, each as sorrowful as the next. *Planhs* for great men and nonentities, bishops and shepherdesses, sailors lost at sea, mothers lost at childbirth. I wish I could remember every one of them, I truly do, but it was all mixed together in this drunken orgy of lamentation, and that song about the lark was somewhere in there. I couldn't remember the rest if you tortured me."

"I haven't ruled that out yet," warned Theo. "Could Vidal be behind this? He knew Folc well enough. Any reason for enmity between them?"

"They were the greatest of friends," said Pantalan simply.

"Damn it, damn it, damn it," sighed Theo. "I guess we have to find Vidal. Any possibility that you know where he is nowadays? And why did this have to be such a secret?"

"That's not the secret," said Pantalan. "Vidal's whereabouts are the secret."

"Where is he?"

"Here," said Pantalan. "He's in Marseille."

"What? Since when?"

"A week ago. Out of the blue, like the last time. Only . . ."

"Only what? He's drunk again?"

"Worse. He's mad. Barking."

"Barking mad?"

"He's mad and he's barking," said Pantalan. "Another romantic disaster. I couldn't get all the details, something about wearing wolf-skins and howling in the mountains and being beaten half to death by shepherds, but he's gone around the bend this time. I didn't want the Guild to know."

"What were you going to do with him?" I asked.

"If he didn't come out of it, then there's a place I know of in Malta. An isolated place, run by the Templars for knights who have lost their reason. I was going to send him there."

"Where is he?" asked Theo.

"West of town," said Pantalan. "A quiet place. There's a family I trust who watch him. He's . . . he's tied to a bed, Theo. I'd hate for anyone else from the Guild to see him like this. That's not how he would have wanted to be remembered."

"Does he have lucid moments?"

"Sometimes, but you never know when they are coming. And he won't talk to me. He only talks to the women, trying to seduce them with his songs. He keeps calling them Adalaïs. They don't know who he means, of course."

"With all his madness, he still sings," mused Theo. Then he looked at me. "But only to women."

"Oh, no," I said, my heart sinking. "That would be cruel. Just to find a song?"

"I don't know what else to do," he said. "The song may be the key. What did this Adalaïs look like? More important, what did she sound like?"

"A low voice, often harsh in rebuke," said Pantalan. "About four notes down from your speaking voice, Claudia."

"Like this?" I asked, shifting my voice down.

"Around there. But not as sweet."

"Do I look anything like her?"

"The height is right," he said, regarding me critically. "She was of fairer complexion, and younger back then than you are now."

"If the room is kept dark, then he might not notice," suggested Theo. "He wants to see her. His madness will make up the difference. We'll have to get you back into your old clothes, Duchess."

"Let me not change until we get there," I said. "I don't want people here to see me like that."

I opened my chest of costumes and dug through them. There, near the bottom, was a dark, green brocaded gown that I used for "The Duchess and Her Forward Fool," a scene that Theo and I had played many times to great success in taverns and markets while secretly enjoying the truth that underlay it. I had worn similar gowns when I had been a duchess, but none of them survived the fires of Constantinople.

I rolled it up and stuffed it into my pack.

"Lead on," I said.

We followed through the quarter until we came to its outer wall. Small mountains rose from the sea to our left and continued in a ring around the city. The road we were on cut through farmland, and after about thirty minutes' walk, Pantalan turned to the right and led us to a small farmhouse and knocked on the door. A woman of perhaps sixty opened it and looked at him silently, then at the rest of us with suspicion. Pantalan nodded, and she jerked her head around to the left. We filed past her and walked to the rear of the house. There was a set of crude wooden steps descending into an earthen cellar. I washed my makeup off and changed.

I heard him before I saw him. Drifting up from the darkness were hoarse fragments of songs, muttered songs, shouted songs, songs of a dozen languages. All of them coarse, obscene, the things sailors sang of what they had done to women or what they would do, given the chance.

And I smelled him before I saw him, for the stench emanating from that hole was foul indeed. Pantalan shrugged as he saw me wrinkle my nose in disgust.

"He's been tied to a bed," he reminded me softly. "For several days."

He took a candle from a shelf and lit it at the cooking fire.

"Put it on that table by the foot of the steps," he said, handing it to me and pointing down. "There will be just enough light for you to see where he is, and for him to know that there is a woman there."

"Take Portia out to see the goats," I said to Helga. "I don't want her to hear this."

"But I want to hear—"

"Do as you are told, Apprentice," said Theo.

She looked stricken, but obeyed.

"Good luck," said Theo. "Be careful. Remember that sometimes he's a wolf."

"All men are wolves some of the time," I said, and I stepped down into the cellar.

He started whimpering as the candlelight flickered into the gloom. The stench grew stronger and fouler with each step. I placed the candle carefully on the table and stood in front of it so that only my shape could be seen.

"Are you there?" I called softly.

As my eyes adjusted to the change in the light, I made out a man, dressed in what might once have been a splendid yellow-and-black tunic and breeches, now in tatters. He was bound to the bed by ropes around his chest, torso, and legs, his hands tied together and connected to the rope crossing his torso.

His face was slightly crumpled, like an old house that was starting to collapse, and his nose was swollen and red. He may have been handsome once.

"Who are you?" he whispered fearfully.

"Don't you know me, Peire? It is I, Adalaïs."

"Adalaïs? Have you come at last?"

"You called me. How could I not?"

Tears ran down the sides of his face to dampen the pallet.

"I have been calling you for so long," he cried. "Where were you?"

"I have traveled far," I said. "It was a long journey."

"Tell me," he begged. "Is this Hell?"

"If it was Hell, would I be here?" I said, laughing lightly. "Would I be asking you to sing for me again?"

"Sing? Oh, Adalaïs, my Lady Pons, there was a time I would have sung to you forever. But this poor excuse of a voice should not be allowed to pass anywhere near your hearing."

"Is this how the greatest troubadour alive responds to the request of a lady?" I scolded him. "Do you not believe that I would prefer the slightest croak from you to all the costumed nightingales of the Court of Love?"

"You have shamed me, Domna," he said, still snuffling. "Of course I will sing for you. But these filthy surroundings—"

"Will be ennobled by your voice," I said. "What care we where we are, as long as there is music to fill the emptiness? Sing to me, Peire, as you sang to me long ago."

"What shall I sing?" he muttered, his eyes flickering back in forth. "So many songs. I can hear them all in my head, all sounding at once, like a flock of starlings screeching in a tree by the window. I cannot find just one."

"Let me name the song, then," I said.

"Very well, Domna. What will you hear?"

I paused. I didn't know its name, just the first two lines, and the second only because of Pantalan's deficient memory.

"There was one I once heard you sing about a lark," I said.

"I know seventeen different songs about larks," he said. "I know three songs by actual larks. Shall I sing them all? Two of them are not fit for a lady's ears."

"There was one in particular," I said. "It began, 'Cold is the hand that crushes the lark.' Do you remember that one?"

He started shaking his head violently back and forth, struggling against his bonds. "Not that one!" he screamed. "It is cursed. It was not meant for you!"

"Who was it meant for?" I asked.

"One that is dead," he said.

"Who?"

"I never knew the name," he said. "But the one who sang it died for it."

"Who sang it?"

"Some other song, I beg of you, Domna, a million other songs!" he said hurriedly, flecks of spittle appearing on his lips. "I know them all; I know the songs of the animals; I have learned the whistles of the birds, the barking of the dogs, the yowls of the cats, the howls of the wolves. I have heard the stars at night singing to each other. No one but me knows those songs, and I will sing them for you, Domna!"

"I will have no other song but this one," I said firmly. "If I had known that you would treat me in this ill-mannered fashion, I never would have come. And if you cannot grant me this simple wish, then I will leave you in this dark cave forever."

"No!" he yelled in panic. "I will sing it. But I don't know all of it. I heard it but the one time."

"Who sang it to you?"

"His name was Rafael de la Tour, a street singer I knew from Montpellier, not even a trained voice, but a natural genius. I heard him sing it in a tavern in Saragossa, and I bought him wine and traded him songs."

"Sing it for me, Peire."

He closed his eyes, and something shifted behind them. He breathed deeply once, and his body relaxed, the tremors ceasing. Then he breathed again, and a voice like a god's spread through the darkness and shivered my soul into a thousand shards.

Cold is the hand that crushes the lark.
Cold is despair unending.
Cold is the rain that douses the spark,
And cold is the grave uncomprehending.
Sweet Lady Lark, why will you not fly?
Fie on the Fates unsparing!
Where lies the voice that made lovers sigh?
And where lies the grace beyond comparing?

He stopped. Time stopped, and I don't know how long it was before I heard anything else, such was the power of that voice in the darkness. Then the candle spat behind me, the spell was broken, and his eyes fluttered open again.

"I am sorry, Domna," he said hoarsely. "That is all that I can summon."

"That was the voice that I remember," I said softly. "Thank you, Peire. What happened to Rafael?"

"Stabbed in an alley a few days later," he said. "I never knew who wrote the song, or for what unfortunate lady it was written. Domna?"

"Yes, Peire?"

"A troubadour is paid for his singing."

"I have gold—"

"No!" he shouted. "No money between us. No payment so cheap as gold. I did wrong to you once, Domna."

"That is long in the past," I said.

"The past is never gone, never forgotten," he said. "I did take from you something that was not mine to take, nor yours to give, and I have been haunted by that sin ever since."

"Then let me forgive you for that transgression," I said.

"It can only be forgiven if I return to you what was yours," he said. "Will you allow me to do that? Will you grant this husk that last favor?"

Somewhere behind me were the men who sent me into this stench-filled darkness. Somewhere up where it was light, and the air was good. I had accomplished the task they had given me. All I had to do was turn away and walk back up the steps, and I would be done.

But I would never forgive myself if I did that.

"Yes, Peire," I said, coming to him. I leaned down and kissed him on the mouth, and he responded hungrily, pressing hard against my lips.

Suddenly, he stiffened. "You are not her!" he screamed, and suddenly he was gnashing at me, trying to seize my flesh between his teeth. I stumbled backwards and he started howling like a wolf with an arrow through its leg, thrashing against the bonds.

"Who are you?" he shouted. "Some demon sent to torment me? To appear in the guise of she who I hold most dear in the world? What Hell is this?"

All I could think to do was to whistle in the darkness. The Guild password. He caught his breath and was silent. I repeated it.

"Who are you?" he asked again, albeit more calmly.

"Give the counter," I commanded him.

He licked his lips, then whistled. It was scratchy and weak, but it was the countermelody to the password.

"My Guildname is Claudia," I said. "Forgive me for this masquerade."

"Why are you here?" he asked. "Why did you do this to me?"

"Because you are held by some madness," I said. "Because you are dangerous to us, and to yourself."

"I don't, I don't . . . ," he started, then he began shaking and gasping. "Where is she? Where is Adalaïs?"

"She died long ago, Peire Vidal," I said. "And you know this."

"No, no, she isn't dead, she lives, you lie!"

"I am so sorry," I said. "I will pray for your recovery."

I turned to take the candle from the table.

"Wait," he said. "Let me see your face. Let me see it in the light."

I turned to face him from a safe distance, and brought the candle in front of my face. Over the flickering flame, I could see him looking at me intently.

"I don't know you," he said.

"No," I replied.

"But I think," he began, then he stopped.

"You think what?" I asked.

"I think that I could have fallen in love with you," he said.

"It would have been an honor," I said softly. "Good-bye, Peire."

"The wolves," he called after me. "The wolves do have their own songs. I know them all."

I blew out the candle and climbed the stairs.

Theo and Pantalan were sitting against the wall opposite, not meeting my gaze.

"Theophilos," I said.

"Yes?"

"Never ask me to do anything like that again."

"I won't. I'm sorry."

"So. 'Lady Lark,' says the song," I said. "The lark is not Folc, but a woman who died."

"In Montpellier," said Theo.

Pantalan raised his hand and pointed west. "That way," he said. "Four days, five rivers."

"Oh, shut up," said Theo.

FIVE

No sai com ni de que chan,
mas quex demanda chanso . . .
[I do not know how, or about what, to sing,
but everyone demands a song . . .]

—FOLQUET DE MARSEILLE, *"CHANTARS MI TORN'AD AFAN"*
[TRANS., N. M. SCHULMAN]

It was an unhappy band of fools trudging back from the farm. Pantalan was unhappy that we knew about Peire Vidal, Claudia was unhappy about the role that I made her play, I was unhappy that we now had to continue this strange journey to Montpellier, which at least was on the way to Toulouse, but that didn't matter, because I would have to bring whatever I found there all the way back to Le Thoronet, and Helga was unhappy because she missed hearing everything.

Portia, on the other hand, was extremely happy, not being fool enough to know that she was supposed to be unhappy, and having just made the acquaintance of a very tolerant nanny goat and her very playful and curious kid. She babbled away, occasionally imitating the sounds she had learned from them and breaking immediately into fits of giggling. I supposed, in her way, that she was telling us jokes.

"Where is Montpellier, anyway?" asked Helga sulkily as we passed through the western gate back into Marseille proper.

"That way, four days, five rivers," we chorused. That started Claudia chuckling, which set the rest of us off, and before we knew it, we were all roaring at the absurdity of our predicament. Portia looked pleased, no doubt believing that she was responsible for a successful punch line.

"I guess we might as well be on our way," I said to Pantalan, wiping the tears from my eyes. "We've troubled you long enough."

"Oh, not until morning, my friends," he replied. "Don't forget that we are performing at the Green Pilgrim tonight."

"That's right. What would you like to do?"

"Oh, some of my stuff, then more of yours, since they haven't seen you before. And to finish—let's see, we have two men, one woman, and a plucked chicken—"

"Girl," protested Helga.

"A plucked girl. How about the Drunken Priest at the Funeral?"

"Perfect," I said. "Helga, you learned that one, didn't you?"

"With Father Gerald playing the priest in class," she said proudly.

"Then you've learned from the best," said Pantalan. "Good. That should be enough to keep them happy, and not so long that they forget that they came to drink."

We ran through a rehearsal in the courtyard in front of his house, the local children watching with glee; then we loaded up our bags and marched down the hill.

The tavern was located a street in from the harbor. I spotted the two guards from the Hôtel de Barral. To my surprise, Laurent, Roncelin's seneschal, was sitting with them. The two guards eyed Claudia with a look I decided to dub approval so I wouldn't have to get into any fights.

"Look over there," muttered Pantalan, nodding toward the bar. There was a clump of soldiers wearing Aragon's colors. "You know any Aragonese songs?"

"I sang one by Giraut de Bornelh to Eudiarde just this morning," I said.

"And she didn't jump you on the spot?" he laughed. "My God,

she must have been drunk. Well, pick something bawdier for those fellows. All right, here I go."

He jumped onto a table at one end of the room and announced his presence with a mighty chord on his lute. The people closest to him clapped. He bowed, then launched into a comic song about a fearful pilgrim trying to muster up the courage to take to the sea. As he sang, he turned the table into a boat and a bench into a gangplank. Despite his girth, he was remarkably agile in his movements, and soon convinced us all that we were being tossed by a storm in the middle of nowhere. He spun the tale out, improvising verses, or at least giving the appearance of doing so. Claudia, Helga, and I picked up the melody and added our instruments to it while Portia took in everything, her eyes wide in wonderment.

He finished to enthusiastic applause, which he milked shamelessly. Then he held up a hand for silence.

"My friends, although it was a shock to learn this, I find that I am not the only fool in Marseille," he said. "An entire family of them has come by to visit, and because of my great love for all of you, and I mean that, even though some of you I've never seen before in my life and never will again, but because of the deep and, dare I say, abiding love that I hold for you, no matter how ugly, depraved, and diseased you may be, but it is still love, I insist, though now that I am thinking about it, perhaps love from a safe distance would be best, yet even that is love, though it may present the outward face of outright loathing—"

"Get on with it!" someone called.

"Such rudeness!" he said, looking wounded. "You have made me forget my place. I will have to start over again—"

There were howls of mock anguish and protest from his audience.

"Oh, very well. I give you Tan Pierre, Domna Gile, and Little Helga—the Fool Family!"

We had a particular routine, suited to the low ceilings of taverns where acrobatics were less effective. The high point was my portrayal of a drunk, which admittedly is never a stretch, staggering obliviously through the clubs being tossed back and forth between my two partners, pausing at one point to drop and then retrieve a coin from the floor, bending down just in time to miss being struck in the head by a high club from one direction, then straightening to avoid a low club from the other.

We then broke into song. I threw in one particularly dirty ditty from Aragon that had the visiting soldiers guffawing. I was glad for Helga's sake that she understood no Aragonese yet.

Pantalan rejoined us in clerical garb, and we segued smoothly into the sketch. It went well, and we finished with a mildly pious local musical tribute to those who would soon be traveling the seas on pilgrimage. All in all, a successful performance, and we were rewarded with many drinks and a bucket of oyster stew from the tavern keeper.

The last round came from the table of Aragonese, who spoke passable langue d'oc as it turned out. We let them pour, as they were marginally more sober than we were by then, and lifted our cups in a toast.

"To your king, the magnificent Pedro," shouted Pantalan.

"To our king!" they bellowed, and one added, "May he go home to his queen tomorrow."

"Why? Where is the stallion of Saragossa?" asked Pantalan.

"Here, damn it," he said. "And I had the finest piece in all Montpellier ready to spread her legs for me when he decided to abandon his bride and come to Marseille."

"He's tired of the countess already?" laughed Pantalan. "I can't believe it. She wore out two husbands before she turned twenty, and now the third is fleeing her after only four months of marriage? I thought Pedro was supposed to be a legend in bed."

"Then he met his match," said the soldier. "Anyhow, as pretty a wench as she is, he didn't marry her for her looks. He married her for Montpellier and whatever money he could suck out of it."

"And now he's here to borrow more?" I asked.

"We don't know why he's here," said another. "We just know that he has some vast plan that means we have to drag our sorry asses from one place to another. Montpellier, Marseille, Genoa, Rome—"

"Rome? Is he going to see the Pope?"

"That's what we hear. Don't know why. It's not like he can marry Innocent off to a spare sister. Say, I bet I know a song that can make a jester laugh."

"Ah! A challenge!" cried Pantalan. "Let's hear it."

And the game commenced, and continued late into the evening. When we staggered home, Portia was fast asleep in Claudia's arms, and I had Helga riding my shoulders.

"What do you think King Pedro is up to?" I asked Pantalan.

"Trying to borrow money," he replied. "Being a king, he owes on a greater scale than ordinary folk."

"Does Roncelin have any?"

"Not really, but the consulat may funnel some through him just to keep up appearances. After all, he's kin to Pedro, thanks to Eudiarde. Did you notice his seneschal there?"

"I did," I said. "I was surprised to see him. You would think he would be busy cleaning the Hôtel de Barral for a royal visit."

"Was that the graybeard sitting with the two men who kept flirting with me?" asked Claudia.

"There were so many men flirting with you, it's hard to know which ones you're talking about," I said.

"Don't be ridiculous," she said, trying not to sound pleased. "There were two soldiers from the Viguerie who said they guard Roncelin, and there was this graybeard with them who never said a word."

"That was him," said Pantalan.

"Something about him bothered me," said Claudia.

"What?"

"He didn't have a single drink the entire evening," she said. "Why would a man come to a tavern and not drink or talk?"

"Because we were so good that he didn't want to miss a word of our performance," replied Pantalan. "Here we are, my friends. Sleep well, and wake me before you leave tomorrow. Here, let me help you with that."

He disentangled Helga, who had fallen asleep while I was carrying her, and placed her gently on her pallet. He looked at her for a moment, then yawned mightily and climbed the steps to his room.

Claudia put Portia in the cradle and sighed.

"Montpellier in the morning," she said. "I've never been there. I suppose that you have."

"Just passing through," I said. "That's what most people do in Montpellier."

A deep snore came from the room above us. We glanced up, then looked at each other.

"Everyone is asleep but us," said Claudia. "Whatever shall we do?"

"I have an idea," I said.

"Why, sir, are you flirting with me?" she said as I picked her up and arranged her on the pallet.

"I'll do that later," I said.

I woke midmorning to a pounding noise that, for a change, wasn't in my head.

Helga popped up from her pallet, glanced at the two of us and casually arched an eyebrow, then peeked out the window. "It's that graybeard from the tavern last night," she whispered.

"Coming down!" called Pantalan from above. He descended in full motley and makeup and opened the door. There was a murmured conversation outside. Helga listened at the door, then turned to us with a grin.

"We're going to . . . ," she began, then she yelped as Pantalan's hand reached through the doorway and grabbed her by the ear.

"Stay on guard, Apprentice," he said, coming inside and releasing her. "And this is my news to give, not yours. My friends, I am afraid that you must delay your departure one more day. We have been summoned to give a performance at—well, let's just say that the frozen conditions in Hell have lasted another day."

"I'm too hungover for riddles," moaned Claudia, pulling the blankets over her head.

"Roncelin?" I asked.

"The same," he replied. "Turns out his seneschal was scouting us for the entertainment. The powers of Marseille are throwing a dinner for the visiting royalty, and they want to impress, so Roncelin will be playing the continuing role of the Viscount of Marseille, and we will be playing fools."

"We can do that," I said.

We arrived at the Hôtel de Barral in midafternoon. Instead of the two guards at the gate, a full company in full armor stood at full attention. Their sergeant in full dudgeon directed us to the servants' entrance.

"Suddenly we've come down in the world," observed Pantalan. "Just because some king drops in for a bite to eat. Now, remember—I left this room yesterday just ahead of a spearpoint, so be careful what you say around Roncelin."

"What about Pedro?" asked Claudia.

"He likes wine, women, mirth, merriment, and more women," said Pantalan. "Anything is fair game."

We climbed a back staircase and went through a narrow corridor that brought us to the Viscount's ballroom. It had been completely transformed since our visit yesterday. An entire layer of grime had been lifted off, revealing the unknown glories of the patterned wood floors. The tapestries had been cleaned to the point where one could actually see the colors, and the shutters at the end of the hall were wide open. A giant log burned majestically in the great fireplace, and torches brought light to all the places the sun couldn't reach.

A quintet of musicians was setting up on a low platform in the corner. Pantalan introduced us all around, then conferred with their leader over the division of entertainment while we unpacked. As music was not to be our responsibility, we left our instruments by the wall and concentrated on the juggling gear.

A team of servants lent to the château for the occasion set up the main dining table, then buried it under a huge damask cloth. Side tables were brought in, and then came giant loaves of bread, carried between two servants apiece.

Eudiarde suddenly swept into the hall, barking orders right and left that made no sense and were otherwise ignored by the staff. It seemed to give her satisfaction, nonetheless.

"It's been a long time since she's had a chance to play the lady," whispered Pantalan.

Just then she caught sight of me. She stopped in midsentence, blushed for a moment, then resumed haranguing a poor girl who was not putting the spoons and knives on the table fast enough.

"And what was that all about?" asked Claudia slyly.

"It looked like a woman remembering something that didn't actually happen," I said. "Clubs or balls, dearest?"

Laurent came up to Eudiarde and whispered something to her. She squeaked in dismay and ran out of the room. He clapped his hands, and the bustle momentarily ceased.

"Our guests will arrive shortly," he said. "If anyone asks, you've worked here for years. Make it look like it. We want the Lion of Aragon to enjoy himself. Then we want him to leave happy. Soon, but happy. Am I understood?"

There were nods all around.

"And it's been a long time since he's had a chance to play the seneschal," whispered Pantalan. "Here they come. Let's start juggling."

"And eavesdropping?" asked Helga.

"Of course," said Pantalan, winking at her.

"Oh, good," she said, and she cartwheeled away.

Portia was looking restless, so I picked her up and carried her in my left arm while keeping two clubs going with my right hand. This proved a great draw for the great ladies and merchants' wives as they arrived. We had her dressed in a tiny little motley tunic with a cap and bells on her head that she kept pulling off and shaking.

"And who is this little fool?" cooed one woman as she chucked her under the chin.

"Don't underestimate her," I said. "She's the smartest of all of us."

"How so?"

"She gets all the attention, eats for free, yet she is the worst juggler in the group," I said. "Drops everything."

The cap and bells jangled to the floor, and the ladies laughed as Portia and I looked down at it in dismay. I stuck my toe under it, kicked it into the air, snatched it with my free hand and stuck it back on the baby's head. Not much of a trick, but it's adorable. The ladies applauded and moved on.

I looked at Portia, and she looked back at me with a big smile.

"Why do I get the feeling that you dropped that on cue?" I asked, and we rubbed noses.

Roncelin and Eudiarde made a grand entrance. He was still in a black robe, but this one was actually clean and richly embroidered. We all bowed, and they promenaded to the center of the room opposite the main doors. Laurent appeared carrying a massive silver tray holding a pitcher of wine and three gold goblets. We stood silent for what became an uncomfortably long interval; then there was a blatting of trumpets outside. A moment later, Pedro appeared in the doorway.

Was it coincidence that his entrance coincided with the sun's rays angling through the windows toward him? Somehow, I doubted it. His pose as he stepped in was designed to dazzle, his golden breastplate reflecting the afternoon light in all directions. He might have been some ancient Roman general returning in triumph from battle, a Mark Antony before his Egyptian depletion, his legs the strongest, his beard the manliest, his voice as he bellowed his greeting the boomiest bass in all Christendom. Every woman in the room buckled slightly and began to sway like a grove in the breeze.

"Roncelin, Eudiarde!" he cried. "I am here!"

The Viscount and Viscountess of Marseille bowed to the King of Aragon as he strode toward them.

"Your Highness, my brother," intoned Roncelin as he took the pitcher and poured wine into the goblets. "Marseille bids you welcome."

He handed one goblet to Pedro, one to his wife, and raised the third.

"Our house is yours!" he said, and they tilted their heads back and drank. The room applauded, and the musicians launched into a celebratory dance.

"Now, that is a very handsome man," observed Claudia as Helga stared unabashedly at the king, her mouth hanging open. I tapped the girl on the noggin with one of my clubs.

"You're here to work, not to drool, Apprentice," I said. "Start juggling. And every club you drop is another meal you cook on the way to Montpellier."

Pedro took Eudiarde's arm and led her grandly to the head table, taking his place at the center. Roncelin trailed them awkwardly, and there was a momentary confusion as to who was supposed to be sitting where that was quickly smoothed out by the seneschal.

The blessing was given by the archbishop in full ecclesiastical finery, his miter rivaling the king's breastplate in gaudiness. Then the dinner began, the servants ladling fish stew into bowls and keeping the wine coming. I signaled Helga to take Portia from me, shook my left arm awake, and began some serious juggling that carried me about the room to the head table. No one thinks you're listening when you have five clubs in the air, but the conversation taking place was meant to be heard by the entire room.

"My wife sends her love and greetings," said Pedro blandly.

"And how fares our former sister?" asked Roncelin. "I am surprised that she chose not to accompany her husband so soon after her nuptials."

"She regrets that she cannot be with us," said Pedro. "But travel would be unsafe in her current condition."

"Oh, dear," said Roncelin sympathetically. "What is the matter?"

"Nothing of concern," said Pedro. "She is with child."

There was applause from the rest of the table.

"Already!" exclaimed Eudiarde. "But you were only just married."

"God has chosen to bless my life," said Pedro. "He recognized the value of my settling down and repenting my wanton youthful ways, and has rewarded me with the continuation of my line. It will be a son, I have no doubt."

"To the future King of Aragon and Count of Montpellier," said Roncelin, lifting his cup in salute. "Long may your lineage thrive."

"And I am hoping to add to that," said Pedro.

"More children would be a multiple blessing," said Roncelin.

"Children?" laughed Pedro. "I was thinking more in the line of adding territories."

The music kept playing, but the other conversations ceased as the diners turned their full attention to the king, who was sopping up his remaining stew with a piece of bread.

"Territories?" queried Roncelin nervously. "Whose territories?"

"Those that the infidel has kept from their true destiny," said Pedro. "God has chosen me to be His steward here on earth, and I would be a most neglectful steward indeed if I allowed His lands to be under the sway of those worshippers of false prophets."

"Do you propose to go to Jerusalem, then?" Roncelin asked, trying not to seem hopeful.

"Neither Jerusalem nor the Holy Land," said Pedro. "At least, not yet. I believe that there are lands and Christians to be rescued closer at hand."

"Certainly, there are lands bordering your own . . . ," Roncelin began.

"The Balearics," interrupted Pedro. "Majorca and Minorca. Rich prosperous islands under the thumb of the Mohammedans."

"Islands," said Roncelin.

"Those things in the middle of the water, milord," Pantalan called out helpfully from one end of the table.

"No, those are called boats," I called from the other.

"The things that don't float, I mean," he said.

"Those are called boats that sink," I said.

"Quiet," commanded Roncelin, glaring. He turned back to Pedro. "Well, the Balearics. Worthy quest. Best of luck with it."

"I'll need more than luck," said Pedro, holding his goblet up to be refilled. He drank, and then sighed. "Ah, marriage. Such a joy. It has taught me a valuable lesson."

"What lesson is that?" asked Roncelin.

"Never marry a city without first checking its port," he replied. "Consider Montpellier. Good location, decent income, but no harbor worth a damn. You have to unload your ships onto barges, and it's still miles up a shallow river before you get there. I let my judgment be clouded by love. Well, you of all people know what that's like, my brother."

"Of course," said Roncelin warily as Eudiarde gulped down her wine. I had lost track of how much she had drunk, but I was sure that there was going to be either an outburst or a collapse soon. Maybe both.

"They have to ship everything through Narbonne," continued Pedro. "But I've never liked the Narbonnese. No family there, at least not yet. I was thinking now that I've added Montpellier to my holdings that maybe I could throw that trade your way."

There was a rustle of excitement among the merchants at the table. One of them caught Roncelin's eye and nodded slightly.

"I am sure that could be arranged to our mutual satisfaction," said Roncelin. "We thank you for your consideration."

"It is nothing," said Pedro. "Are we not family? Do we not show our love for each other in every possible way?"

"Every possible way?" repeated Roncelin. "What do you want?"

"Want? Your love is enough," said Pedro.

"Well, then we thank . . . ," Roncelin began.

"Now, I would like you to show that love publicly when I am in Rome," continued Pedro.

"Rome?" said Roncelin.

"Minor city in Italy, milord," called Pantalan. "I think the Pope lives there."

"Take him away," said Roncelin irritably, and there was a minor ruckus down at that end of the room as the servants threw the fool out, his protestations echoing down the stairs.

"Why are you going to Rome?" asked Roncelin. "And what does it have to do with me?"

"I am inviting you to be present at my coronation," said Pedro.

"Coronation? But you are already the king. Everyone knows—"

"Everyone knows nothing!" shouted Pedro. "I am God's anointed messenger, sent to carry out His will, and I cannot even scrape together enough ships to make a decent escort on these little social calls. Great plans cost money, my brother, and your fat merchants do not adequately recognize their moral obligation to my cause. So, I am going to Rome to be anointed and crowned by the Vicar of Christ himself, and then I will go forth and do God's bidding with proper support from my flock. And I am inviting you to be present at this tremendous honor."

"We could visit Rome?" breathed Eudiarde. "Travel? Leave this place?"

"It would be a great sacrifice to leave my responsibilities to my people," said Roncelin.

He glanced down the table as he spoke. The merchant who had caught his eye before had a brief whispered conversation with his brethren, then shrugged and nodded again.

"But our love for you is greater than those responsibilities," continued Roncelin hesitantly.

"Then it is done," boomed Pedro. "Let's have some music! Something jolly. And let that pretty lady who juggles so deftly come where I can see her better."

I bounded up, batting my eyes at him. He broke into laughter.

"Not you," he growled. "That one."

Claudia came up.

"Milord, allow me to introduce you to my wife," I said as she bowed.

"Wife," he repeated, sounding disappointed.

"Yes, milord," she said. "And may I be so bold as to congratulate you on your ascendance to matrimony. It is a holy sacrament, sanctified by God. May you be blessed forever in His sight."

"Of course, of course," he said, sighing. "Let me see you perform. I have never seen a woman juggle before."

"All woman juggle," she said, launching into her patter. "Say this club is marriage . . ."

She had matters safely in hand, so I wandered about the room. Helga came up, the baby asleep in her arms. "Who is the merchant who is pulling the strings of the viscount?" she asked.

"I would guess the head of the Anselme family," I said. "We'll have to ask Pantalan. Damn him for getting thrown out and leaving us on our own."

"That king certainly doesn't act like a man who just got married," she said, watching Claudia keep her clubs between her and Pedro.

"Kings don't behave any differently than the rest of us," I said. "They just get away with it more. Keep Portia with you at all times."

"Why? Is she in danger?"

"No, but you may be," I said. "If Pedro wants to dally with a female fool, and Claudia is unavailable, he might look your way."

"But I'm only twelve!" she protested.

I patted her shoulder. "Just keep holding Portia," I said. "She'll protect you."

I kept working the room, but heard nothing of use. Toward the end of the evening, Laurent signaled me to join him by the entrance. We walked into the hallway and he led me to a small room that served him as an office.

"I trust that you will be seeing Pantalan tonight," he said, unlocking a drawer with a key from a bunch at his waist and pulling out a handful of coins.

"I will."

He sorted through them, then handed me four pennies.

"One for each of you," he said.

"Then there should be five," I said.

"How so?"

"The baby. She earned her keep tonight."

He flipped me one more. "Only because I like babies," he said.

"Thank you, milord," I said, bowing.

"Am I to understand that you will be leaving Marseille in the morning?" he asked, sitting down at the desk and motioning me to a chair across from him.

"You are remarkably well-informed," I said.

"One overhears things when one is a servant," he said.

"Especially when one is trying to overhear things," I said.

"Just so," he said.

"Well, there's no reason to hide it," I said. "We go to seek our fortune in Montpellier next."

"Do they lack fools in Montpellier?" he asked.

"On the contrary, there is a surfeit, but it takes a professional such as myself to point that out to them."

"I wonder if they will appreciate the information," he said. "Well, since you are going, I was wondering if you would be so kind as to deliver something to a friend of mine."

"What sort of something, and what sort of friend?" I asked.

"A letter," he said.

"Are there no couriers you can use?"

"Not leaving tomorrow."

"What's in the letter?"

"It's personal," he said. "It will be sealed."

"And who is its intended recipient?"

"My counterpart there. His name is Léon, the seneschal to the Countess. It would have the advantage of gaining you a valuable connection upon your arrival."

"That would be useful," I said. "Very well. I'll do it."

"Thank you," he said. From the desk he took a piece of parchment that had already been written upon, then dipped a quill in a jar of ink and jotted down a few lines that I couldn't make out, blotted them, then folded the parchment in thirds. He turned to take a candle from a shelf behind him, and I slipped my hand into my pouch. He turned back to melt some wax onto where the folded edges met, then pressed a signet ring into it. When it hardened, he handed it to me.

"Have a safe—," he began.

"Two pennies," I said.

"What?"

"Two pennies more for the extra weight."

"What weight?" he scoffed. "A piece of parchment will add nothing to your wain."

"The weight of the responsibility," I explained. "It sits heavily on a fool's shoulders."

"Oh, for Christ's sake," he muttered, handing the coins to me.

"A fool's blessing upon you for your generosity," I said, pressing his hands fervently between mine as he did so.

"What is that worth?" he said, extricating his hand from mine.

"Two pennies," I said, tossing them into the air and catching them.

We returned to the dinner, which was at its end. My wife was at the other end of the room, her virtue successfully defended. Pedro was in intense conversation with Anselme, having sniffed out the real power in the room, and Roncelin sat moodily as his wife berated him loud enough for all to hear. The subject seemed to be his inability to provide her with children. The guests were practically fleeing the room.

We quietly gathered our gear and slipped out, waving to the poor musicians who were forced to play to the bitter end. Pantalan was waiting for us by the wharf, skipping pebbles across the harbor's waters.

"Roncelin is one of the sorriest excuses for a man I have ever seen," he said, fuming. "Not one smile the entire night. And to throw me out! The nerve. What does he think he is, a viscount? Please tell me that he got drunk, picked a fight with Pedro, and got beaten to a pulp."

"No, no, and no," I said. "Let's go back to your place. We need to pack for tomorrow."

When we were done packing, I tossed Pantalan his share of our payment for the evening.

"A penny," he sighed. "The price of my humiliation. Who paid you?"

"Laurent," I said. "And he asked me to deliver a letter to Montpellier for him."

"Really? That's odd."

I pulled it out of my pouch.

"It's sealed," said Helga.

"You know, a friend of mine was once asked to take a sealed letter somewhere," I said. "His curiosity got the better of him, and he decided to break the seal and see what was inside. It turned out to be a warrant for his execution."

"I suppose he decided not to deliver it after that," said Helga.

"You suppose correctly, Apprentice."

"So, open it."

"Ah, but what if it is a letter that we do want to have delivered?" I asked her.

"Then you can deliver it—Oh, but what about the seal?"

"There's the problem," I said. "Fortunately, seal-stealing is a specialty of mine. Observe."

I reached into my pouch and pulled out a small lump of clay.

"Make sure that it's quite moist before you put it in your pouch," I said. "Then, you can use it to make an impression of a seal or key."

I turned it toward her to show her the impression of Laurent's signet ring. I had gotten it while pressing his hand between mine when giving him my blessing.

"Now, all we have to do is find a smith of dubious propriety and get him to cast a new seal for us," I said. "Pantalan, you must know such a man."

"I do," he said. "But he's probably out drinking right now."

"Well, I think we should find him, don't you?"

"I wouldn't bother," he said. "He's mean and useless when he's drunk, and you don't want someone like that handling molten metal."

"But this could be important," I insisted.

"I agree," he said. "Wait here."

He climbed the steps to his room. We heard some rummaging noises; then he came back down with a small bronze coffer. He opened it and spilled two dozen seals onto the pallet.

"Let's see," he said, sorting through them. "Roncelin, Eudiarde, Anselme—oh, that big one is my favorite. It belongs to Hughes de Fer, he's the chief of the Viguerie, very grandiose, took me ages to get hold of it. Ah, here we are. Laurent's signet ring."

He held up a small chunk of iron with the seneschal's seal re-created on one end.

"I didn't know," I said.

"Because you didn't ask," he said. "Now, if you would like, I could have you teach my grandmother to suck eggs. But first, open that damn letter."

I took my knife and slid it carefully under the seal, making sure the parchment was undamaged. Then I opened.

" 'To my Lady Marie, Countess of Montpellier,' " I read. " 'Your husband attempted to raise money from Anselme and other members of the consulat, but has been unsuccessful. He has, however, prevailed upon Roncelin to accompany him to Rome, where he intends to have himself coronated by Innocent. I shall attend the Viscount so that I may further learn of your husband's plans. I remain, as ever, your obedient servant.' "

"No execution this time," said Claudia. "Interesting. He addresses it on the outside to this Léon person, but it is clearly meant for the countess herself."

"He said he was a servant," I commented. "Now we know who he's serving. Any idea how he knew the countess?"

"Well, we all knew her when she was here," said Pantalan. "Laurent has been with the house of Barral for over thirty years, so naturally he would know her well."

"But in Marseille?" I asked.

"Of course," said Pantalan. "She lived here for several years."

"Wait," said Claudia. "Do you mean that she's the same Marie who married Barral?"

"Yes," said Pantalan. "I thought you knew that."

"I never made the connection," she said. "But then Folc would have known her."

"Here and in Montpellier," said Pantalan.

"And if Folc knew her," she said, starting to pace back and forth. "And the timing. Let me think. Yes, the timing works out."

"Where are you going with this?" I asked her. "Do you think Marie has something to do with the message to Folc?"

"Look, when Barral died, she was pregnant with his child," she said. "So the child would have a claim to being the next in line to become viscount, and maybe Marie could have been regent until it was of age. But Folquet comes up with the idea of bringing in Roncelin. Did Marie protest when this happened? They basically dispossessed both her and the child."

"She didn't utter a peep, as I recall," said Pantalan. "It seemed very noble of her at the time."

"Let's say that Folc had something to do with her staying quiet," said Claudia. "Maybe he had some information on her that kept her from asserting her claim. She goes back home to Montpellier because there is nothing left for her here. When her father dies, she becomes Countess of Montpellier and then marries the King of Aragon. That was when?"

"This past August," said Pantalan. "And she didn't become countess when her father died. Her brother was count, but he renounced the title and entered a monastery at the beginning of the summer."

"Lot of that going around," I said.

"So, she has just become more powerful than any woman since Eleanor of Aquitaine," continued Claudia. "But maybe she still considers Folc to be a danger. Or maybe word reached him and he sent her a letter reminding her of what he knows. She sees it as a threat, and threatens him right back. Hence, the warning in the librarium. And that's why it only surfaced after all these years. It was Marie's marriage that brought it on."

She stopped, grinning triumphantly. We looked at each other.

"Well?" said Claudia, looking at me.

"It's possible," I said. "The timing of the marriage is certainly suggestive. And it's not like we have any better leads to follow."

"I still like my idea about the pilgrim captured by pirates," said Helga.

"It sounds far-fetched to me," said Pantalan. "But if it will fetch you far from here, I'm all for it. I could use the peace and quiet."

"Then it's to Montpellier in the morning," I said.

"What will we find there?" asked Helga.

"A flock of wild geese," said Claudia. "And we are going to chase every single one of them."

SIX

Mas vos, Domna, que avetz mandamen . . .
[But you, Lady, who are in control . . .]

—FOLQUET DE MARSEILLE, "*AMORS, MERCE! NO MUEIRA TAN SOVEN!*"
[TRANS. N. M. SCHULMAN]

Portia let out a squeal of delight as Theo drove Zeus and the wain into the courtyard, and the horse whinnied in return. I brought her carefully within petting distance of his head, and she reached out with both hands, straining against my arms to stroke the monster's muzzle. Zeus submitted to her inexpert attentions with unbridled affection, nuzzling her gently. I never understood how this great horse could be so loving with one infant, yet so carnivorous toward everyone else.

Theo and Helga took advantage of the distraction to load the wain. Pantalan stood and watched, occasionally picking up one of the lighter items and handing it to our beleaguered apprentice, all the while offering a stream of useless advice.

A voice hailed me from the entrance to the courtyard, and I turned in surprise to see Julien Guiraud hurrying toward me, waving. "Oh, good, I have caught you," he said. "I have found him!"

"Well done," I said. "Found who?"

"Marin Itier," he said. "He lives, or at least did until recently."

"Itier? Who is he again?" asked Theo, coming over.

"Ah, you must be the lucky husband of this remarkable lady," said Julien, shaking his hand enthusiastically.

"Itier was the merchant that Folc ruined," I explained. "I told you about him."

"Ah, yes," said Theo.

"I remember him," said Pantalan, coming over to greet Julien. "He sailed off to Acre after that, didn't he?"

"He did," said Julien. "After that pilgrimage, he disappeared, and Marseille never heard from him again. But I made some inquiries among some sailor friends of mine, and it turns out that he ended up in Toulon! He's a peddler there, fallen on hard times, but he still lives."

"Toulon," said Theo. "That's east, down the coast a ways."

"Exactly," said Julien.

"Well, we'll look into him if Montpellier proves fruitless," said Theo. "And it may very well be a barren town for us. Thank you for the information, friend Julien."

"Give my warmest regards to your sister," I added. "If our path takes us through Gémenos again, I promise to visit her."

"I am sure that she would enjoy that," he said, taking my hand and bowing over it.

Theo rolled his eyes over the display of gallantry. I stuck my tongue out at him before Julien straightened up.

"Then all I can do now is wish you a safe journey," said Julien.

"Thank you, Sieur Guiraud," said Theo, and the merchant departed.

"I guess this is good-bye," said Theo, turning to Pantalan.

"It was, if not fun, at least a change," said Pantalan, clasping his hand. He turned to me and bowed with ten times as much flourishing as had Julien, then kissed my hand.

"That's how it's done properly," I said to Helga. "It was a pleasure meeting you, Brother Fool. Take care of our troubadour friend."

"I will, Domna," he said. He waved and wrinkled his nose at Portia, who giggled and waved back.

"Oh, I almost forgot," said Helga. "I have a question for you."

"Ask away," said Pantalan.

"Why do you live here, when everything that's happening is down by the harbor?"

He was taken aback for a moment, and I could see some easy quip forming in his mind. Then his eyes softened. "There is a garden by a church up here," he said. "A wall around it shuts out the world. A jester's life is filled with constant chatter and noise. If I didn't go there and enjoy the stillness every once in a while, then it would be me up in the mountains singing to the wolves instead of Vidal."

"Oh," said Helga.

She held out her hand, expecting him to kiss it. Instead, he shook it so heartily that it nearly came off.

"Good-bye, Little Chick," he said merrily. "Come back and visit when you're fully fledged, and maybe I'll marry you. This town needs more fools."

We clambered onto the wagon. Theo flicked the reins, and Zeus trotted out of the courtyard. I looked back, and Pantalan was waving until we lost sight of him.

We took the western gate out of the Ville-Haute, the same that we had taken to see Vidal. This time, however, we took the main road west, the sun following behind us.

Helga was uncharacteristically quiet as she perched in back, watching Marseille gradually disappear from view.

"Do you think he meant it?" she said suddenly.

"Meant what?" I asked.

"About marrying me. Was he serious?"

"When is a fool ever serious?" I asked.

"When he talks about marriage," said Theo. "It's a very frightening subject. It will make any fool turn sober."

"You didn't turn sober when we got married," I said. "Much the opposite."

"The subject turns the fool sober," he explained. "The actual marriage will drive him right back to drink."

"That's the male fool speaking," I said. "I, on the other hand, got drunk one fine night, and when I sobered up, to my horror found myself married to this one. That's the only explanation for it."

"What about Pantalan?" persisted Helga.

"If you think he's serious, feel free to go back there and find out," said Theo. "Once your apprenticeship is complete, you should be old enough."

"But he's so old!" she said. "He must be over thirty."

Theo and I glanced at each other.

"Do you want to throw her over the side, or shall I?" I asked.

It was a four-day journey, although I don't know if I would count five rivers. One or two were merely streams, easily forded. The Rhône, on the other hand, was wide and full of boats, and we waited in line for two or three hours before the ferrymen were able to accommodate us. The price of crossing was exorbitant, but one look at their massive arms was all it took to dissuade us from haggling.

"The name of the fool in Montpellier is Grelho?" I asked my husband as we broke camp on the fourth day.

"Right," he said. "I've never met him. I was last here back in '79, long before I ever met you. Grelho has been there about twenty years, I think."

"So he would have known Folc."

"Folc the merchant did business in Montpellier, and Folquet the troubadour rode the circuit from Marseille and back. If the answers to our quest aren't found in Marseille, then they may very well be here. Unless it is that Itier fellow."

"Or somebody else we haven't even thought about," piped up Helga helpfully.

"You can look for him," said Theo.

"Or her," I said. "The Lark is a woman, after all."

"You know, one thing about your theory bothers me," he said.

"What is that?"

"Why would Folc join the Cistercians when he did? Everything that happened with the succession in Marseille happened several years before that. You also don't account for the sudden fear and haste that your gallant merchant described."

"Maybe it had something to do with her second marriage," I said. "Maybe we should go back and question Folc some more."

"Maybe I should have thought of that before we came all the way to Montpellier. Look! You can see the bell tower from here."

There was one more river to cross, a broad but shallow one that supported only barges and flat-bottomed boats. There was a bridge over it, and a road leading to a gate protected by a tower that soared some sixty feet. The combination might have been intimidating to the casual invader were it not for the fact that no walls fanned out from them, nor were there any soldiers guarding them. One solitary man sat on a stool to the right, leaning back with his eyes closed, enjoying the morning sun. He was wearing a leathern apron over his clothing, and an enormous hammer with a thick handle the length of a man's arm rested against the stool.

Theo looked at the gate, which was closed, then glanced to the open sides. "I'm guessing we go around," he said.

"And I'm guessing you don't," said the man, his eyes still closed, but his right hand now resting on the hammer.

"We go through the gate?" asked Theo.

"Yes," said the man.

"But the gate is closed," said Theo.

"It is; that's the plain truth of it," said the man, yawning, then stretching like an immense cat.

"How are we to pass through the gate if it's closed?" asked Theo, smiling slightly.

The man finally opened his eyes, stood, and walked over to us. He turned to stare at the gate, apparently in deep contemplation.

"I could open it for you," he offered finally.

"That would be a kind and Christian thing to do," I said.

"But I can't just yet," he said. "There are things I am supposed to say first."

"Some ritual incantation?" I asked. "Is it a magical gate?"

"Ooooh," sighed Helga, lost in the idea.

The man looked her and the baby, and a broad grin split his grimy face. "First, I am supposed to say welcome to the cloture commune of Montpellier," he said. "At least, it will be a proper cloture when they finish building the walls."

"I would think a gate without walls would be fairly useless," said Theo.

"It is, and that's the plain truth of that," agreed the man. "But it is much easier to connect the walls after you build the gates and towers than it is to build the walls all the way around, then tear down the spaces for the gates and towers and build them, especially since the gates and towers are the tricky parts. Any fool can build a wall."

"I can't," I said. "But I'm not just any fool."

"So that's what you are," he said, peering at our faces. "I thought as much. Introductions, then. I am Reynaud, the blacksmith."

"I am Tan Pierre, the fool," said Theo. "My wife, Domna Gile, and our daughters, Helga and Portia."

"I'm Helga," clarified Helga. "She's just a baby."

"Two daughters," said Reynaud. "A world of trouble faces you. My sympathies. A pleasure meeting you. The Blacksmiths' Guild welcomes you to Montpellier."

"We thank you," I said. "Why are the blacksmiths manning the gates?"

"It's Wednesday," he said. "Each of the guilds has their gates and days to watch them. When the walls are built, we'll hire more soldiers to do a proper job. But there's not much point in paying soldiers when anyone could just go around."

"Like us, for example?" asked Theo.

"Not like you, for I can see that you have the proper respect due to a gatekeeper," said Reynaud. "Even a once-a-week gatekeeper like myself. And I would think that people hoping to make a living as entertainers would want to make a noticeable entrance into a new city."

"True enough," said Theo.

"Now," continued Reynaud. "The next thing that I am supposed to ask you is if you will be staying or passing through?"

"Staying for a while," said Theo. "Then leaving when the while is up."

"Does that constitute passing through?" I asked.

"I would say not, but it all depends on the length of the while," said Reynaud. "Is a fool's while the same as most people's?"

"I think a fool's while is probably longer," said Theo.

"It depends on the wiles of the fool," I added. "How long is the while of a blacksmith?"

"That would depend on the circumstances," he said. "Sometimes my wife asks me to do something that I would rather not, but because I love and fear her, I will say, 'In a while, my sweet.' And that while can be a very long time indeed. Therefore, I will put you down as staying. Now, if you are escaped serfs, and I'm not saying as you are, but if you were, then you have no protection against being returned to your master should he request it. But if you are escaped serfs, and it's really none of my business whether you are or you aren't, and you succeed in staying here for a year and a day, our laws consider you to be free, in case you weren't before."

"A generous policy, whether it applies to us or not," I said.

"We need people to populate the city once the walls are finished," he said. "Otherwise, what's the point of expanding?"

He took a small paintbrush from a bucket of whitewash that sat near his stool and marked our wagon with an *x*.

"Three pennies for the entrance fee," he said. "I'm not charging you for the baby."

"Thank you, kind Reynaud," said Theo. "Now, could you tell us the whereabouts of a fool named Grelho?"

"He lives just off the herberie," said Reynaud. "And that's just past Notre Dame of the Tables. Ask when you get there. Hey, now that there's more than one fool in town, maybe you could form your own guild."

"There's an idea," said Theo, smiling at me. "What do you think, wife?"

"Not a good idea at all," I said firmly.

"Why not?" asked Reynaud, disappointed at my quick dismissal of his plan.

"Because if there was a Fools' Guild, then we would have to take a turn guarding the gates," I said. "You wouldn't want your city to be guarded by fools, would you?"

"A good point," he said. "All right, let me open them for you."

He walked over and swung them open easily. Theo flicked the reins, and Zeus pulled us through.

"No lock on the gates," Theo noted.

"What would be the purpose?" asked Reynaud. "People can just go around them."

"Good-bye, friend Reynaud," I called. "We'll be sure to come to you if we have any iron that needs, um, hammering."

We had come to the city from the southeast, and a broad road ran northwest from the newly fashioned gate we had just encountered, moving uphill toward the church of Notre Dame, whose bell tower had a double set of arches piled one upon the other. It was this road, I would come to learn, that carried the pilgrim traffic from the west to Marseille, while another road, the via Francigena, ran north to south, taking a different group of pilgrims from France to retrace the steps of James of Compostela. Where the two roads crossed was a place of holy gossip as those returning shouted their good news to those on their way, and great was the misinformation thereof.

It was in these two crossing rivers of pilgrims that the good citizens of Montpellier cast their nets and hooks, trawling for whatever sustenance they could find. Fishers of men abounded in Montpellier, though not what Our Savior had in mind when he used that description. Fishers of pockets and purses, more the like. What would the inhabitants of Montpellier and Marseille do for a living if these quests for absolution ever stopped?

We passed by the church of Notre Dame. Directly in front of it were the tables of the money changers, taking the coins of whichever direction people were coming from and trading them for slightly less of those of the opposite compass point. We exchanged some of our dwindling Guild funds for local coinage, then sought out the herb market.

This turned out to be a short distance west of the money changers, a small rectangle of space with a number of narrow twisty streets radiating out from it. It was a lively place, filled with gossiping wives and cooks with bunches of green dangling from their baskets, and the mingled scents from the different stalls greatly eased the fatigue of our journey.

Theo inhaled deeply as we passed through, his eyes closed for a moment. Then he looked at me and smiled sadly. "My mother kept an herb garden," he said. "Or so I was told. I always imagine her holding me when I smell fresh herbs." He sighed. "But she never did, did she?"

"Let's find our colleague," I said softly.

Half the streets in Montpellier were barely wide enough to allow passage of our cart, and the other half weren't. We kept scraping against the walls of the buildings, most of which were two-story structures with a vaulted store at street level and a single room above. Light was at a premium—windows were angled to catch as much of it as they could, and many of the houses seemed tilted in their construction, ready to follow the passage of the sun like a flower over the course of a day.

Grelho lived in a particularly dark and grubby little street that probably saw daylight only at noon in good weather for three days in midsummer. The road ran down a hill, and sloped on both sides down to a central gutter that carried a sickly stream of water. The house itself was indistinguishable from the others. A blotch of black paint covered the door. Nothing would have alerted a passerby to the presence of a jester within. Theo touched the black blotch on the door gingerly with his forefinger.

"Still tacky," he said. "He's painted over his sign. Wonder what's going on?"

"One way to find out," I said.

He pounded on the door.

"Go away!" came a muffled voice from inside.

"Open up, Grelho," called Theo, pounding on it again. "Don't make me start singing."

An eye appeared for a moment at a peephole. "Christ on a crutch," moaned the owner of the eye. "Why me? Why now?"

The door opened, and a skinny man dressed in gray rags dashed out and started grabbing our gear from the cart.

"Get it inside," he muttered. "Quickly, you bastards. Oh, God, a horse. Wonderful. Is he safe?"

"Not particularly," said Theo as we lugged in our gear in as few trips as we could. Portia started crying.

"All I need, all I need," said the man. "Shut her up. Give her a rattle, stick a teat in her, whatever you do, just get her quiet. Is that everything? You, Fool, throw something over your motley and get rid of your bells. What were you thinking?"

"Who are you?" asked Theo.

The man stopped and glared. "I'm Grelho, as you very well know," he said. "That's why you're here, isn't it?"

Theo whistled the first part of the password.

"No time for that," said the man; then he squeaked as my gentle good-natured husband took him gently by the collar and slammed him good-naturedly into the wall.

"There's always time for a melody," said Theo, smiling.

The man looked at him, his eyes bulging; then he tried to whistle. A few faint notes came out. Then he licked his lips frantically and tried sounding a few more.

"That's enough," said Theo, releasing him. "You are Grelho the Fool."

"Your confidence is appreciated, I'm sure," gasped Grelho. "Now, throw a hat on, and we'll get rid of this damned horse and cart. The rest of you get inside and don't breathe until we're back."

He practically shoved Helga and me into the store and closed the door. We looked at each other in the dark. Portia continued to cry.

"What should we do?" asked Helga.

"You keep watch," I ordered her. "I'll nurse."

Portia snuffled a little, but latched on quickly. The subsequent burp after she was done would have won her a round of drinks at many a tavern.

"How does she do that so loudly?" wondered Helga. "Wait. They're coming back." She opened the door quickly and the two men slipped in.

Grelho pushed the door shut and slid a bolt into place. He turned to face us in the gloomy space. "Welcome to my humble hospitalum," he said. "Now, tell me why you are here."

"First, light a candle or something," said Theo. "We didn't travel all this way to talk to a fool in the dark."

"Candles cost money," said Grelho.

Theo grabbed at his pouch in disgust and stuck a coin in front of Grelho's face. "This is a penny," said Theo. "It will buy you a couple of boxes of candles. Light one now, you cheap bastard, or I will shove a wick up your ass and see how long you burn."

"Oh, I'd taper off in the end," said Grelho. "Stay here."

He vanished up a steep set of stairs at the rear of the storeroom.

"If he hadn't made that last quip, I'd still be wondering if we had the right man," commented Theo.

"I wonder what put him into this state," I said.

A glimmer appeared at the top of the stairs; then Grelho descended, carefully holding a lit candle in each hand.

"Catch," he said, suddenly tossing one to Helga.

She snatched it from the air without batting an eye and spun it through her fingers while keeping the flame going.

"Well done, Apprentice," he said. He took a small table from a nail in the wall and set it down in the middle of the room, then placed the candle at its center, and held out his hand. Helga tossed back the other candle, and he put it by the first.

"Welcome to Montpellier," he said bitterly.

"Some welcome," said Theo. "What's going on?"

"The whole city has been turned upside down," said Grelho. "Ever since the She-Serpent married the Devil's Spawn."

"The new broom has been sweeping?" I asked.

"More like the new scythe has been reaping," he said. "Haven't you heard?"

"We've been on the road," said Theo. "We knew about Marie marrying Pedro, but we haven't heard the latest. Bring us up to date."

"Where to begin, where to begin?" muttered Grelho. "It started going wrong with the second-to-last Guilhem."

"The what?"

"Montpellier has been ruled by a long series of Guilhems," explained Grelho. "The second-to-last was Guilhem the Seventh, an absolute prince of a man, even if he was only a count. Cultured, witty, played the harp rather well, always had some revelry going at the palais royal. Oh, the Guild did fine by him, I can tell you. I was there practically every day, and there were usually a couple of troubadours hanging about. He kept the peace with everybody inside town and out, and kept the Bishop happy down at Maguelone, so the Church never bothered sticking another bishop here to keep an eye on things."

"And this was Marie's father?" I asked.

"Correct. By way of Eudoxie, this high-strung Byzantine witch who everyone thought was the Emperor's daughter, only she turned out to be a niece or a cousin or some such thing. And that was a problem, because she was constantly putting on airs, and belittling everyone she considered inferior, which was basically everyone else. But her fatal flaw was that after she produced Marie, she couldn't come up with a son."

"Let me guess," I said. "The second to last Guilhem wanted another Guilhem."

"Yes," said Grelho. "Off goes Eudoxie into holy orders, off goes little Marie to an advantageous marriage in Marseille, and in comes the new younger wife."

"I've heard this song before," I said. "She was pretty and soon pregnant."

"And produced the last Guilhem," said Grelho. "Lovely boy. Serene, thoughtful. I taught him to play the harp myself."

"Good for you," said Theo. "So, why isn't he Guilheming about the town?"

"Because when old Guilhem died two years ago, young Guilhem was only twelve. Back comes big sister Marie, fresh out of her second marriage. She played her little brother like a harp. She convinced him that she was the rightful heir to the town, not him. And she praised his contemplative side to the Heavens, brought in the Bishop to do a little holy cajoling, got Rome to do some righteous threatening over the propriety of the second marriage, and before we looked up, the boy had renounced Montpellier in her favor and was off to Maguelone to become a monk."

"Lot of that going around," I said, stealing Theo's line.

"Pedro was lurking about, waiting for the right moment," continued Grelho. "He makes his move on our lusty single countess, and now Montpellier is learning to speak Aragonese."

"But what happened to you?" asked Theo.

"What happened to me was what happened to everybody," said Grelho. "The old families were allied with the Guilhems. Marie and Pedro linked up with the newer money, made some strategic promises, and started revoking charters that had been with the old families since they were new." He shuddered. "She has a long memory, this one does. Every slight from someone at court has become an exilable offense. A score of scores are being settled, my friends, and the entire town is living in fear."

"Are you one of the scores?" I asked.

"I was the friend of her father, the teacher of her brother," he said sadly. "I had enough of a jester's immunity to avoid the worst. I'm too lowly to exile from the town, so she simply exiled me from the court. I'm ruined. A jester with no access to the court is worthless. I'll be juggling for drinks again, and I'm getting too old for that."

"Have you tried getting back in her good graces?" asked Theo.

"I can't even get through the door," he said.

"Maybe I can," said Theo. "I have this letter to deliver to her seneschal. That at least gets me inside."

"You won't get past him," said Grelho. "Even if she wanted a fool, she won't see you. The word is that she's been on a general rampage against men ever since her new husband popped a baby into her and promptly left town."

Theo looked at me. "I knew there was a reason I brought you along," he said.

I glared at him.

"A second reason," he amended hastily.

In the morning, Theo handed me Laurent's letter, and I handed him Portia. He held the baby out in front of him with both arms, and they looked at each other quizzically.

"What is this?" he asked.

"That is your child," I said. "Try not to drop her until I return."

"And then I can?"

Portia immediately looked worried.

"No," I said.

"Why can't Helga take care of her?" he asked.

"Because Helga is coming with me," I replied.

"I am?" exclaimed Helga in delight.

"She is?" exclaimed Theo in dismay.

"She is," I said. "She's an apprentice, not a nanny, and this is an excellent opportunity for her to get some experience. We'll see you later. Brother Grelho, will you be our guide?"

"Shouldn't you wash off your makeup and change into something normal?" he asked.

"If I did that, then I would be something normal," I said. "And the truth is, I am something extraordinary. Lead on, former Fool."

Theo had begun telling him about our quest, and I filled in the rest as we walked along the main road to the western part of the city.

"Folquet," he said, shaking his head. "I knew he would bring us trouble someday."

"How well did you know him?" I asked.

"Oh, he was a fixture here back in the eighties," he said. "Left his family behind in Marseille when he came here, so he felt so unshackled that he practically floated above the city. The seventh Guilhem loved his singing, and Folquet loved to sing and loved to be loved by the royalty, so he was at the palais all the time."

"Doing the Guild's business, of course."

"The Guild's business, and his own business, and lots of little businesses on the side," said Grelho. "Handsome bastard. I wouldn't bring his name up with Marie."

"Why not?"

He sighed. "This was only a rumor, mind you," he said. "He did the troubadour bit with Eudoxie, writing songs that sent her fluttering about like a deranged pigeon. Everything you would expect a practitioner of the art of courtly love to do."

"And the rumor?"

"That maybe it wasn't just courtly love he was practicing."

"No! With the countess in the palais itself? Incredible."

"Well, it wasn't just incredible; it was completely untrue," he said. "But truth never stops the rumormongers from mongering rumors. Someone may have whispered in Guilhem's ear that Marie may not have been his daughter, and that may be the real reason he got rid of

Eudoxie and brought in the new wife to give him an heir of certainty. Folquet stopped doing business here around the same time, which was an interesting coincidence that added fuel to the fire."

"When was that?"

"About '87, I think. The last Guilhem was born a year later."

"Does Marie resemble her father?"

"I see his face in her," said Grelho. "In temperament, however, she can be her mother's daughter. We are coming to the Peyrou quarter. That's the palais royal up ahead."

"I thought it might be," I said.

It must have been a comedown for Eudoxie, I thought. Once you've been raised in Constantinople, no other city will seem so impressive, nor will any small city palace compare to Blachernae, the abode of the Byzantine emperors. But there were no Byzantine emperors in Blachernae anymore. I saw the last one flee as the city burned behind him, and now Blachernae was filled with French and Italian soldiers. So much for palaces.

And, if you asked me, the local palais royal was good enough for everyday purposes, built of blocks of white stone that gleamed in the sun and must have come from the mountains nearby. It was on a hill, with a fosse surrounding it, and the view was splendid, with gardens and vineyards just below and farmland stretching out into the distance until it met up with the mountains. The gates were open and guarded by actual soldiers. Grelho tapped me on the arm.

"This is as far as I go," he said. "Good luck."

Helga and I looked at each other, took a deep breath, and passed through the gates into an enormous paved courtyard. The central building rose four stories into the air, with marble columns that harked back to old Rome, their capitals carved with intertwining grapevines. The wings reached around us to the front wall, containing guardhouses and stables on either side, and a blacksmith's forge down in one corner. The new cloture wall had been completed here first, of course, so the rear of the building was well protected from the west, with towers soaring every hundred paces.

Laurent's seal got us through the front door, where a haughty manservant led us to an even haughtier man in an office to the right of the entrance. He sat behind a grandiose mahogany desk that was covered with neatly stacked papers. He was dressed in a magnificent red surcoat with gold threads woven into its brocaded front. A large seal hung from a silver chain around his neck.

"Give me the letter," he ordered me.

"I may give it only to its intended recipient," I said. "I am Domna Gile, the Fool, and this is my daughter, Helga. Pray tell me, Sieur, who it is that I am addressing?"

"You will address me as Sieur, and nothing else," he sneered. "Give me that letter."

"Well, Sieur Andnothingelse, this letter is to be given to the countess's seneschal, whose name is Léon and whose surname, I believe, is And-no-one-else-but. A surname very close to your own. Perhaps he is a relative?"

"Do you see this?" he said, holding out the seal.

Helga and I leaned forward and looked at it.

"It's lovely," I said. "Goes with your outfit quite handsomely."

"And it brings out the gray in your hair," added Helga.

"You are impudent," he said, rising to his feet. "I shall have you both whipped."

I stood quickly and moved to the fireplace, holding the sealed letter near it.

"We were told by your counterpart Laurent that we would receive a cordial reception for doing him the favor of delivering this," I said. "I suspect that your lady is the true recipient. I think that she might not appreciate it if she was denied this letter because it accidentally was burnt to a cinder thanks to the rudeness of her servant."

He looked at the letter, the fire, and my expression. My hand was getting uncomfortably hot. Then, to my relief, he sat down.

"I am Léon," he said. "My apologies for my incivility. May I have the letter?"

"No whipping," I said. "Your word."

He hesitated, and I let go of the letter, then snatched it from just above the flames.

"You have my word," he said quickly.

I walked up to him, gave him the letter, then made a show of blowing on my hand. Helga hid a smile behind her hand, then recovered and restored her expression to one of complete serenity.

He inspected the seal briefly, then broke it and read the letter. Score one for Pantalan's seal collection, I thought with relief. He glanced up when he was done. "You may go," he said.

"But I want to stay," I said.

"What?"

"We are traveling fools, Sieur Léon, and travel requires funds. Your friend Laurent assured us that you would present us to your lady so that we might entertain her."

"She does not want entertaining," he said.

"That is not what they say in town," I said. "Anyway, she might be interested in what I have to say about her husband."

"What is that?" he asked suspiciously.

"Something that should only be discussed between women," I said. "The fewer women, the better. I would hate to be the cause of any vicious gossip."

"I promised not to whip you," he said. "I said nothing about having your tongue ripped out."

"Nor have I promised not to cut off your balls," I said. "But being in such gracious society, I thought such things were understood. No threats, Sieur. I think the countess will want to speak with me. Everyone wants entertainment, despite what you believe."

He stood. "Stay here," he ordered, and left the room.

"What do you think? Should we run?" asked Helga.

"He's a coward," I said. "I had a steward with a real spine who knew how to stand up to people without threatening them every other sentence. This man blusters, but he won't actually do anything. Listen at the door—I'm going to see if there is anything useful in his desk."

I rifled through it like a good little burglar, but found nothing but accounts. I left things as I had found them. When the seneschal returned, Helga and I were tossing six balls back and forth. He looked at them, and nodded.

"She will see you," he said. "Impressive, juggling six balls like that."

"We can do eight," I said. "But for the life of me, I cannot find two more around here. Would you be so kind as to show us the way?"

His brow furrowed; then he turned and beckoned us to follow him. We went down a hallway with a black marble floor, up a grand staircase, then up a less grand staircase, and to a set of white wooden doors.

He paused briefly and looked at us sternly. "She is to be addressed as milady, and nothing—" He stopped short. "Just call her milady."

He pushed open both doors and strode in, announcing, "The fools are here, milady."

We paraded in and bowed low, waiting. Nothing happened. I risked a quick peek. There was an ornate oaken chair with a red cushioned seat and back by a small writing table, and divans and cushions scattered about, but no countess. We straightened up slowly and looked at the seneschal, who was looking around just as puzzled as we were.

"She was just here," he began, but then a door opened at the rear of the room and the countess dragged herself in.

She was a tiny woman, shorter than me, and her face was pale without the benefit of makeup. She was clad in a green silk dressing gown, and her hair was unplaited and poorly combed. She walked unsteadily to the chair and plopped into it with a sigh. With some simple care, she would be a beautiful woman. As it was, she looked like a beautiful woman after an all-night carouse.

She focused blearily on the two of us, then looked at her seneschal. "Get me some hot cider," she said, hoarsely. "Them, too."

"But, milady, you shouldn't be alone with—"

"Now! I want some cider now!" she screamed.

He backed out of the room, bowing rapidly, and closed the doors. Helga and I turned back and looked at her as she leaned onto an arm of the chair.

"Men never understand morning sickness, do they, milady?" I said sympathetically.

"I wish it on every single one of them every minute of the day," she moaned.

"I had a terrible time of it with this one," I said, patting Helga's head affectionately. "The last one wasn't too bad. I must be getting better at carrying children."

"My first, I barely knew what was going on," she said. "I was fourteen when she was born. No one told me anything until the midwife showed up to stay with me for the last month. I learned more from her than anyone in my life before or since."

"Well, you won't learn much from a pair of fools like us," I said.

"Then why are you here?" she said, a sudden sharpness in her voice. "Léon said that you had information for me about my husband. You just came from Marseille?"

"We have, milady."

"And you brought the letter from Laurent?"

"Yes, milady."

"And you saw my husband there?"

"We did, milady."

She hesitated. "How was he?" she asked softly. "How were his . . . appetites? His humors?"

"He was . . . merry, milady," I said.

She looked at me with something like fear for a moment, then picked up a silver bell from the writing table and rang it. A maidservant ran in from the door at the rear.

"Sylvie, is Guilhema dressed?" she asked.

"Oc, milady," replied the maid.

"Take the girl to her rooms," said the countess. She turned to Helga. "My daughter, Guilhema, is about your age. Amuse her."

Helga bowed low, then followed the maidservant out of the room. Léon came in with a tray on which sat a large pitcher of cider and several cups. He placed them on the writing table, then at the countess' gesture poured one for each of us.

"Come sit by me," she ordered.

I approached and sat on a low stool that materialized through some mysterious move by the seneschal.

"Leave us," she said to him.

He did the backwards-bowing thing again, and closed the doors as he left.

She sipped slowly from her cup, looking me over as she did. "Merry, you said," she prompted.

"Yes, milady."

"He ate well?"

"There was a feast in his honor, and he honored the feast."

"And he drank?"

"Like a master of revelry, with a different toast every time."

"He should have been miserable," she said bitterly. "He should have been despondent. It's the first time he's been away from me, and we've been married only four months. Not even. How can he be merry when I'm not at his side?"

"He may have only been pretending," I said. "To respect his host."

"He flirted, didn't he?" she asked. "That's what you came here to tell me."

"He flirted, milady."

"With what woman?" she demanded.

"With me, milady."

She started, and I calmly sipped my cider.

"With you?" she whispered incredulously. "You have the audacity to flaunt it to my face?"

"I thought it best that you hear it from me rather than through rumor," I said. "Wasn't it in Laurent's letter?"

"Why—yes, of course, it was," she said. "I was just testing your honesty."

"I hope to pass all such tests," I said. "Including the one set before me by your very attractive husband. I refused him, naturally."

"You refused him?" she exclaimed. "You must be the first woman who ever did so."

"I thought we married women should stick together, milady," I said. "If we don't help each other, who will? Certainly not the men."

"What is your husband?" she asked.

"A fool," I said. "Professionally, I mean. When he's not practicing his foolery, he's generally passed out drunk."

"And you have another child?"

"Oh, yes. A baby girl named Portia. Nine months old and already a mischief. She'll probably be smarter than all of us."

"I think this one will be another girl," she said, patting her belly. "I dread the prospect."

"Why, milady?"

"I've already failed Pedro so much," she said, her eyes tearing. "And to not give him a son—"

"Nonsense!" I said. "You'll be giving him the future queen of Aragon."

"Only if he still wants me," she said. "Men are so easily disappointed. My father renounced my mother just because I wasn't another Guilhem."

"A galling lack of gallantry in one who fancied himself a gallant, if you don't mind my saying so."

"I don't," she said, pouring some more cider. "Everyone before you has been afraid to say anything about my father. It's refreshing to hear someone actually say what I have thought all those years."

"One of the advantages of being a fool, milady," I said. "And you continued living here after he sent your mother away?"

"For a little while," she said. "Then he married that Castilian bitch and decided to trade me to Marseille for some shipping agreement or other. And in Marseille, I became the bitch that Barral married after renouncing his barren wife."

"How horrible," I said, patting her knee sympathetically. "And you were only thirteen?"

"Barely," she said. "But at least, I was a viscountess. Papa may have thought he could take Montpellier from me, but I had Marseille, as long as I could keep that old goat of a viscount happy."

"And you did," I said. "Until he died."

"You can overdo happiness," she said, sighing. "You can die from it. And you can kill with it. That's another lesson I learned too late." She glanced at the lute slung over my shoulder. "Do you sing?"

"Of course, milady," I said, tuning it. "What would you like to hear?"

"A woman's song," she said. "Something for mothers."

"Then it will be a strong song," I said.

I had been traveling with my fellow fools for so long that I had forgotten what it was like to sing by myself.

It was glorious.

She shifted over to one of the divans and lay down, her feet propped on a cushion, waving her hand aimlessly to the rhythms of the songs. And so we passed the time.

After I finished a third song, I heard applause from the rear of the room. I turned to look, and saw Helga standing with a smaller girl who might have been a toymaker's attempt to capture the countess in miniature.

"That was lovely!" said the girl, dashing forward to embrace the countess.

I stood and bowed to her, and she giggled in delight.

"Careful, darling," warned the countess. "When a fool bows to you, it may only mean you are the queen of fools."

"I would like that, Maman," she said. "And I truly love this Helga. May we keep her?"

The countess glanced at me, and I laughed.

"Tempting, but she is not for sale," I said. "However, we will come and visit tomorrow so that you may play together again."

"May they come again, Maman?" begged Guilhema. "Please?"

"By all means," said the countess, hugging her. "If it pleases you, it pleases me. But now, Maman needs her nap."

"Then we will take our leave of you, milady," I said, and Helga and I bowed and withdrew.

Léon was waiting for us and escorted us out. As we reached the front entrance, he handed each of us a penny. We bowed and thanked him, then passed through the courtyard and out the gates.

"Well, how was it?" I asked Helga.

"I have something to tell you," she said, grinning.

SEVEN

The white sheet bleaching on the hedge,
With heigh! the sweet birds, O, how they sing!
Doth set my pugging tooth on edge;
For a quart of ale is a dish for a king.

The lark, that tirra-lyra chants,
With heigh! with heigh! the thrush and the jay,
Are summer songs for me and my aunts,
While we lie tumbling in the hay.

—WILLIAM SHAKESPEARE, *THE WINTER'S TALE,* ACT IV, SCENE 3

When I was little, I lived with Mama in a house full of women and children. There were many rooms, but we weren't allowed to use most of them because they were for business, so we all slept jammed into one room in the cellar. As I got older, I learned to amuse the men when they came to the house. They would tell me to sing and dance, and I would, and I was good at it. I started doing somersaults and cartwheels, and could do real flips by the time I was eight. The men would give me candy, which I would share with the other children, and sometimes a penny, which the Master would take from me as soon as the men were out of the room. I soon learned how to palm the pennies so I could give them to Mama, and she would say, "Helga, little angel, soon I will have enough to buy us out of here."

But she started getting sick, and the Master wanted to throw her into the street. She begged him to let her stay. He told her that he would if she would let the men bid for me. I was nine. I told her I would do anything to help her. She told me how proud she was of me. Then, in the middle of the night, she carried me out of there and brought me to a funny-looking man wearing oddly colored clothes. She told me to sing, and I sang. She told me to dance, and I danced. She told me to fly, and I ran and jumped, doing a somersault in midair. The man clapped, and asked if I would like to do all that instead of living with all the women and children crammed into the cellar, and I said, Yes, I would. Mama hugged me hard and cried and told me to go with the man, and she would come see me as soon as she could. Then the man took me to another funny-looking man in another town, and he brought me to the Fools' Guild.

I never saw Mama again.

At the Guildhall, the old one in the Dolomites that we lived in before the Pope chased us out, I slept in a room with all the girl novitiates. There were less of us than the boys, but we were still packed like salt fish in a barrel, and the Dolomites were cold, so we huddled together in the big beds for warmth, and it was much nicer than the cellar room where I was before. When we went to the haven in the Black Forest, we all slept in the hayloft of the barn, girls on one side, boys on the other, and horses down below.

Then I became apprentice to Theo and Claudia, which meant I either slept in one room with them, or, if we were lucky, in a separate room with Portia.

I have never had one room to myself in my entire life. That's how I knew this girl Guilhema had to be one of the wealthiest girls in the world. She had three rooms, just for her.

She was having her hair brushed by a maidservant when the woman Sylvie brought me to her. She was seated on a cushion by a window that overlooked a garden, and had a tabby cat sleeping on her lap.

She looked at me, and her eyes lit up. "A girl fool!" she squealed. "What do I call you?"

"You call me Helga, milady," I said. "What do I call you?"

"Well, I was supposed to be Viscountess of Marseille," she said, considering the question. "And I am going to be the Countess of Montpellier someday, and I'm the stepdaughter of the King of Aragon."

"Well, all I am going to be is a fool," I said. "I can't possibly remember all of that. How about I just call you Guilhema?"

"Nobody calls me that but Maman," she said indignantly.

"What about your friends?" I asked. "What do they call you?"

"My—That's none of your business," she said. "But you're not my friend; you're a fool. You can't call me Guilhema. It's not proper."

"Look, if you are going to be a lady someday, then you have to have a fool," I said. "It's very fashionable."

"Is it?" she asked.

"Oh, yes," I said. "And everybody who is anybody knows that fools treat nobody with respect."

"They don't?"

"That's right. So, I will call you Guilhema."

She thought about that for a minute. "That's fine," she said. "I can play the harp."

"I can play the lute," I said. "And I can wiggle my ears."

"Can you really?" she breathed.

"Watch closely," I said. I scrunched up my face and clenched my teeth, and my ears wiggled a little.

"That's wonderful!" she laughed. "Can you teach me how to do that?"

"I'm not sure it can be taught," I said. "But I'll try. Let's sit in front of that mirror there."

We sat side by side, and she watched my reflection as I did it, which made her giggle, then tried to imitate it, which made me giggle, and soon we were making all kinds of silly faces and laughing until we were weak. The two maidservants stood by the door and never smiled once.

"What else can you do?" she asked, gasping.

"I know lots and lots of songs," I said, then I leaned forward and whispered, "and lots of stories that I'm not supposed to know."

Her eyes grew big; then she turned to the maidservant and said, "Sylvie, you and Marianne go away for a little bit."

The two maids curtsied, looking relieved, and vanished silently from the room.

"Tell me!" she cried as soon as they were gone.

I told her a mildly naughty story that they had taught us girls at the Guildhall for just such an occasion, and she was in hysterics by the end of it.

"I love it!" she said. "I wish I had someone to tell it to."

"Are there no other girls here to play with?" I asked.

"Not really," she said. "A lot of the girls had to leave after Maman became Countess because Maman didn't like their parents. I felt bad for them. It wasn't the girls' fault that their parents were so mean to Maman and had to be punished like that. Now all the other girls are scared when they come here."

"I'm not scared," I said.

"No, you're not," she agreed. "I'm glad. I'm not a scary person. My servants like me just fine, and so does my kitty, and so do my birds. The birds have only known me for a couple of months, and they like me!"

"You have birds?"

"Lots of them. Want to see?"

"Oh, yes."

She grabbed my hand and we ran through a door into a long, narrow room with windows all along one side and a dozen birdcages on the other. There was no singing. Half of them were asleep, and the others were hopping about the floors of their cages pecking at seeds scattered around.

"That's a *bergeronnette,*" she said, pointing to a yellow bird the size of my hand that was wagging its tail as it ate. "He likes bugs, especially crickets. He'll eat them out of my hand. Maman doesn't like me to touch bugs, but I think it's fun."

"He's pretty," I said. "That's some kind of finch, isn't it? I've seen those all over."

"It's a chaffinch," she said. "And that's a dunnock, and that's a chiffchaff, and that's a thrush, and that's a linnet, and that's a warbler, and that's a warbler, and that's another kind of warbler."

"Why aren't they warbling?" I asked.

"I don't know," she said. "They sing in the morning, sometimes, but my room faces west, so I think they get confused or something."

"Maybe they're lonely," I said. "You have just one in each cage."

"I could try that!" she exclaimed. "Put them together, or get lady birds and they could all get married and live together like Maman and Pedro, only Pedro isn't living here right now. This one is a tree creeper."

She poured some seeds into her hand and held it by the bars of one of the cages. The bird inside had unusually long claws and clung upside down to a log leaning against the side of the cage. It pecked at her hand, and she whistled at it. It did not reply.

"Where did you get them?" I asked.

"They all came from the houses of the people Maman didn't like," she said. "Everybody liked to keep songbirds, so she just took one that she liked from each place."

"Like hunting trophies."

"I suppose so," she said, pausing at one cage which had a small bird that was streaked with different shades of brown and had a short beak. "This one made her laugh when she got it, I remember."

"What kind is it?"

"A lark," she replied.

Oh, if Father Gerald could have seen me at the moment. *Full marks for the nonreaction, Helga,* I could hear him say.

"Why did it make her laugh?" I asked, looking at it. "It's not a very funny-looking bird."

"She was just saying how that's the right bird to take from *that* house," she said.

"Why? Which house was it from?"

"I don't know, and I don't care," she said. "It's mine, now. I wish I could hear it sing, though. I don't think I ever will."

"Why not?"

"Maman said that larks only sing when they fly free," she said.

"Maybe you should let it go," I suggested.

"No!" she said, stamping her foot. "It's mine, and I am going to keep it. And if it dies, I'll bury it in my garden with the other ones that died and I'll make a little stone to mark its grave. Would you like to see my dolls?"

"Please," I said.

We walked into another room.

I once had a doll that was just some sticks tied together with some scraps of cloth, but it was my favorite thing in the whole wide world because it was my only toy, and then a little boy I was playing with got mad at me and threw it into the fire. I cried for a whole month.

Guilhema had a room with toys and games, and one entire wall had shelves built just for dolls. She must have had a hundred.

"Which ones shall we play with?" she asked me.

"You pick," I said.

"All right," she said, taking down several. "Let's make a wedding. I can read and write, can you?"

In five languages so far, I wanted to say, and Claudia was teaching me Arabic. But Father Gerald's voice echoed in my head again: *What you know is a weapon, and what they don't know you know is a better one. When people think you can't read, they may leave something worth reading in front of you.*

"No," I said. "Someone showed me once how to make my name."

"That's the most important thing," she said. "Here's the Princess. Should she marry the brave knight, the monk, or the pirate?"

"I don't think monks can get married," I said.

"But he'll be a greedy evil monk who really wants to be Viscount," she said. "So he'll quit being a monk just to get married to do that."

"All right."

"I think I'm going to marry a king someday, just like Maman."

"That's a very good idea."

"Only I don't want to marry other people first like she did. Do you want to marry a king?"

"I don't think I can," I said. "I'm not noble like you."

"Who will you marry?"

"I had a proposal just last week," I said.

"You did! How exciting! What's he like?"

"A fool," I said. "Like everyone else I know."

We played for a while. I actually enjoyed it. Then she decided we should go see her mother, and we ran down to the room where I first saw the Countess. I could hear Claudia singing as we came to the door. I held a finger to my lips and we stood silently by the door and listened.

Claudia is a wonderful singer, and the smartest woman in the world, and had a wonderfully romantic marriage to a duke, and then her husband died and she met Theo and became a fool because she loved him so much. All the girls at the Guild kept looking at Theo and wondering what was so special about him, because he wasn't a very handsome man, but when he came back from Constantinople with Claudia and Portia and taught some classes, we could see what a good jester he was. Father Gerald said he was one of the best when he was sober, and Father Gerald didn't say that about just anybody. I listened to Claudia sing and thought Theo must really be something if he had Father Gerald's praise and Claudia's love, and how lucky I was to be apprenticed to them.

We said our good-byes, and Guilhema asked if I could come back, which pleased Claudia, I'm sure. We left, and the seneschal paid us, and we bowed and thanked him.

When we were outside the courtyard, Claudia turned to me and asked, "Well, how was it?"

"I have something to tell you," I said, grinning.

EIGHT

There are three degrees of bliss
And three abodes of the Blest,
And the lowest place is his
Who had saved a soul by jest
And a brother's soul in sport . . .
But there do the Angels resort!

—RUDYARD KIPLING, "THE JESTER"

"Let me get this straight," said Grelho when he returned from escorting my wife and apprentice. "You have traveled a hundred miles to track down an obscure song that may contain an obscure reference to an obscure someone who is probably dead because an obscure someone else killed another obscurity so he could splash some blood on some books."

"Yes," I said. "Although when you put it like that, it seems like a waste of time."

"No, that's fine," he said, shrugging. "I just wanted to make sure you had a good reason for all of this. I still haven't heard the song from either of you."

I sang it to him, and he started nodding by the second line.

"I know that song," he said when I finished. " 'The Lark's Lament,' I remember hearing it."

"When and where?"

"When? Who knows? It was a long time ago, and there have been a lot of songs," he said. "But where and who, that I can tell you. It was in a tavern near the Blancaria that has long since burned down, and the singer was—"

"Rafael de la Tour."

"Well, yes," he said, crestfallen. "You shouldn't step on a fellow jester's punch lines like that."

"Tell me about him."

"A simpleton, barely capable of keeping himself alive," he said. "But with one amazing gift that made his fortune. He could hear a song once, then sing it forever, and with a better voice than any troubadour in the Guild, including Folquet and Peire Vidal. When all of our other entertaining was done, we would repair to this tavern and listen to him sing into the early morn. We would take visiting Guildmembers to hear him, and their mouths would hang open the entire time. Then one day he disappeared from Montpellier, and nobody knew what had happened until we heard about his death in Saragossa."

"Did he leave town before Folquet did?"

He thought for a moment.

"I think it was a year or two after," he said. "Folquet was last here in '87. I remember being surprised that Rafael left the one place where he had enough of a reputation to keep himself in bread and wine, but I didn't give it that much consideration."

"Did he write 'The Lark's Lament'?"

"He wrote nothing," said Grelho. "He was an idiot with a glorious voice. Troubadours would hire him to sing their work, and other people passed songs along to him. I taught him a few myself."

"Who wrote it, then?" I asked.

"Don't know," he said. "It had a brief vogue, and then Rafael vanished, and the song vanished with him."

"Any idea who the Lady Lark was?"

"None," he said. "Sounds like a private name for someone by whoever wrote it, but that's obvious. I never heard it used to describe anybody around here. Maybe there's something in the second verse that could help you."

I stared at him.

"What?" he asked nervously.

"There was a second verse?"

"I'm certain there was."

"By Balaam's ass, why didn't you tell me that before?"

"You were the one who knew the song," he said. "I just assumed you knew the whole thing."

"Tell me you don't remember it."

"It's a lament!" he protested. "I'm a jester. I've never had a need for laments. At least, until lately, and that's for my own pitiful existence, no one else's. And that song was so specific—you couldn't really adapt it for other occasions. How many Lady Larks are going to drop dead and require this particular song to be sung over their graves? Even Rafael only sang it a few times. You don't get drunks buying you drinks for dirges."

"All right," I said. "Let's go. I'm tired of sitting in the dark."

"Go where?" he asked.

"What's a good market for local gossip?"

"Any of them, although you don't want to be going by the fish market this late in the day. I'll watch the baby while you change out of your motley."

I grabbed my kit and pushed the door open. "I'm not changing," I said.

"You're going out in motley?"

"That's what we do," I said. "The town already knows we've arrived. It would be stranger if we didn't perform. Why don't you get yours on and join me?"

"Sorry," he said. "Let me hold your daughter while you work. I might as well do something useful."

"Then you've become nanny for the day," I said, handing Portia to him. "I'll juggle, you see what you can find out."

"And when the Viguerie take you away, I'll be able to inform your wife," he said. "Unless she's already been thrown into a dungeon."

"In that case, raise my daughter with foolish values," I said.

"Come on, you spineless coward. All you have to do is chat up the ladies."

He followed me, Portia clinging to him placidly.

"She resembles you, I think," he observed. "Although I haven't seen you with your makeup off."

"I haven't seen you with yours on, so that's a fair trade."

"What am I supposed to do?" he grumbled. "I'm not the one who banned me from court."

"No, but you took it lying down," I said. "What kind of a jester lets that happen? When they threw you out the door, you should have hit the ground tumbling and rolled right into the markets to make fun of them."

"I would have been kicked out of town."

"No," I said. "You're a jester. The town would have been on your side. You should have kept popping up all over the place, and sooner or later the Countess would have given up bothering you. She might still let you back in. I would work on her daughter. Appear at some of the other great houses to amuse their children—Guilhema would get wind of it and demand a private performance."

"Maybe," he said. "Here's the Orgerie. That's as good a place as any."

"Good," I said, pulling my clubs out of my bag. "Find some knowledgeable women. Use my daughter as an introduction—she enjoys being the center of attention."

The Orgerie was the grain market, where farmers and merchants displayed both unmilled grain and flour in huge burlap sacks, the open ones containing their most presentable products, the rest sewn tightly shut. God help the careless housekeeper who purchased a closed sack without inspecting it first.

I started with three clubs. Any fool can do three clubs. In fact, many people who are not fools can juggle three clubs, but you have to start with the basics. I had them spinning easily, and began tossing them behind my back and under my legs. Then my nose itched, so I tossed all three of them with one hand and scratched my nose with the other.

The itching persisted and spread across my body, and soon my hands were frantically alternating between juggling clubs and clawing at increasingly inaccessible parts of my body, some of which required me to fold into strange contortions while still keeping the clubs aloft. I grabbed a fourth club and used it as a backscratcher, but when that proved ineffective, I began literally beating the itch to death with the club, each blow causing me to stagger and the tossed clubs to spin in ever more chaotic patterns.

All of this to try to attract enough people for Grelho to do his part. Out of the corner of my eye, I could see him chatting up some women, but they seemed uninterested in sharing much conversation. Indeed, there was a general lack of response in the whole area, whether to my performance or to each other. The haggling by the grain-sellers was listless; deals were closed without ceremony; women hurried in to get what they wanted, and hurried out again, rarely making eye contact with anyone else. I launched into my patter, but it might as well have been a crowd of deaf-mutes for all the reaction I got.

After an hour of this, I caught all my clubs and bowed to scattered applause from the grain sellers. A few pennies came my way, but nothing like I am used to.

"Thank you, kind people!" I shouted. "I am Tan Pierre, of the Fool Family. We are available at reasonable prices for your entertainment. Come let us bring joy to your homes."

I walked over to the edge of the square. Portia reached out to me eagerly, and I took her from Grelho.

"Tough crowd," he said.

"I disagree," I said. "There were not enough of them to be a crowd."

"That's the way things have been lately," he said as we walked back to his place. "Everyone's afraid. With so many of the great houses in ruins and new people taking over, no one knows what's happening anymore, who to depend on, who to bribe, who to trust. All because Marie felt slighted and Pedro needed money."

"Any useful gossip?"

"No gossip of any kind," he said. "I couldn't even get a smile from the maids I flirted with, and I am a damn good flirt. Used to be, anyway."

"You used to be a lot of things," I said.

Portia pointed at everything she saw, saying, "Ooo?" at each one. I named them as we passed by.

"Smart little girl," said Grelho.

"I think so," I said.

"The older one, what's her story?" he asked. "She's not your daughter."

"No," I said. "She was born in a whorehouse in Swabia. She'd be working there right now, but her mother smuggled her to us. Father Gerald says she's the best pupil he's had in years."

"He must hold you in high regard to make her your apprentice," he said. "Unless he did it so she'd learn from your wife. Where is her mother now?"

"Died a month after saving her," I said. "Helga doesn't know."

"I bet she does," he said. "Somehow, children always know."

We ran into Claudia and Helga at the top of his street. Portia squealed and squirmed, and her mother came over to take her.

"You haven't been juggling the baby, have you?" she asked suspiciously.

"Not with anything sharp," I replied. "Any luck?"

"Not for me, but our apprentice mined a small nugget of gold," she said. "Let's go inside."

We sat down and listened to Helga give an account of her day, complete with imitations of everyone she saw.

"Good work, Apprentice," I said, and she beamed.

"A caged lark from one of the banished houses," said Grelho. "That's the best lead we have?"

"It's more than we had before," said Claudia. "And Marie knows something about it, I'm willing to bet."

"You know all of the families who were evicted since Marie's ascension?" I asked Grelho.

"Of course," he said. "I used to . . . Yes, I know them."

"Then you've just become our local spy," I said. "See if you can find out if the Lady Lark was with one of them."

"We are talking about a dozen families, most of whom have been banished or scattered," he said. "That's a lot of work."

"Then it is well that you have so much time on your hands," I said. "It will be good for you, getting out of this stuffy dark hole and into the open air."

"And what will you be doing while I am doing all this work?" he asked.

"He'll be going to Maguelone," said Claudia.

"Yes, I'll be going to Maguelone," I agreed, then I turned to her. "Why am I going to Maguelone?"

"Because there is one other person who has inside knowledge of the goings-on at the palais royal," she said. "The last Guilhem."

"That's why I'm going to Maguelone," I said. "I knew there was a good reason. How do I get there?"

"Go through the Lattes Gate, ride out a mile, then it's a straight shot south," said Grelho. "You can see the cathedral from the roof of the house at the top of this street. You can get there and back in one day on a decent horse."

"Then Zeus can have you there and back by noon if you get up at dawn," said Claudia.

"I am not getting up at dawn," I said. "I plan to sleep off tonight's performance."

"We're performing? Hooray!" cheered Helga. "Where? I hope it's a tavern."

"Maybe she really is your daughter," said Claudia. "Where are we performing?"

"In a tavern," I said.

"Which one?" asked Grelho.

"Where do the guards like to go drinking when their watch is over?" I asked.

"The Cormorant, up near the Tanners' Quay," said Grelho. "How did you manage to get invited there?"

"I don't have an invitation," I said.

"You plan to barge into a tavern full of drunken soldiers and tanners without permission?" he asked. "That's akin to suicide."

"Well, if we have to die tonight, at least we'll know that we'll be in good company," I said. "You're coming with us."

He winced.

We could smell the Tanners' Quay long before we saw it. It was north of the town, on a small river that fed the Lez to the east.

"Where's the tavern?" I asked.

"There, about fifty paces upstream," said Grelho, still in his civilian attire. "If it was downstream from the tanners, no one would live after drinking their beer."

"Unless they had leather insides," said Claudia. "I'll stick to wine, undiluted and unpolluted, thank you very much."

The tavern was a two-story wooden structure raised up from the ground several feet so that drinking could continue unabated during times of flood. As we drew nearer, we heard a constant roaring from inside. A crude carving of a cormorant adorned the roof over the entrance. The roar increased suddenly, and we heard a bottle break. Then someone came flying through the front door, missing the steps neatly to land facefirst in the mud near us. Claudia considerately turned his head to the side so that he would not drown, then stepped over him daintily.

The three of us in motley ascended the steps first, with Helga in the middle.

"On three, we go in," I said. "The usual tavern routine."

As I spoke, I reached behind Helga to tug on my wife's elbow. She nodded slightly.

"Ready?" I asked.

"Ready," said Helga.

"Ready," said Claudia with a slight smile.

"One, two, three!" I counted.

Then Claudia and I stood there as our young apprentice barged into the tavern by herself. Grelho came up to join us.

"You didn't just do that," he muttered. "Not here."

"Let's watch what happens," I said.

Helga stood in the middle of the tavern, blinking uncertainly as she realized she was alone. That is, alone except for a couple of dozen soldiers and other rough-looking sorts, who all looked at her and licked their lips.

"Excuse me," she said. "I'm looking for my father."

"And who might he be, little girl?" said the tapster, leaning over the counter to leer at her.

"Well, knowing my mother, it could be any one of you," said Helga, which brought astonished laughs and a few worried looks from the men. "But the man she tells me is my father is a disreputable foul-smelling lout who consorts with the worst sorts of men in the worst sorts of places. Naturally, I came straight here."

"Impressive," said Grelho, as the men caught on to the joke and began laughing.

I nodded at Claudia, and she bustled in.

"There you are, you little scamp," she scolded Helga. "I have been in every tavern in this city looking for you."

"I was looking for father," she said. "He's already been to every other tavern. He's bound to show up here."

"Only if he can still walk," said Claudia.

With that cue I fell through the doorway. I grabbed my shoulder with one hand and pretended to pull myself up with it. Then I stared at Claudia and Helga. "Wife, daughter," I said in surprise. "Good, then I must be home. What's for supper?"

"You missed supper," said Claudia icily. "You missed the last three suppers."

"They were quite delicious," piped up Helga.

"Where were you?" demanded Claudia, pulling out a club and slapping it menacingly against her palm.

"I wasn't with you?" I asked.

"No."

I scratched my head, puzzled, as she pulled out more clubs. Helga had hers out as well.

"Then who was that woman?" I asked her.

The clubs came flying at me from both females, and I caught and returned them as fast as I could, my feeble protests ineffective against the invective of my good wife. Duchess she may have once been, but she could outcurse any sailor when she was in character, and the combination of clubs and obscenities flying out of her had the men in the room guffawing and cheering within seconds.

Grelho slipped in unobtrusively and took a seat by the front door, watching us. I caught one club and, instead of returning it to Helga, flipped it over my shoulder in his direction. He was holding Portia in the crook of his right arm, so he caught it with his left hand.

"My pardons, Sieur," I called to him. "Would you be so kind as to toss that back to me?"

He didn't look happy about having any attention directed his way, but did his best to appear like a casual onlooker and threw it clumsily in my direction.

I sent it back, then sent another one right after it. He caught each in rapid succession, and returned them as Portia bounced happily. I now held three clubs in my left hand as I kept returning the ladies' throws with my right. I grinned at Grelho.

He sighed. "Hold this," he said, handing Portia to a soldier sitting by them. Then he stood up with a grimace and beckoned to me with both hands. Claudia and Helga tossed me their remaining clubs so that I had a total of eight. I tossed four to Grelho.

"First one to drop buys," I said.

"You're on," he replied, and the game began in earnest. Around us, men were frantically betting. The clubs went back and forth between us in a blur. He was good. He was very good. Too good, in fact. I lost after about fifteen rounds.

"The great Grelho!" I cried, holding up his hand in triumph. "And we are the Fool Family!"

There was applause; there was drinking. I bought Grelho his first, but that was the last coin to leave our pouches that evening.

"Grelho, where have you been hiding yourself?" asked a captain of the Viguerie, coming over to our table to slap him on the back.

"Oh, you know what it's been like lately," said Grelho. "I didn't think there was much call for my services."

"Ah, don't let that bitch and her new man get you," said the captain. "We missed seeing you. Where's the makeup and costume? I didn't even know it was you until this other fool introduced you."

"Well, I—," began Grelho.

"Part of the act," I interrupted. "Sieur Grelho kindly agreed to play an innocent member of the crowd."

"Quite generous of him to share the room with us," added Claudia. "Always a privilege to work with a master fool."

"Stop, you're embarrassing me," said Grelho, pleased in spite of it.

"We'll have you at the barracks Saturday," said the captain. "It's payday, and we always have a party. Bring your friends. That little girl is a pip."

We celebrated with our new friends until midnight, then staggered back to Grelho's place. He continued carrying Portia, putting her up on his shoulders and galloping about as she shrieked in laughter and terror.

"Apprentice," I said when we arrived. "Front and center."

She stood before us.

"There are a number of tests you have to pass before becoming a jester in full," I said. "You passed one tonight. Congratulations."

She beamed as the rest of us applauded, including Portia.

"Now, let's all get some sleep," I said. "We'll wake when we wake."

Grelho handed Portia to Claudia, smiled, and waved a weary good night as he climbed the steps to the upper floor. Helga was practically out on her feet, and needed little coaxing to go to sleep. Claudia nursed Portia, then put her down.

"Grelho has a nice smile when he uses it," she said.

"Nice to see it come out," I said.

"I've never seen you lose a juggling challenge when there's a free drink on the line," she said. "One might almost believe that you let him win."

"First time for everything," I said. "I'm going to sleep. I'm riding to Maguelone at a lady's behest in the morning."

The Lattes Gate was being manned by the Tanners' Guild when I passed through it, and the leathery-looking fellow standing guard recognized me from our performance at the Cormorant and waved me through. Zeus saw open road ahead and bucked a couple of times to see if I was paying attention. I tugged on his reins to let him know that I hadn't fallen off; then I flicked them gently, and the landscape became a blur.

Fortunately, the Mediterranean presented an obstacle large enough that even Zeus knew better than to try to leap it. A narrow island spread out before us, and dominating its western end was the cathedral. The island was well-protected by walls and fortifications seaward, but was connected to the mainland by a low wooden causeway to our left. The tide was out, however, so we simply rode across the exposed sand flats, scattering shorebirds who were stabbing at the crabs and shellfish with their long pointed beaks.

The cathedral itself was a cross between a house of God and a fort against Muhammad. It was Romanesque in style, made of blocks of white sandstone, with a white tiled roof. The island was the principal defense for the area against attacks by invaders or pirates, which was why the Church chose to place the bishopric here rather than in Montpellier proper. Still, once on the island, with its gentle beaches and its ample vineyards, I could see the seductive aspects of renouncing the world for the cloth. If they only had a decent tavern . . .

The door to the cathedral was carved with vines and grapes, and had a tympanum over it with a frieze depicting Our Savior welcoming one and all, surrounded by some adoring animals. I rejected the possibility that that meant I could bring Zeus into the cathedral itself, and tied him to a rail nearby. There was a wooden post standing there with an iron bell suspended from it.

There was an inscription over the door: *To this haven of life come those who are thirsty. In crossing this threshold, pray for your life. Always weep for your sins. Whatever is wrong is cleansed by the fountain of your tears.*

I have never been much for weeping. But then, I have never been much for cathedrals, either. Still, this one lacked the wasteful extravagance of the Gothic monstrosities that were being built everywhere, so I renounced my pride and crossed the threshold. I did pray for my life, albeit dry-eyed. There were not enough tears to cover my sins.

It was dark, the narrow windows stingy with what they let in from the outside. The layout was a simple rectangular box, the altar at the far end just a stone slab of a table. Plain wooden stalls lined both sides. Probably no more than a dozen clerics here, all told. At the base of the altar was a curious-looking fan made of peacock feathers. As I looked at it, someone cleared his throat. I turned to see a priest standing there.

"Why the fan?" I asked, pointing at it.

"To protect the Host from contamination," he said. "The mosquitoes can be something fierce around here. May I help you, my son?"

"Forgive the intrusion," I said.

"We can forgive far worse things," he said, smiling.

"I am looking for one of your newer monks," I said. "Guilhem of Montpellier."

"Brother Guilhem should be attending to our gardens," he said, pointing to the north side of the cathedral.

"Thank you, Father," I said, starting in that direction.

"Should be, I said," he continued. "But I would first check the beach. It might save you a trip."

"Thank you again," I said. I placed a penny in the collection box and went back outside.

I passed through groves of almonds and date trees, restraining myself from plucking anything that didn't belong to me. There was a brick wall at the other side, and I followed it until I came to a door. I opened it, and the bright blue Mediterranean dazzled before me, separated by a short stretch of sand. A young man was stretched out on top of his discarded cassock, his sandals discarded next to a football. He had been swimming recently, if the wet tonsure was any indication. His eyes were closed, but he was humming, so I assumed he was awake. I decided to put that theory to the test.

"Brother Guilhem," I said sternly.

He sprang guiltily to his feet, gathering his cassock.

"Forgive me, Father, I'll get right to—" he blurted, then stopped as he saw me.

"Forgive me, Brother Guilhem," I said, chuckling. "It was too good an opportunity. I am Tan Pierre, the fool."

"And you have made me another," he said, laughing at his embarrassment. "Let me reassemble myself."

"Oh, don't bother on my account," I said. "I came to see Guilhem of Montpellier, not Brother Guilhem of Maguelone."

"Really? Why?"

"Curiosity," I said.

"Oh, is that all?" he said petulantly. "Come see the boy count who gave it up to be a monk before he could even shave."

"That patter is much too long," I said. "You'll get more tourists if you come up with something short and catchy."

"But they'll come because I'm an oddity, isn't that what you're saying?" he said, kicking the ball in my direction.

I blocked it, then kicked it up and juggled it back and forth with my knees.

"Hey, you're good," he said. "Kick it back to me."

And suddenly, we had a game going. I quickly learned that the accumulated skills of a middle-aged jester are no match for the energy of a fourteen-year-old boy. After about ten minutes, I held my hands up in surrender.

He picked up his cassock and threw it over his head, then tied the cord around his waist. He picked up the ball and his sandals. "Good match," he said. "Walk me to my penance. I detest gardening."

"That's why they have you do it," I said.

"No doubt," he said cheerfully. "You should join us. No one else here plays football. They're all too busy praying."

"Isn't that the point?"

"I suppose," he said, tossing the ball up and heading it a few times. "But they're all so old. They don't know what it's like to have someone young here. They've forgotten how to dream. It's a romantic place, in many ways. Do you know the legend of Maguelone?"

"No. Tell me."

"Maguelone was the daughter of the King of Naples, a rare and virtuous beauty. A brave knight fell in love with her, and entered a tournament to win her. After many heroic battles, he was victorious and they pledged eternal devotion to each other. He gave her three golden rings in a cloth bag to keep by her heart. But a seabird swooped in and stole the bag. The knight promptly pursued it by boat, and was lost at sea."

"How sad."

"But it didn't end there," he said. "She searched for him, and ultimately ended up here, where she founded a hospice for the sick and abandoned. Meanwhile, it turned out that he had been captured and made the slave of a sultan. After many years, he grew ill and unrecognizable, and the sultan cast him off by a miraculous coincidence at this very spot. He was carried to the hospice and nursed back to health by Maguelone, who didn't recognize him. When he recovered his health and memories, he revealed himself to her, and they were married and lived happily to the end of their days running the hospice. Now, many come to Maguelone to ring the bell outside the cathedral to be blessed by her before marrying in the cathedral."

"Did she ever get her rings back?"

"The story doesn't say," he said. "Probably not."

"Why did you join?" I asked. "You don't seem to be the monkish kind."

"That's that curiosity of yours," he said. "Do you know Grelho?"

"I'm staying with him in town," I said.

"He was my father's fool, and mine, too," he said. "I remember his telling me the story about the fool who wanted to find his identical twin. Do you know that one?"

"No," I lied.

"He saw him at the bottom of a well, and drowned trying to embrace him," he said.

"And what is your exegesis of this foolish parable?" I asked.

He sat down to put on his sandals. "Ever since I joined here, men have journeyed from the city to see me," he said. "Powerful men. Rich men. All wanting something from me, because I am the last of the Guilhems. I have nothing to give them, but they won't accept that. And, although they don't know it, they end up giving me something valuable and dangerous."

"What is that?"

"That they came to powerless me, knowing that my sister is the countess. Which means that they are a threat to her."

"And being a good brother, you pass that information on to her."

He nodded.

"Will you be telling her about me?" I asked.

"I don't know yet," he said. "You are neither rich nor powerful. And you played football with me. I like that. And, I confess, you have aroused my own curiosity. I've never been sought out by a fool before. I reserve judgment. Tell me what you want to know, and remember that lying is a sin."

I bowed briefly. "I have no interest in your sister, or the affairs of Montpellier," I said. "I am tracking down an old story, probably from before your time. Ever hear of the troubadour Folquet of Marseille?"

He stopped.

"I thought you had no interest in my sister or the affairs of Montpellier," he said. "Folquet is a forbidden topic."

"Ever hear of the Lady Lark?" I asked.

"The Lady Lark," he repeated. "A ghost of a rumor. I once heard my father referring to a lady at court by that name when I was young. Someone who died before I was born."

"Did you know her real name?"

"No. But he said that she sang like a bird until someone put her in a cage, then she pined away and died."

"A sad story," I said. "Was Folquet part of it?"

"I don't know," he said. "Perhaps it was just another parable. Is that all you wanted?"

"Yes."

We climbed over a stile into a large vegetable garden. He picked up a sack and a hoe and sighed. "I really don't mind gardening," he said. "Life is so much simpler now."

"There was simplicity in the Garden of Eden," I said.

"And when they chose knowledge and exile, they bred and produced a fratricide," he said. "I chose to return to ignorance and innocence."

"Why?" I asked.

"Because if I hadn't, either my loving sister would have killed me, or I would have been forced to kill her," he replied. "A mortal sin was avoided either way. Will you be leaving Montpellier once you find what you need?"

"Yes."

"Then I won't tell Marie about your visit," he said. "Thank you for playing with me. Go with God."

"And you, Brother Guilhem," I said, bowing.

I left the garden, retrieved my horse, and got the hell out of there.

❦

It was close to sundown when I returned Zeus to the stable. He had barely broken a sweat with only me for his burden, but I treated him to a bath and a thorough brushing, which he pretended not to enjoy. I patted him on the neck and gave him a bunch of carrots as a final treat, then went back to Grelho's. I ran into my family at the door.

"Well met," said Claudia, kissing me. "Take Portia."

"Has she been to the palace?" I asked as the baby clung to me like a monkey.

"She has," said Claudia. "Made quite the impression on the countess. I barely had to do anything."

"You are proving to be a great help," I said to my daughter. "Pity you can't stay this age. We'll just have to keep having more babies."

"That is not going to happen," said Claudia in a voice that had steel in it. Very sharp steel.

"Just a thought, good wife," I said meekly. "And how was your day, Apprentice?"

"I have been playing with dolls for hours," said Helga. "I had no idea fun could be so wearying. But I didn't learn anything helpful."

Grelho opened the door. We looked at him and cheered. He was in motley and makeup. "Come in, come in," he said merrily. "I have dinner prepared."

"You actually spent money?" I said in mock astonishment.

"I'm celebrating my comeback," he said. "I had a good day in the markets. Some people actually threw sausages, which I hope was meant as a compliment."

There was fresh cheese and superb wine to go with the sausages. We were sated and happy in a very short time.

"Did you find Guilhem, husband?" asked Claudia.

"I did," I said. "He likes to play games, although he's left the main game to his sister."

"That was a prudent move for him, I think," said Grelho. "But it would have been better for the town had he stood up to her. Did he know anything?"

"He said the Lady Lark had been a woman at his father's court who died before his time," I said. "Does that narrow things down for you?"

"A recently banned family with a lady who died say in the late eighties," mused Grelho. "I can think of three who meet those characteristics. But before we go gallivanting after them, I have found someone who might help us even more."

"Really? Who?"

"Turns out Rafael de la Tour had a younger sister," he said triumphantly. "Turns out she's still in the area. And best of all, they say she sings like an angel."

"So the gift ran in the family," said Claudia. "She might know more about 'The Lark's Lament.' Where is she?"

"Married to a farmer a few miles north of town," he said. "We can go tomorrow."

"Well done," I said. "All right, we should—"

A pounding on the door interrupted me. We sprang to our feet, the senior fools with hands to weapons and Helga picking up Portia and retreating to the stairs at the rear. I nodded at Grelho.

"Who is it?" he called.

The pounding repeated, but weakly this time. Then there was a soft thud. Grelho slid back the bar on the door and pushed it open a crack.

"There's a man lying in the street down near the bottom of the hill," he said. "He's moaning."

"Let's see who it is," I said. "Helga, stay here with Portia."

For a change, she didn't argue.

It was near midnight, and there was only little moonlight to guide us. We stepped quietly toward the prostrate form, guarding against attack from where the alley met the next street.

The man was on his back, one arm feebly beckoning to us for help. Grelho and I stepped past him to make sure no one was waiting for us around the corners, then turned to look back at him. He was a large man, and cloaked. Claudia knelt by his head.

"It's Brother Antime!" she exclaimed.

"Who's he?" asked Grelho.

"Did Folc send you?" I asked, kneeling by him.

"Told me to come here," he said hoarsely. "To find out what you've learned."

"What's wrong with him?" asked Grelho, nervously looking up and down the street.

I ran my hands across his chest and felt something thick and wet. "He's been stabbed," I said. "What happened, Antime?"

"The other man," he gasped, and I heard a bubbling sound as he did.

"What other man?"

"The other man following you," he whispered. Then he coughed twice and fell silent. I felt his neck for a pulse.

"Let's get back inside," I said. "He's dead."

NINE

En chantan m'aven a membrar
so qu'ieu cug chantan oblidar!
[It happens that, by singing, I remember
that which I thought, by singing, to forget!]

—FOLQUET DE MARSEILLE, *"EN CHANTAN MA'VEN A MEMBRAR"*
[TRANS. N. M. SCHULMAN]

We sat in darkness by the barred door, listening.

"Who was Brother Antime?" asked Grelho.

"He was a Cistercian monk at Le Thoronet," said Theo. "He was the cellarer."

"The big monk?" whispered Helga. "He's dead?"

"Stabbed," said Theo.

"And you just left him there?" she asked incredulously.

"If anyone had seen us, I would have called for the guard," said Theo.

"No one saw us, so we left him for the nightwatch to find," said Grelho.

"I don't understand," she said.

"They would have suspected us in his death," I explained. "Even if we could have talked our way out of it, it would have made our mission more difficult."

"Isn't it anyway?" asked Helga.

"No question," said Theo. "I think we made it safely inside. Let's go to bed as if nothing happened."

"How can we possibly do that?" asked Helga.

"Lie down, pull up the covers," I said. "When the nightwatch bangs on the door, we will sound like we'll be getting out of bed because we will be."

"I'll be upstairs, then," said Grelho. "We'll talk in the morning. When there's light."

He slipped upstairs, and the rest of us crawled under our blankets.

There was no sleep to be had for Theo and me. We carried on a silent wake for the dead monk, waiting for the first shout of discovery, the alarm, the rousting of the tenants house by house, inexorably approaching our own as we prepared our startled expressions, our shock and horror that murder had struck so randomly and so near.

Only for us, it wasn't random.

"Helga's asleep," said Theo softly. "In spite of everything, she can sleep."

"She's still a child," I said. "And she didn't see the body."

"Right," he said.

We lay silently for a few minutes.

"This is embarrassing," I said.

"Extremely," he said. "Bad enough that we've been followed by one man ever since we left Le Thoronet without spotting him."

"But to be followed by two is shameful," I said. "Father Gerald would have us back in class with the beginners. Antime must have been a very good soldier in his time."

"Good enough to follow us, but not good enough to watch his back," said Theo. "And now his time is over."

I shivered suddenly, and he pulled me close and held me.

"The rats will be at him by now," I said. "Maybe the dogs. And the crows will be out at daybreak."

"It's hours before dawn," said Theo. "I must say, I'm not impressed with the watchfulness of the watch."

Then there was a shout, and a flurry of footsteps. A horn blew, was answered in the distance. More footsteps, more shouting, then shutters being thrown open, cries of anger, surprise, fear. Boots tramping up the street, doors struck with mailed fists, protests of ignorance and innocence.

Theo got up.

"Too much noise to feign sleep," he said wearily. "I'll open the door and wonder what's going on."

He poured some water in a basin and quickly scrubbed his whiteface off. I did the same, then mussed my hair so it looked slept in. He pulled open the door, looking tired. A soldier was just getting to Grelho's house.

"What's going on?" asked Theo as I peered around him, squinting as the torchlight hit my eyes.

"Someone's been killed," said the soldier.

"Killed?" I gasped, crossing myself. "Where?"

"Down at the next street," said the soldier. "Far as we can tell from the blood, he got stabbed in the chest, fell, then managed to pick himself up and get as far as here before he collapsed and rolled back down the hill."

"Who was he?" asked Theo.

"Don't know," said the soldier. "Nothing on him. Must have been a robbery. Want to take a look, see if you recognize him?"

"If it will help," said Theo. "Shall I wake Grelho? That might not be easy. He had a lot to drink last night."

"Oc, if you can," said the soldier. "We're running everyone in the neighborhood past the corpse just in case."

"I'll get him," I said, and I went upstairs.

"The watch is here," I whispered.

"I know," said Grelho. "I've been listening. Give me a minute."

I came back down.

"He's on his way," I reported.

"Thanks, Domna," he said.

Grelho stumbled down the stairs and caught himself before hitting the wall. "Jacques, is that you?" he said, shading his eyes. "What's this about someone getting killed?"

"Take a look," said the soldier.

We trooped down to where a small crowd of people had joined seven of Jacques's companions who stood in a circle facing away from the body, their spears held horizontally to form a barricade.

"Anyone know him?" asked a sergeant. "Anyone see anything? Hear anything?"

We all shook our heads. I don't know who there besides us was lying.

"Of course," grumbled the sergeant. "We'll catch the bastard who did this. And if it turns out any of you was in on it, we'll make sure we have lots of fun before you swing. Go back to your safe warm beds while we do our jobs."

"If you were doing your jobs, he wouldn't be dead," snarled someone in the pack.

The soldiers rattled in anger, but no one saw who had spoken. The crowd slowly dispersed. We went back to Grelho's. I checked on the baby, who had slept through everything, then kissed Helga on the forehead. The older girl shifted uneasily in her bed, muttering something that was too garbled to understand.

"In the morning," yawned Grelho, and we all went back to our beds.

Outside, we could hear the search progress, then recede. Finally, there were just the sounds of the night, the wind through the shutters, a solitary dog barking somewhere. The snoring of my husband.

"Damn you for a cur without conscience," I muttered, including both dog and husband in my curse, but the dog kept on barking and the husband kept on snoring. I sighed, and stared into the darkness. Eventually, I fell asleep.

"Folquet sends you on this investigation," said Grelho. "Then he sends his bodyguard—"

"Cellarer," corrected Theo.

"His giant to follow you," said Grelho. "What's his game?"

"He wants to know what we've found out," said Theo.

"Or he's worried about what we've found out," I said. "Maybe he had second thoughts about sending us. Maybe there's something he doesn't want us to know about."

"So he sends the giant to do what, exactly?" asked Grelho. "To stop you? To follow you and report back to him?"

"I don't know," said Theo. "He wasn't exactly forthcoming with information."

"Which brings me to my main concern," said Grelho. "Our late giant was strong enough to take a fatal wound and still climb the hill to pound on my door. He was sneaky enough to follow two experienced fools without being caught. Yet this strong and sneaky fellow was stabbed to death practically on my threshold, which means that whoever killed him was even stronger and sneakier. And that even stronger and sneakier man is on our collective tail right now. That unnerves me."

"Brother Antime might not have been following us," I said.

"How do you figure that?" asked Theo.

"Maybe something occurred to Folc after we left," I said. "He might have remembered something that was here in Montpellier. He couldn't know if we would come here, so he sent Antime directly."

"And Antime learned of our arrival, and sought us out," concluded Theo. "That conjecture pleases me, mostly because it means that I did not fail to see a giant following us."

"No, you only missed the man who killed him," said Grelho.

Theo fumed silently.

"Why was he killed?" asked Helga, who had followed the conversation while bouncing Portia on her lap.

"He must have learned something," I said. "And someone killed him to keep him from telling us what he learned. Which means that there is one positive note in all this."

"Forgive me for not seeing anything positive here," grumbled Theo. "What is this glorious ray of sunshine?"

"We're in the right place," I said. "Whatever there is to be found is in Montpellier."

"Hooray," said Grelho. "I hope you live to find it."

"Which brings me to my next thought," said Theo. "Claudia, I want you, Helga, and Portia to leave the city and go back to Marseille."

"What?" cried Helga.

"Are you mad?" I shouted.

"It's too dangerous here," said Theo. "That monk killed at the abbey was a chance encounter. Bad luck for him, but there was no reason to think we were potential targets. But now, we know the killer is on our trail, and he has no compunction about spilling more blood to stop us."

"I've seen blood spilled before, as you very well know," I reminded him. "I've spilled some myself, usually while saving your foolish noggin. Or have you forgotten our journey to Constantinople?"

"I've forgotten none of it," he said. "You are the most courageous and resourceful woman I have ever met, no argument. But things are different now."

"Why?"

"Because we have a baby," he said. "And I will not put her in harm's way. Let Folc's abbey burn to the ground and the Guild be scattered to the four corners of the world, but I will not risk our daughter."

"I see," I said. "So, to keep us safe, you would send us back to Marseille."

"Yes."

"There I'd be, a solitary woman traveling with a twelve-year-old girl and a baby, with a dangerous killer dogging us for the entire distance."

"The killer would be in Montpellier, trying to stop us," said Theo.

"Unless he thought we had already learned the great secret, and were on our way back to Folc with it."

"That's a nasty thought," commented Grelho.

"There we are, on the open road, four days and five rivers," I continued. "Lacking your manly protection. One less fool for keeping watch, one less fool for fighting off predators. But if you are so concerned for your daughter's safety that you must insist upon us making this perilous journey, then by all means, husband, send us back to Marseille."

Theo sat there, trying to think of some retort, and failing miserably.

"I think this is the part where you concede," said Grelho.

"You're not helping," said Theo.

"We can't go back to Marseille," said Helga. "Not now."

We turned to look at her.

"Why not?" asked Theo.

"I'm not old enough to marry Pantalan yet," she said. "I need a couple of years."

"Well, then that settles it," said Theo. "It was a stupid idea. Whose was it, anyway?"

"Yours," we all said.

"Then don't let me have another," said Theo. "Good. Now that we've cleared that up, let's move on to our day. You three are off to the palais royal?"

"Yes," I said.

"Then Grelho and I will poke around and try to find where Antime was staying," he said. "We'll meet you after the noon meal and go find this de la Tour woman."

"Very well," I said.

"One more thing," said Theo. "From now on, none of us goes anywhere alone. Not to the market, not to the stables, nowhere. We watch each other's backs."

"Antime was stabbed in the chest," pointed out Grelho.

"Again with the not helping," said Theo.

"I could watch your chest," offered Grelho.

"That will make a nice change," I said. "You've been staring at mine often enough."

"And I've got nothing to stare at," complained Helga.

"A watched pot never boils, Apprentice," I said.

"Enough," said Theo. "Let us escort the ladies to the palais."

We walked up the main road to Peyrou, a small parade of motley. Helga cartwheeled and flipped ahead of us, Theo juggled, and Grelho greeted everyone he saw by name and had a quip for each one of them.

I carried the baby.

When we came to the gates of the palais courtyard, Theo and Grelho stood at either side and mimed holding heraldic trumpets, sounding a triumphant fanfare that might have been more impressive had it not been done by them blatting raspberries as loudly as they could.

"It's like walking through a gauntlet of farts," I said.

"Good-bye, O manly men," said Helga, waving. "We'll put in a good word for you at the palais."

I walked over to Theo to let him kiss Portia.

"Be careful in there," he said.

"We're the ones inside the fortifications," I said. "You be careful. And that was a lovely speech about letting Folc's abbey burn down. Only one problem."

"What's that?" he asked as we ladies passed through the gates.

"It's made of stone!" I called.

Léon, still surly with us, led us to the Countess. Guilhema wanted to play with Portia, so the three girls went off with a maid, leaving the two of us alone with some good wine. Marie had a near-empty cup in her hand.

"You have started without me, milady," I scolded her.

"It is the prerogative of the privileged," she said grandly, tossing back the rest of it and holding her cup out.

I filled it, along with one for myself.

"Your health, milady," I said, raising my cup.

She nodded graciously. "What gossip in town?" she asked.

"Did you hear about the murder?" I replied, leaning forward.

"No," she exclaimed. "Where? Who was it?"

"Not a hundred paces from my doorstep," I said excitedly. "Some large bald man was stabbed in the street in the middle of the night. The guards were everywhere, banging on doors and looking for the killer, but I don't think they found him. Didn't your captain tell you?"

"No, and I will have a word with him about that," she said sternly.

I had the sense that this was indeed news to her. Not that I truly suspected Marie of being involved in Antime's death, but it never hurts to be alert to any possibility.

At the moment, I was alert to the fact that our cups needed refilling. I took care of that immediately. Marie held her cup before her eyes, looking intently at the glimmering wine.

"Whom shall we toast this time?" she asked.

"To our daughters," I said. "May they rule the world."

"Our daughters!" she cried, gulping it down. "Sing me a song about daughters."

I sang a ballad of two heroic sisters who set off on a journey to rescue their kidnapped mother from a sultan's harem. After many verses and many adventures, they succeed. Marie applauded when I was done.

"How you managed to memorize all of that, I don't know," she said, slurring her speech slightly.

"Part of my profession," I said, bowing. "Here's another one."

I sang one about a mother cat and her kittens that had the Countess mewing along with the chorus by the end. Then I sang a paean to the Virgin Mary.

"How many songs do you know?" she asked, massaging her belly absentmindedly.

"Oh, maybe a hundred and fifty by this point," I said.

"So many!" she exclaimed.

"Not when you think about it," I said. "Merchants know their stock, priests know their prayers, jesters know their songs and jokes. My husband, when he's not drinking, knows far more songs than I. He knows so many that he has forgotten how many he knows."

"Does he write them himself?"

"Some," I said. "Most of our songs we learn from each other, or from passing troubadours along the way. That last one I sang was an old one from Marseille."

"Marseille," she said, frowning slightly.

"Yes, by a troubadour called Folquet," I said, prattling on as if I hadn't noticed. "Never met the man; apparently he went into holy orders, but he was quite the songwriter in his day. They say he was a marvelous singer as well. He—is something the matter, milady?"

She was pulling away from me, her teeth bared. "How dare you?" she growled.

"Excuse me, milady, in what manner did I offend you?" I asked.

"To say that name in my presence," she said, practically spitting.

"Who? Folquet?"

She shrieked.

"Milady, a thousand pardons. I had no idea," I babbled. "I am in Montpellier but a few days. No one told me that I was never supposed to say Folquet, oh, I beg pardon, milady," for she was shrieking again. "That slipped out by accident. It's the wine talking, not me. I would never do anything to cause anyone grief, especially one as gracious as you. But surely it was the job of your steward to advise me of subjects that were forbidden."

"Léon did not tell you?" she said.

"He never did, milady," I said. "And that is the steward's duty when a new fool comes to court. Why, when I was with the Byzantine court—"

"You were in Constantinople?" she said in astonishment.

"Well, surely I was the fool to the Empress Euphrosyne, wasn't I?" I said. "Your steward must have told you that. Didn't he look into my past before passing me along to you?"

"Yes, of course he did," she said. "He did mention something about the Byzantine court, come to think of it."

"Then you would know, naturally, that a fool must be prepared if she is to perform before royalty. Oh, there can be so many nuances of behavior and preference to account for. Why, I was given two full days of instruction by the Empress's steward before I even plucked one string of my lute before her."

Actually, I barged in and made myself at home in seconds, but this was a better story.

"You know, I am related to the Imperial Throne of Byzantium," she said in her most regal tones.

"Well, of course," I said. "Your mother was of the Imperial family, was she not?"

"She was," said Marie. "I am related to both Euphrosyne and Alexios. It was terrible what happened to them, to be forced into exile like that."

"Yes, it was," I said. I did not think it politic to comment on my role in their overthrow. "It must have been difficult for your mother, leaving Constantinople for a foreign marriage. Did she speak langue d'oc before she came here?"

"She did not," said Marie. "She spoke only Greek when she first married my father. He used to say he liked her a lot better when he couldn't understand her."

"She must have been very lonely," I said.

"And she was never comfortable speaking langue d'oc," she continued. "She spoke to me in Greek when no one else was present. She would regale me with stories about Constantinople. Tell me, what was Euphrosyne like?"

"Oh, mad but magnificent," I said. "Prone to sudden fits of anger, but then generous to a fault, and at all times with a sense of grandeur and style like no one I have ever seen. She must have had a new pair of earrings for every day of her life while she was Empress."

"Earrings," sighed Marie. "I do love them so. And you were her fool!"

"Yes, and she appreciated the value of having a fool at court," I said.

"I appreciate having you," she said.

"You do, and yet you don't, milady," I said.

"How don't I?"

"Any noble worth her salt knows that a proper fool can and will say anything at any time," I said. "Not just in private, but for all the world to hear. It shows that her master, or mistress, is unafraid, and why should anyone be afraid of things that are merely spoken by a fool? The more the fool says, the more confident is the face shown to the world by the fool's master. Or mistress."

"I see," she said.

"Now, whatever there was about this Folquet that upsets you, I don't know and I'm sure I don't care," I said as she bristled again. "But if you forbid the gossip, you'll only encourage people in believing it's all truth. They won't talk about it in front of you, but it will spread like a weed behind your back. There is no power on earth that can stop a rumor."

"Then what can I do about it?" she asked.

"Have me seated at your feet at some function," I said. "Let me sing Folquet's songs, and show no reaction."

"As simple as that?"

"As simple as that."

She poured another cup of wine. "I am having the new ladies of the town to midday meal on Friday, two days hence," she said. "Will you be so good as to provide the entertainment?"

"I will, milady," I said, smiling.

"Sing anything you like," she added.

"With all my heart, milady," I said, rising and bowing. "Now, it is time for me to rejoin my husband. I will see you on Friday."

Our two men were in position with the guards when we emerged.

"Company, salute!" bellowed Grelho, and the soldiers drew their swords and held them high, grinning as Theo and Grelho repeated their fake trumpet fanfares.

"Good soldiers, you do us great honor," I said, gesturing to them in exaggerated noblesse. "Were my husband not here, I would show you such favor as a lady of my worth may do for a soldier. But, alas, he is here."

"I could leave," offered Theo.

"Did you earn anything today?" I asked him.

"A little," he said.

"Then I shall go with you," I said. "Valiant men, we will see you Friday evening."

"Company, at ease!" commanded Grelho, and the guards returned to their duties, waving to us as we departed.

"How was your search for our late monk?" I asked.

"We found where he was staying," said Grelho. "He arrived the day before you did, so you are absolved for not seeing him. But what he did in town after he arrived is unknown. So, we will leave it to the Viguerie to investigate, and go off to see de la Tour's little sister."

"Where is she?" asked Theo as Grelho veered to the left.

"North, and out of town," replied Grelho. "Her name is Jacquette. She married a farmer about three miles past the river."

"How old is she?" I asked.

"Must be about thirty," he said.

"So, she must have been about eleven or twelve when Rafael left Montpellier," I said. "Are you certain she remembers the song?"

"If she has any part of her brother's gift, she'll know it," said Grelho. "Along with every other song she's ever heard."

"How is it that you didn't know about her before?" I asked.

"From what I heard yesterday, her mother kept her talents quiet," said Grelho. "Rafael was an embarrassment to the family, being an idiot and all, so when he left, she decided not to let Jacquette follow in his footsteps. The only place anyone ever heard her sing was in church."

"Pity," I said. "Is she simple like her brother?"

"I don't know," he said. "There was enough to her that someone was willing to marry her."

"Don't say it!" I warned my husband immediately.

He closed his mouth and looked disappointed.

We crossed a footbridge upstream from the Cormorant and followed a heavily rutted road, passing one farm after another. It was past harvest time by now, and the fields were covered with drying stalks or mounds of hay. Flocks of linnets were hopping about, poking under the stalks and snatching seed from the ground.

"What do they grow here?" I asked.

"Flax, mostly," replied Grelho. "Some barley, but flax is what keeps them going. They grow it all year, then spend the winter weaving linen and pressing linseed oil. You should see the fields in bloom. All blue flowers, and the linnets twittering away. It's quite pretty."

He stopped to look at an old stone marker at a place where a road ran east from the main road.

"Over there, if my directions are correct," he said, pointing to a small wooden farmhouse with a thatched roof. There was a well-maintained stone wall running around the farm's border, with a simple wooden gate nearby. We went through it and closed it carefully behind us, then walked to the farmhouse.

"Ho, there, is anyone about?" called Grelho as we approached.

There was a scurrying inside; then a thickset man appeared at the door, a spear in his hand. "Go away," he said.

"Are you Salh de Lez?" asked Grelho.

"Who's asking?" returned the man, raising the spear.

"I could have sworn it was me," said Grelho. "I didn't realize the matter was open to debate. But I will repeat the question, just to clarify in my own mind that I have, in fact, asked it of you: Are you Salh de Lez?"

The man looked at him slowly, then at the rest of us. Something resembling realization dawned on his face. "You're that fool from town," he said.

"I am. Grelho by name. And these others are fools as well."

"We'll be having no foolery here," said the man. "Earn your keep in town and stop bothering us working folk."

He turned and started to close the door.

"Actually, we might be able to help you earn your keep," Theo said.

He stopped and turned back to face us. "How's that?" he asked.

"We have heard that your wife has a talent that interests us," Theo began, then held his hands up placating the farmer as he hoisted the spear into throwing position. "Not that kind of talent, I assure you, good friend. But if you are Salh de Lez, and if your wife is named Jacquette, born de la Tour, then that might be worth a little money to you both."

"How much money, and for what?" he asked suspiciously.

"A penny for a song, if she knows it," said Theo.

"And a penny for your time, no matter what," I added.

"She doesn't sing," he said. "Singing is the Devil's work. It led her brother into Perdition."

"Then we will add one more penny that she can give to the church to remove the sin," I said.

He wavered.

"And one more that you may donate to remove the sin of allowing her sin," said Theo. He held up four pennies. "I swear that our intentions are good and just."

The farmer nodded suddenly, then turned back to the house. "Jacquette, there are fools to see you," he called.

"I'll bet those last two pennies never see the inside of a church," murmured Grelho.

A woman emerged, looking at us fearfully. She was brown, whether from the sun, from the dirt, or by blood, I could not say. She wiped her hands nervously on her apron; then her eyes lit up when she saw Grelho.

"You're that fool," she said. "The one that taught Rafael those bawdy songs. I remember you."

"And I remember a pretty little girl with big brown eyes," replied Grelho smoothly.

He remembered nothing of the sort, but the lie pleased her inordinately. She looked at him dotingly while her husband looked back and forth between the two of them and smoldered.

"They want a song out of you, Jacquette," he said harshly.

"A song," she whispered. "I'm not supposed to sing. Maman and Rafael made me swear to it. Never sing anymore, they said, and I promised on the Virgin."

"When was this?" asked Theo.

"Right before he left," said Jacquette. "Told me the bad men might do things to me if I sang, and he had to run before the bad men found him. He couldn't stop singing, so he had to run. He loved singing more than life, Maman used to say."

"He was a wondrous fine singer," said Grelho. "We are looking for a song I heard him sing once or twice. If you know it, it is worth money to you. It was called, 'The Lark's Lament.' Do you know it?"

But her hands were pressed hard against her mouth, and she started to rock back and forth. "That's the one he said most of all not to sing," she said, a keening wail starting to emerge. "That's the one they killed him for."

"Who killed him?" asked Theo.

"I don't know, I don't know, I don't know," she cried.

"Stop that whining, woman," shouted Salh. "Sing the fools the song, and we'll eat well these next two months."

But that only set her wailing louder. The farmer stepped toward her, ready to clout her one.

I ran to her and held my hand up. "Please," I said to her. "I know you promised your brother. And you've kept his promise all these years, and that is doing him honor. But the bad men who killed him are back. They have killed someone else, and they may kill again if we cannot stop them. You're the only one who knows the song. If you sing it to us, then we will be able to stop the bad men, and that would be the opposite of a sin, don't you see?"

She stopped crying and looked at me. "You'll stop the ones who killed my brother?" she asked warily.

"We will do everything in our power," I said.

She wiped her nose on her sleeve, then looked at her husband.

"Wait," he said.

He held out his hand to Theo, who crossed it with the four pennies. He nodded at Jacquette. She stood with her feet apart, looking to the west, then drew a deep breath.

The voice that came out was purer than a mountain stream and had all the songbirds of the world in it.

Cold is the hand that crushes the lark.
Cold is despair unending.
Cold is the rain that douses the spark,
And cold is the grave uncomprehending.
Sweet Lady Lark, why will you not fly?
Fie on a fate so unsparing!
Where lies the voice that made lovers sigh?
And where lies the grace beyond comparing?

High flew the arrow, missing its mark.
High was the tree unbending.
High was the branch and smooth was the bark
That kept this poor creature from ascending.
Sweet Lady Lark, why flew you so high,
Tempting the Hawk with your daring?
Ta'en in his claws and pluck'd from the sky
While all passed below and watched uncaring.

She stopped. There was silence all around us. Even the birds seemed to have stopped their twittering to listen.

Jacquette stood there, frozen, expressionless.

"Was that all there was?" I asked.

"That is all that I know," she said bleakly.

"Who wrote it?" asked Theo.

"I don't know," she said.

"Who was it written for?" I asked.

"I don't know," she said.

"That's enough," said Grelho. "Thank you for singing for us. Your voice surpasses your brother's. It was an honor to hear it."

"I must confess my sins," she said. "Salh, take me to the church."

"But—," began the farmer.

"Now," she said.

"You lot," said the farmer to the rest of us. "Leave here."

We left.

"It's a pretty verse," commented Theo. "I still have no idea who it's talking about."

"That's all right," said Grelho. "I do."

TEN

Ab bel semblan que fals'Amors adutz
s'atrai vas lieis fols amans, e s'atura . . .
[With the fair appearance that false Love produces,
it attracts the enamored fool and he sticks to it . . .]

—FOLQUET DE MARSEILLE, *"SITOT ME SOI A TART APERCEUBUTZ"*
[TRANS. N. M. SCHULMAN]

"We'll need more wine," said Grelho. "Good wine, and lots of it. I know a decent wine-seller. We can make it back into town before sunset, stop there, then head back to my place."

"You can't just tell us on the journey home?" asked Claudia.

"The best part of a story is in the telling," said Grelho. "We'll do this my way."

"Shouldn't we be looking for the Lady Lark?" I asked.

"We cannot do anything more today," said Grelho. "We have time enough, believe me."

The mountains to the west were poking at the sun by the time we crossed the river and reentered Montpellier. The wine-seller was closing up shop when we came in. He grumbled once to see there were late customers, and again when he saw Grelho, but the fool promptly slapped some coins in front of him.

"That covers what I owe you," he said, and the wine-seller brightened. "Two skins of the good Syrah, sirrah, and if I approve, I will make your reputation as the greatest of the grape purveyors."

The wine-seller returned from the back with two bulging wineskins. He opened one and handed it to Grelho to sample.

Grelho took a swig from the skin and nodded. "The other one now," he said.

The wine-seller smiled coldly and gave it to him. "I hope these meet your exacting standards," he said.

"Not bad, not bad at all," said Grelho after his second taste. "I shall spend the rest of the night composing a special encomium in your honor."

"Compose it before you start drinking, if you don't mind," said the wine-seller. "I have heard what songs you come up with when you're drunk."

"Perhaps I should compose it in the morning," agreed Grelho.

"Late morning, after the hangover fades," said the wine-seller.

"Done," said Grelho.

He handed one skin to me, and we walked quickly back to his place before the sun had fully set.

"This is a miracle," I said as we went inside. "We have witnessed Grelho opening his purse on two consecutive days. They'll never believe us back at the Guild."

Grelho went upstairs, then came back down with an actual lantern, which he lit and placed on the table.

"Hail, Diogenes," said Claudia. "The extravagance of this evening abounds. I wonder if your tale will be up to two wineskins and a lantern."

"It's an old tale, and requires a libation to invoke it properly," said Grelho, laying out plates of cheese and sausage. He filled four cups and passed them around, then raised his.

"To Bacchus," he said.

"To the Maenads," responded Claudia, and Grelho glanced at her nervously before drinking his.

"The Lady Lark?" I prompted him.

"I don't know anyone by that name," said Grelho.

"But you said—"

"Peace," he said. "This is my tale, and I shall unfold it as I choose."

He stirred the wine around in his cup, sprinkling a little cinnamon into it from a clay jar. He watched the swirling patterns for a minute.

"I came here in '82," he said. "Down from Cologne, where I did my apprenticeship. The fool who was here before me had died, and although there were a couple of troubadours who were regularly at the court, the Guild wanted a proper jester in town.

"Folquet was here then, or as frequently as his merchanting would bring him. He was riding the Marseille–Montpellier circuit, but I had the impression that he spent much more time here than there. I knew he had a wife back home, and maybe that was the reason, but he never talked about her.

"Eudoxie, the wife of the second-to-last Guilhem, liked having the troubadours about because they knew Greek songs, which made her feel less homesick. Guilhem, to his credit, tolerated their attentions. At first, anyway. As I told you, he himself was a decent harpist and loved to sing, so half the time Folquet was here, he was accompanying Guilhem, praising his voice, his exquisite taste in music, and so forth."

He paused to sip from his cup.

"I never liked Folquet; I confess it," he continued. "He was a toady and a climber. I know that his access to Guilhem benefited the Guild, but his naked ambition to be one with the nobility was repellent. He flattered, he posed, he laughed too loudly at Guilhem's feeble jokes, and treated the rest of us like inferiors. And he was a handsome devil with a beautiful voice and knew it all too well. There were many women trapped in loveless arranged marriages, and he had an eye for trapped wives. He would strut amongst the ladies, preening and displaying like a peacock, playing the gallant so beautifully that they competed for his favors, the Countess included."

"I thought you said he did not woo the Countess," said Claudia.

"He did not allow himself to conquer her in bed," said Grelho. "He knew that was a line never to be crossed. But he danced close to it endlessly, causing no end of scandal. There were also other ladies of lesser rank and looser morals to be won, and he would permit himself to win them. He would return to us from his little visits and never quite boast, but would casually mop his brow with a handkerchief that we had previously seen peeping from a lady's sleeve. Then he would drop an unsubtle hint, and we would all laugh uncomfortably."

"He must have made some enemies back then," I said.

"Of a certainty," said Grelho. "But he had Guilhem's love and protection, at least for a few years."

"But the song—"

"Patience! I am coming to it," Grelho admonished me. "Now, when I was trying to remember families who fit the pattern you suggested, three came to mind. But when I heard de la Tour's sister sing the second verse, I realized that there was one more candidate."

"You remembered who the Lady Lark was?" I asked.

"No," he said. "As I said, I have never heard of any lady called by that name. Not by Folquet, not by another troubadour, not by any rumor flitting about the back alleys of this town, and I have been collecting gossip for over twenty years here. How the Guilhems knew it is beyond me. But the Hawk—that was a name I recognized. Antoine Landrieux. A nobleman, from a family that went back as far in Montpellier as did the Guilhems. A tall, thin, cruel man, he lived for the hunt, and it didn't matter what he hunted or how, so long as there was some beast or fowl to be tracked and slaughtered in the wild. He could spit a full-grown boar with a single thrust while riding at the gallop, then in the next breath shoot a dove down from the sky with a swiftly drawn bow. Or so they say. The things that amused him were not the sort of things a jester provides, so he never asked me to join him. Those that pretended to be his friends called him the Hawk. They called him that to his face, and he reveled in it."

"Did Folquet ever ride with him?" asked Claudia.

"Folquet ride to hunt?" laughed Grelho. "Far too dangerous. He would watch the parade of virility trot off, serenading them as they passed the gate, and be waiting for their return with a flagon and a song at the ready. But in between, while the Hawk and his companions pursued their prey in the forests, Folquet pursued his prey in town. A hunt would last for an entire day, plenty of time for an assignation. Even two."

"The Hawk had a wife," I said.

"The Lady Mathilde," he said. "A quiet woman, which made her stand out among the gabbling geese of the court back then. In the whole time that I saw her here, I don't think that I heard her speak more than a dozen sentences. But when she did speak . . ."

His eyes grew dreamy and far away.

"She had a voice that would turn a man's head toward her with such violence that he'd be lucky it didn't snap off," he said. "Melodious, mellifluous, melancholy Mathilde. She was not a woman whose beauty you would see at first, but hear her speak once, and Cleopatra would seem a shrill scold by comparison."

"Where was she from?" asked Claudia.

"I never knew her history," said Grelho. "She was already married to Landrieux when I came to Montpellier, and Landrieux, as I said, was not one to have a jester over to entertain."

"How about a troubadour?" I asked. "Was she one of Folquet's successes?"

"That's the thing—I don't know for sure," he said. "I never heard of anything between the two of them. If Folquet did love her, then she was someone he kept quiet about. And that would have made her the only one."

"Interesting," said Claudia. "Could it have been true love? If such a thing was possible from such a philanderer."

"She appeared in all respects to be a virtuous wife and mother," said Grelho. "She did not participate in the contests of flirtation that were the principal hobby of the ladies of the court. And her husband, for all his brutish ways, was devoted to her."

"When he was home," said Claudia.

"When he was home," said Grelho.

"You said she was a mother," I said.

"Yes," said Grelho. "A boy, Philippe, was born in '85. Joy abounded at the Landrieux household. It lasted for two years. Then, one day, the house was draped with black cloths. Mathilde had died."

"How?" asked Helga.

"A fall down a flight of stone steps," said Grelho. "Tragic, for one to reach the end of her tale so young, leaving a grieving husband and a bewildered toddler behind."

"In '87," I said. "That was the same year that Folquet left Montpellier for good."

"If good was what he left it for," added Claudia.

"As I said, I never knew for certain that there had been anything between the two," said Grelho. "He left a few days before she died. I never thought to connect the two events until now."

"He left before she died?" I repeated.

"Yes," he said. "At the time, I just assumed that was part of his regular business. It wasn't the leaving for Marseille that was strange. It was his failure to return."

"What happened to his business here?" I asked.

"He sent a subordinate to take over as his agent. He confined his Guild duties to Marseille, claiming that the traveling had affected his health, and that he wanted to be with his wife and sons more. It was sudden and inconvenient, but not so startling a decision. After a period of scrambling, the Guild found another troubadour to take over that route, and we were back to normal."

"If he left just before she died, then how—?" I shook my head. My thoughts were muddied, and the wine wasn't helping. "Did you go to her funeral?"

"Why would I?" asked Grelho. "They never had me entertain them in life. The talk of her death lasted a few days, then some other topic moved in, and that was the last I thought of her until now."

"Could her husband have killed her?" wondered Claudia. "Could the Hawk have threatened Folquet to find out the truth, and then kill his own wife after the rage became too much to bear?"

"It would not have been out of character," said Grelho. "In fact, he would have taken her to the woods, given her a head start, then hunted her for sport. But I never heard anyone suggest that anything untoward had happened. He observed all of the proper mourning, and never said a word against her after."

"His family was one of the ones dispossessed by Marie, wasn't it?" I asked.

"Yes," said Grelho.

"Do you know where he is now?"

"I do," said Grelho. "I will take you to see him in the morning. He isn't far."

"I wonder," I started, then stopped.

"Wonder what?" asked my wife.

"I wonder if Folc killed her," I said.

A stupid random thought that popped up unasked for, then refused to leave. Just like we had with our host, I thought. Served me right. But if this was some long-delayed vengeance for a death, then the Hawk might be our man. Or maybe his son—he would be nineteen. Nineteen is old enough to kill.

I was thirteen the first time I did it.

Claudia looked at me with concern when we emerged from Grelho's house in midmorning.

"Are you all right?" she asked softly while Grelho put Portia up on his shoulders and chatted with Helga.

"I had trouble sleeping," I said.

"That hasn't happened in a while," she said.

"Some old memories came up. You know."

"I know," she said, taking my hand and squeezing it for a moment.

"This way, fools," called Grelho.

He led us south, to the gate that led to the Béziers road.

"Didn't Landrieux keep his house in town?" I asked.

"He used to," said Grelho. "But he resides in the faubourg de la Saunerie now. That's this neighborhood. Not quite as fashionable as his old place, but things change."

"This is where he settled after being dispossessed by Marie?"

"No, he settled here some time before that," said Grelho. "His family was dispossessed more recently."

"He left his family to come here? Why did he do that?"

"I don't think he had much choice in the matter," said Grelho. "Ah, here we are. Show proper deference, fools. We are about to see a great man."

We were standing before a small church.

"Welcome to the parish of Saint-Barthélemy," said Grelho.

"Another one for the priesthood," groaned Claudia. "This is getting to be a veritable plague of religion."

"No, he's just as damned as he ever was," said Grelho. "We don't have to go inside the church if you don't wish it. He's around back."

"I see," I said, finally understanding the fool's riddles. "Lead on."

We walked around to the rear of the church. There was a graveyard there, filled mostly with simple headstones, but with a couple of large mausoleums. He brought us to one, built like a small Roman temple. On the lintel, the name LANDRIEUX appeared. On its roof perched a marble sculpture of a hawk, scanning for prey.

I had the eerie feeling that it was looking right at us.

"When did he die?" I asked.

"Take a look," he said, pushing open the door.

There were three large sarcophagi in the center of the room, and lesser relatives were stacked against the sides, with shelf space available for future tenants. The sun shone through a circular window at the back, enough for us to read the name and dates on the central sarcophagus. The Hawk had ceased flying in 1195.

"Nine years ago," I said.

"I guess he is no longer a suspect," said Grelho. "Unless you think the dead walk among us. That might explain the lack of reaction to some of your jokes the other day. Or maybe they just weren't funny."

"If not the Hawk, then who?" I wondered aloud. "And why now? He dies in 1195. . . ."

I stopped.

"What?" asked Grelho.

"That's the same year Folquet renounced the world and put his entire family into holy orders," I said. "That cannot be a coincidence."

"Yes, it can," said Grelho. "Folquet has not been seen in this town since '87. Why would the Hawk's death have any effect on him whatsoever? Much less plunging him into monasticism."

"Someone else," I said. "Someone connected to the Hawk, to his family. His son? His son, in 1195 . . ."

"Would have been nine or ten," said Grelho. "Hardly a threat, even if he was a precociously violent person, which he wasn't, by the way. Nice young man in all respects. Took after his mother."

"Where is she?" asked Claudia, who had been looking at the other vaults.

"What do you mean, where is she?" asked Grelho. "She's dead."

"But she's not here," said Claudia. "Every one of these has a name, and I don't see Mathilde Landrieux anywhere."

"But I know she's dead," said Grelho. "Everyone knows she's dead."

"You didn't go to her funeral," said Claudia. "You didn't see her body."

"Well, no," he replied. "But—"

"Then you can't say for certain that she's dead," concluded Claudia triumphantly.

"Found her!" called Helga from outside.

Grelho and I looked at Claudia.

"So I got excited," she said, shrugging.

We trooped out to the open air. Helga was standing by a grave about ten feet from the mausoleum, a simple stone at its head. The engraved words read, MATHILDE LANDRIEUX. 1163–1187.

"I told you she was dead," said Grelho. "Now, back to the question of—"

"Why isn't she in the family mausoleum?" asked Claudia.

"I don't know," said Grelho, exasperated. "Maybe wives didn't get in because they were only related by marriage."

"There were four Landrieux wives in there," said Claudia. "And space for several more family members. The Hawk had her buried here, where that bird could watch her until Judgment Day. No loving sentiments on the marker, no biblical inscriptions. Not exactly the most affectionate interment I have ever seen. I thought you said that he showed nothing but tender affection during her life and proper mourning after her death."

"To my eyes, yes," said Grelho. "I admit, this puzzles me."

Claudia slowly walked around the headstone, looking back and forth at the sculpture of the hawk and frowning. Then she squatted down and peered at the headstone more closely.

"Come here," she said.

"What did you find?" I asked as we gathered around her.

She pointed to the back of the headstone. Someone had scratched a crude design into it.

"Looks like some kind of bird," said Grelho.

"It's a lark," said Helga. "Isn't it?"

"Could be," I said.

"I think it is," said Claudia. "Who do you think put it there?"

"Whoever wrote 'The Lark's Lament,'" I said. "Grelho, you know every troubadour who passed through this town. Consider this lament. Whose style is it most like?"

I knew the answer as soon as I asked the question. Grelho looked down at his feet.

"Folquet's," he said. "I thought that as soon as I heard the second verse."

"Because of the Hawk?" asked Claudia.

"No," he replied. "All of that business about the branch on the high tree, and how he was unable to climb it. That was one of his favorite metaphors when he was wooing a wealthy woman. Cheap flattery from a cheap climber, I thought, but it worked for him, so he used it often. Beat it to death, really."

"Speaking of Death," said Helga. "Isn't that him coming right now?"

A gaunt old man in a black tunic was shambling toward us, carrying a scythe in his right hand. What kept his appearance from being completely spectral was the spade and hoe he carried in the other. He stopped upon seeing us, as puzzled by our manifestation as we were by his.

"Did some fool die that you've come to arrange the funeral?" he asked in a screechy voice.

"My friend here has some failed jokes he'd like you to bury," said Grelho, pointing to me. "Are you the sexton?"

"Oc, that I am, going on fifty years now," said the man. "You're Grelho the Jester, aren't you?"

"I am," said Grelho. "Forgive me for not knowing your name. I don't recall seeing you in town."

"Don't go there much," said the sexton. "Got my tending to do, and my legs hurt from the walking, so I save the hurting for here. My name is Otz."

"This is a lovely graveyard," said Claudia politely. "You have kept it beautifully."

"I thank you for that, Domna," he said, bobbing his head. "It keeps me up, so I keep it up. Might as well be married to it these days."

"You're a lucky man, having such a quiet and well-behaved spouse," I said.

"Oh, she's not so quiet as all that," he said. "I hear her speaking to me, especially at night."

"You live here?" I asked.

"I sleep in the back of the church," he said. "Father Aimerie's got one room; I got the other."

"At least you have someone living to talk to," said Grelho.

"Oh, we don't talk, the Father and me," said Otz. "He's new. He thinks he can save me because I'm around all the time, but he's just the latest one to try. They all move on eventually, and I'm still here."

"You hear her speak," said Claudia, indicating the graveyard. "Have you ever heard her sing?"

"Sing?" repeated Otz, scratching his head idly with the tip of the scythe's blade. "No, can't say I have. Only singing I've heard is over the graves, not from inside them."

"Ever hear anyone sing by this one?" I asked.

"By Lady Mathilde? That was a troublesome grave," he said.

"How so?"

"I had to bury her twice, didn't I?"

"Now, that sounds like an interesting story," I said, pulling out the second wineskin from the previous evening. It was half-full. "I propose a fool's trade: share your story, and we'll share our wine."

"But I've got my tending to do," he protested feebly, eyeing the wineskin with interest.

"We can take care of that while you talk," I said. "Helga, ever wanted to learn how to use a scythe?"

"Oh, ever so much," said Helga. "Where shall I start?"

"Anything that looks too tall, cut it down," said Otz.

She held out her hands, and he gave her the scythe. She took it and trudged past us. As she did, she glanced up at me. "You're tall," she muttered, hefting it speculatively.

"That patch there could use some of your loving care," I said, pointing helpfully. She headed over to a clump of weeds and beheaded them, grumbling.

"Shall we sit here?" I asked. "It looks comfortable enough."

"If I sit on the ground, I won't be able to get up again," said Otz. "There's a bench yonder."

We accompanied him to a weather-beaten wooden bench. He sat down slowly and beckoned for the wineskin, which he then upended for a good long time.

"That's as good as I've had in many a year," he said when he emerged, wiping his mouth with his sleeve. "What were we talking about?"

"Burying Lady Mathilde twice," I prompted.

"Oc, that was the one," he said. "Well, I had to bury her twice."

Then he sat there, blinking, while we waited.

"There is more to the story, isn't there?" asked Claudia finally.

"Not really," he said, and blinked some more.

"How was it that she came to be in need of a second burial?" she asked.

"Ah, well, someone dug her up," he said. "Two nights after she was buried, so the ground was still loose."

"Grave-robbers?" I said. "After her jewelry?"

"Don't know that she was wearing any," said Otz.

"Surely you could have seen if the body was disturbed in any way," said Grelho.

"Oh, the body was disturbed all right," said Otz. "They disturbed it right out of the graveyard."

"They took her body?" shrieked Helga from across the graveyard.

"Good ears on that one," said Grelho. "Not to mention lungs."

"Why do you suppose she was taken?" I asked.

"Who knows?" he said. "Maybe one of them schools where they pretend to teach medicine. Maybe a trick. Maybe, well, they say she was a pretty lass. Maybe they wanted her for something else."

Claudia shuddered.

"Do you remember the condition of the body before she was buried?" I asked. "Were there any signs of violence?"

"I never saw the body," he said. "I usually don't. They bring it into the church and do their praying while I'm out here digging the hole. Then they bring the coffin out and drop it in, and I cover it up."

"Who came to her burial? Do you remember?"

"Well, there was that Landrieux fellow," he said, considering. "Two of his men, one named Berenguer, he's the one who paid me, and the other was a big fellow, limped a bit—"

"Rocco?" guessed Grelho.

"Oc, that was him. And the priest, that was Father Firmin back then. Nice man. Him, I talked to."

"And that was it?" I asked. "No one else came?"

"No," he said. "The two men brought the coffin out on a cart, lowered it into the grave, Father Firmin said a few words, we got paid, and I buried her. Then I had to do it again, and I didn't get paid for that one."

"Where is Father Firmin these days?" I asked.

"Over there," he said, pointing to a simple wooden cross marking a grave on the far side of the fence enclosing the cemetery.

"Why isn't he buried inside the fence?" asked Claudia, crossing herself.

"Killed himself," said Otz tersely.

"Why?" I asked.

"Don't know," he said. "He wasn't the type, but one night I come back from the tavern, and there he was, swinging by the neck in the church. Surprised me."

"I remember hearing about that," said Grelho. "It surprised everyone."

"Do you remember if anyone sang at her funeral?" I asked.

"Nah, no one did that," he said.

"Well, that was a long shot," I said as we rose.

"The singer came a week later," he said.

We looked at each other, then sat down again. Helga gave up all pretense of working on the weeds and came over to join us.

Otz lifted the wineskin and contemplated it mournfully. "Not much left," he said.

"Finish it," I said.

He bobbed his head again, then drained the wineskin to the last drop. "Damned good wine," he pronounced. "What were we talking about?"

"The singer at Lady Mathilde's grave," I said, trying very hard not to jump on him and shake the remainder of the story out.

"Right. Maybe two weeks later, I hear someone singing. I go out here to look, and there's this young fellow, used to sing up in that place in town, you know the one I'm talking about?"

"Near the Blancaria," said Grelho. "His name was Rafael."

"That's the one," agreed Otz. "Singing his heart out. Don't have an ear for music myself, but he sounded real good."

"Was he with anyone else?" I asked.

"I didn't see no one about," said Otz. "None of my business what people want to do around here, except digging them up again. That's just extra work for me."

"And you didn't tell anyone about the grave being robbed?" I asked.

"Oh, no," said Otz. "People hear there's grave-robbing going on, they won't want to be buried here. Then I'm out of a job. This is all I know. Been here going on fifty years."

"So we've heard," said Claudia, picking up Portia from where she had been playing in the grass and putting her in her sling. "Thank you for your time."

"All I got is time," said Otz. "Where did you get that wine, anyway?"

"In town," said Grelho. "At that place. You know the one."

"Hmm," said Otz wistfully. "I ought to go into town more."

"Here's your scythe," said Helga, giving it back to him.

We left him sitting on his bench, starting to drift off.

"Possibility," I said as we walked. "Folquet leaves; Mathilde dies. It takes a week for word to reach Folquet in Marseille. He comes back here and gets Rafael to sing 'The Lark's Lament' as a final personal tribute to her."

"Sounds romantic," said Grelho.

"Possibility number two," said Claudia. "Folquet is threatened, leaves town, but in a fit of jealous rage sneaks back and kills her. Then, in remorse, he composes his lament."

"Sounds less romantic," said Grelho. "And it shares the same problem. Why was the body stolen? And who did it?"

"It was stolen because he couldn't bear to have her share eternity with her husband," said Claudia. "He rescues her from the grave and buries her in a place only he knows."

"Then he comes back to this grave to have Rafael sing the lament two weeks later, knowing that she isn't there," responded Grelho. "It still doesn't make sense."

"Do you think they killed the priest?" asked Helga.

"It crossed my mind," I said. "I just don't know how to fit that in with the little that we know. Grelho, whatever happened to the two men who came with Landrieux?"

"Berenguer and Rocco? They're still in town, to the best of my knowledge. I think they latched on to other houses after the Landrieux family was dispossessed."

"Who became guardian for Philippe Landrieux when his father died?"

"Guilhem himself," said Grelho. "He let the boy live in the family house. He appointed Berenguer as the steward for the family finances until the boy became of age."

"What happened to Philippe after he was disenfranchised?"

"I don't know," said Grelho. "But I can find out."

"Theo," said Claudia.

"Yes?"

"Why didn't Folc tell you that he wrote 'The Lark's Lament'?"

"That's the first question I am going to ask when I see him," I said.

"Because if he did kill Mathilde, then it would be natural for him to deny it," she said. "It would be even more natural for him to send us off on what he thought would be an impossible quest. And then he panicked and sent Brother Antime to Montpellier to find out if someone here knew what he had done, and to intercept us if we showed up."

"Only someone intercepted Antime first," I said. "Yes, that certainly seems plausible. But if Folc was covering up an adulterous affair from his past, he could have reacted the same way. I have no doubt that he has some dark secret to hide, but how dark it is, we have yet to learn. Grelho, let's go find Berenguer and Rocco and see if they will be willing to talk to us. Berenguer first, I think. He was the steward."

"Right," said Grelho. "I think he lives up in the Saint-Mathieu parish. I remember seeing him come out of a house there once, and saying hello."

"You were the master conversationalist even then," I said.

"Oh, I want to solve all of this, if only to get rid of you people," he said.

He led us back through town, once again taking us past the markets. We came to a square filled with flower-sellers, peddling mostly dried bouquets and a few late bloomers. We turned into the narrow twisty streets north of there, and Grelho stopped at a crossing, looking uncertain.

"It was somewhere around here," he said. "He actually had his own place, as I recall."

"Maybe it's the one with all the Viguerie clustering about it," said Claudia, pointing to the right.

We looked in that direction. Sure enough, a group of guards was gathered in front of a house, spears in barricade position, while others were fanning out and pounding on doors in a way that was becoming all too familiar.

"Unfortunately, you are correct," sighed Grelho. "Let's go ask. Nothing unusual about being curious in these circumstances."

We walked up to the perimeter of the barricade.

"Ho, Jacques, since when are you working days?" called Grelho.

I recognized the guard who had rousted us two nights before. He nodded at us. "They woke us up for this one," he said. "Remember Berenguer? Used to be the Landrieux steward?"

"Vaguely," said Grelho. "What's he done?"

"Done? He's done nothing," said Jacques grimly. "Someone's done him. Stabbed in the chest."

Gasping and crossing from us all.

"How horrible," said Grelho. "Isn't that what happened to that fellow you found near my place the other night?"

"It is," said Jacques. "And we're going to turn this town upside down and shake it until the rat who did this falls out. Until then, I would advise you to be careful. Don't go walking anywhere on your own at night."

"Good counsel, and we will abide by it, friend Jacques," promised Grelho.

We watched for a few minutes as if we had nothing better to do, then moved on.

"I'll have to ask around about Rocco," said Grelho. "I don't know where he lives."

"We have to find him as soon as possible," I said.

"You think he's in danger," said Claudia.

"Let me put it this way," I said. "You know that man we thought was following us?"

"Yes?"

"I think he's ahead of us now."

ELEVEN

. . . me sui conogutz
del gran engan qu'Amors vas mi fazia;
[. . . I now know the terrible trick Love played on me;]

—FOLQUET DE MARSEILLE, "*SITOT ME SOI A TART APERCEUBUTZ*"
[TRANS. N. M. SCHULMAN]

My first instinct when my husband said, "I think he's ahead of us now," was to go for my dagger and fling it at any man I saw in front of us. Luckily, my reason seized hold of my hand before I did so.

"Who did Rocco go to work for after the Landrieux family?" asked Theo.

"The Conque clan," said Grelho.

"Would he be in the actual house?"

"Not likely," said Grelho. "Rocco isn't a servant. He's a guard, more muscle than brains. But the Conques don't keep him at the house—he's too new to their service. They've been using him at their warehouse."

"We passed a group of warehouses when we crossed the river Lez," I said. "Was the Conque warehouse one of them?"

"Yes," he said.

"Let's go," said Theo.

The warehouses were downstream from the bridge we had crossed on our journey to Montpellier, about a mile east of town. When we reached them, we saw a group of men loading crates onto a barge to be sent down the Lez for transfer to a ship at Lattes. Grelho scanned the group quickly.

"He's not here," he said. He cupped his hands and called out, "Hey, Gombal!"

A man turned and waved to us, then came up, wiping his brow with his sleeve. "Grelho, what on earth are you doing this far from a tavern?" he asked, slapping the fool's shoulder. "Come to see real men do real work?"

"Every now and then I need reminding why I chose a jester's life, so I come watch you," laughed Grelho. "But I am actually looking for Rocco. He loaned me some money last week, and I want to pay him back before I forget and spend it on wine. Know where he is?"

"He didn't come to work today, damn him," said Gombal.

I felt a pang of apprehension.

"All this walking for nothing," grumbled Grelho. "Where's he staying nowadays? I know he's not at the Landrieux place anymore because nobody's at the Landrieux place anymore."

"Oc, sad that," said Gombal. "He's at the house of the widow Gervaise."

"Off Rue de la Potterie? The place with the green shutters?"

"That's the one," said Gombal. "And someday you must tell me the story of how you managed to get that miser to pry open his purse."

"Sorry, it's a trade secret," said Grelho. "Thanks, Gombal."

We trooped on back to town.

"I don't like the idea of him missing work," said Grelho.

"Today of all days," agreed Theo. "Let us hope that he's only deathly ill."

But when we got there, Rocco was not deathly ill. Nor was he dead. He just wasn't there.

"He's not at the warehouse?" was the widow Gervaise's response when I asked.

"No, Domna," I said. "They figured he had taken sick."

"Him, sick!" she said indignantly. "He's never been sick a day since I've known him. Strong as an ox."

"And about as smart," muttered Grelho.

"Could he be with any family members?" asked Theo. "Or some sweetheart, perhaps?"

She turned beet red and slammed the door in our faces, screaming.

"Let me guess," said Theo wearily. "She is the sweetheart."

"Well, if he isn't dead yet, you may have sealed his fate," said Grelho cheerfully. "Maybe you could volunteer to taste his food when he returns."

"If he returns," I said. "He's not here; he's not there. All that leaves is everywhere else. Where do you suppose he is?"

"Did you notice that his route would have taken him by the street where Berenguer lived?" asked Theo. "Maybe he saw the commotion, found out that someone did for his former colleague, and went to ground."

"I hope that's the case," said Grelho. "My money's on him joining the ranks of the recently punctured."

"Until we know that for sure, we keep looking for him," said Theo. "No one has told us that anyone else sought him out first, so we may have a little bit of a lead this time. Grelho, this is your town. You have to know a way to find him."

"I am trying to think," said Grelho. "I know some other former servants of the Landrieux household. One of them might be able to help us."

"That's a start," said Theo. "Anyone else have any suggestions?"

"I have one," I said. "Grelho, do you happen to know any grave-robbers?"

"As a matter of fact, I do," said Grelho.

It was no surprise that Grelho was acquainted with someone from one of the seedier criminal professions. Those of us on Guild business can find ourselves performing all manner of unpleasant tasks, and although I personally have never yet resorted to digging up a grave, that's only because the bodies I've had to poke through and crawl around didn't have the benefit of burial at the time. When we lived and worked in Constantinople, Theo and I had more than once relied upon an uneasy alliance with the dominant criminal organization there, and grave-robbing was certainly one of their sidelines.

The surprise was that when Grelho named his grave-robbing acquaintance, we realized that we had already met him.

"Do you really think this line of inquiry is necessary?" asked Theo in a tone indicating that he did not.

"It may very well lead to nothing," I said. "But it gnaws at my curiosity. Anyhow, there isn't much point in all of us following Grelho around while he searches for Rocco. If I'm going to be lugging Portia about town, I might as well be doing something productive."

"Do you want me to come with you?" he asked. "I could have Helga go with Grelho."

"No, this is a task that calls for a woman's touch," I said. "I'll bring her with me. It shouldn't take me more than an hour or so. Where shall we meet?"

"At the Orgerie," said Grelho. "One hour, then."

Helga carried Portia. As the senior fool, I wanted to keep my hands free just in case. I would have liked to have my sword handy, but jesters don't normally carry swords, nor do women, so the two daggers I had concealed in my sleeves had to suffice.

The man we were seeking lived and worked close to the gate that we had passed through on our arrival in Montpellier. It was a good location, close to the via Francigena. A blacksmith gets most of his work from horses, and horses on long journeys are more likely to need shoeing. The smithy was far enough from the crowded streets and buildings to keep from being a fire hazard, and close enough to the nearby forests to receive its regular diet of wood.

Reynaud was hard at work, making iron nails, which he threw into a crude metal box by the wall. With all the clanging, he didn't hear us come up, and Portia's excited squeal when she saw the fire nearly made him hit his finger with the hammer.

"What the blazes?" he started, then he saw us and smiled. "Oh, it's you. Having a profitable while in Montpellier?"

"We are, Sieur, and thank you kindly," I said. "We had some free time, so I thought I would take the children to see what a blacksmith does. Portia, that's the baby here, loves horses."

"Ah, pity I'm not shoeing any today," said Reynaud. "Whenever I have free time, I make nails, so I'm never wanting 'em when I need 'em."

"Most prudent of you, Sieur," I said. "That is one of the differences between a blacksmith and a fool. We never think about the future."

"Well, prudence is something I've only come by over time," he said. "It didn't come natural, and that's the truth of it."

"Indeed, if half the stories I've heard are true, you had quite a misspent youth," I said, winking at him.

"Oh, you shouldn't believe even half of the half," he said, laughing. "But a man who didn't have a misspent youth squandered it, if you ask me. I know many a stolid successful fellow in his forties who regrets not having his wild days when he had enough strength and energy to be wild. Remember that, young lady."

"I will, Sieur," said Helga solemnly.

"Now, I heard one story about you just today," I said. "I must say I found it shocking."

"Which one was that?" he asked.

I leaned forward so that I could shield us from outside ears. "That you were a grave-robber," I whispered.

"Ridiculous," he snorted. "An old wives' tale."

"Which is why I know it," I said. "A good fool, of course, is as much a collector of old tales as an old wife. We take them, melt them down, and hammer them into new shapes and forms. By the time a talesmith like me is done, I could tell you your life history in such a way that you would never recognize yourself."

"I am beginning to wonder about the purpose of your visit," he said, resuming his hammering. "The past is long gone. What happened then is tales now, and then the tales stop getting told, and that's the way it should be, if you ask me."

"Sometimes that past rears up again," I said. "Sometimes the tales need to be retold. And those who tell them may profit by the lessons in them."

"Profit, you say," he said slowly, tossing another nail into the box.

"As I said, I am a collector. I give value for value. And, in truth, I only want a small part of a larger tale, most of which I already know."

"A small part?"

"The tail of the tale, if you will."

"What does the rest of the dog look like?" he asked.

"Old and shaggy," I said. "But its teeth are still sharp. Would you like to hear it?"

"If you tell it, must I pay you?" he asked.

"I am not working right now," I said. "I would not charge you for an incomplete story, any more than you would charge me for half a nail."

"Go on, then," he said. "I'll see if it's a story I know."

"There was a lady of this town many years ago," I began. "Possessed of a rich husband, a small son, and a beautiful voice. Her name was Mathilde, wife of Antoine Landrieux."

"I remember her," said Reynaud. "I remember her voice even now."

"Then her voice was stopped. She died, victim of an accident, in 1187. She was buried in the cemetery of Saint-Barthélemy, south of the city."

"A brief tale, quickly over," said Reynaud. "Scarcely worth the telling."

"But there was a coda," I said. "Two days after being laid to rest, the grave was dug up, and her body was carried off. No one knows whatever happened to it."

"And you think I had something to do with that," said Reynaud.

"I am merely searching for the missing piece of the story," I said.

"It's not just a piece that's missing," he said, starting to grin. "It's the whole body."

"So it seems."

He started to chuckle, then to laugh loudly. It was infectious, even though we didn't know why he was laughing. "You like a good joke, don't you?" he said, trying to catch his breath.

"A good joke is one of the principal tools of my trade," I said.

"This story of yours," he said. "It's a joke, and you don't know the punch line. It's one I've known for nigh on eighteen years, and I've never been able to tell it to anyone. Sometimes I've been like to burst holding it, for it's a funny one, though not to all ears."

"Funny is my life's work," I said. "Tell your joke, and I will render you my professional opinion."

"But you never heard it from me," he said. "That must be your oath."

"Easily taken," I said. "A jester is loath to give credit to others anyway. I swear by my baby's smile, which I hold dear above all things, that your part in this will be anonymous."

"Then here it is," he said. "Let's say that there once was a young fellow in desperate need of money. Someone in the middle of an apprenticeship to an honorable trade, but with a sickly widowed mother and three younger sisters to support."

"A good beginning and a sympathetic fellow," I said. "One's heart reaches out to him immediately."

"Now, thinks this fellow, there's all these people who have gone on to their just rewards. Their souls are in Heaven, their bodies await Judgment Day, yet their pernicious relatives laid them to rest with jewelry, gold and silver and gems that good men broke their backs wresting from deep within the earth, only to see them buried again. Where's the sense in that?"

"A reasonable argument made by this sympathetic fellow," I said. "There is only one possible conclusion."

"Concludes this desperate fellow, 'The dead have no need of adornment, and no jewelry is worn in Heaven. Why not put these buried trinkets to use for the benefit of the living?' "

"It would, in fact, be a blessing to do so," I agreed.

"So, he embarks on this second profession to his profit. One day, he hears of a rich young lady who has met a tragic fate. He decides to pay his respects but, alas, is unable to attend the funeral."

"Schedules can be so difficult," I said.

"So he shows up at his next free moment, which happens to be shortly after midnight maybe two nights later."

"And he notices that the ground is still loose. . . ."

"And by coincidence, he's carrying a pick and shovel. . . ."

"And nobody else is about. . . ."

"So, why not?"

"No possible harm that I can see."

"And he puts himself to work. . . ."

"And it's no small task."

"It's much harder to dig up someone than to bury her."

"But hard work carries with it a reward."

"Normally," said Reynaud.

"Normally?" I asked.

"All of the graves this fellow ever dug up gave him value," he said, starting to laugh again. "All of them but this one. He reaches the coffin, kind of a cheap one for such a wealthy family, but there it is. He pries open the lid, having taken the care to tie a kerchief over his mouth and nose because that first rush of decay can be something awful. But there is no such smell."

"She was that well preserved?" I asked. "Was she a saint?"

"Perhaps even holier than that," he said. "There's not much of a moon, and he's below the surface without a light to see by. He's done this before, however, so he grits his teeth and reaches into the coffin. He comes away with nothing."

"No jewelry on the body?"

He laughed grimly. "No body," he said. "And that's the punch line."

"You don't think she was like Our Savior, do you?" asked Helga quietly as we walked to the Orgerie. "His body disappeared from the Holy Sepulchre after three days."

"And she only took two," I said. "No, Apprentice, I see no miracle here. Miracles aren't wasted on grave-robbers who keep them quiet. They are placed before us to bring us faith."

"I didn't really think it was a miracle," said Helga, sounding disappointed. "But if it wasn't that—"

"Then it may have been something far worse," I said. "Look, they are already there."

The two fools were carrying on a mock debate in learned gibberish with broad gestures that made them look like apes at one moment, cats at the next, and so on through the catalog of beasts. When they saw us, they barked a greeting, and we barked back. We waited while they collected their gear, then walked to a quiet side street to confer.

"We know where he is," said Theo with smug satisfaction.

"And we know where she is not," I said.

"We already knew that she is no longer in her grave," said Theo.

"She was never in her grave," I said. "She might not have had any need for one."

"What?" exclaimed Grelho.

"She's still alive!" burst out Helga.

"Tell us everything, and tell it quickly," demanded Theo.

I recounted Reynaud's tale.

"Why bury an empty coffin?" wondered Grelho.

"To make the world believe she was dead," said Theo.

"But why would the Hawk want that?" asked Grelho. "If he wanted to get rid of her that badly, he could simply kill her."

"Maybe he didn't want to kill her," I said. "Maybe he wanted her to suffer first. To suffer for a long time. And if the world thought she was dead, then no one would come looking to rescue her."

"What a horrible thought," said Theo, looking sick under his whiteface. "Could the Hawk have been capable of doing something like that?"

"With sufficient provocation, yes," said Grelho.

"My apologies, wife," said Theo. "Not a waste of a trip at all."

"Accepted, husband," I said. "Let's visit friend Rocco."

More carvings of hawks, set on the pillars of the gates to the courtyard of the château. They were padlocked.

"We spotted a wisp of smoke from the chimney," explained Theo.

"No one has taken the place since the Landrieux clan was evicted," said Grelho. "Apparently Pedro is asking too high a price for it."

"Could it be a caretaker?" I asked.

"The lady across the street says there is none," said Theo. "It's a good place to hide temporarily."

"Is there another way in?" I asked.

"Servants' door around back," said Theo. "Bolted from the inside. We could pick the padlock here, but that might alert the Viguerie, and I don't think we could talk our way out of that one."

We strolled around to the back of the château. The servants' door looked quite formidable from this side. I looked up at the windows of the second floor.

"He left one unshuttered," I observed. "Careless."

"It's rather high up," Grelho pointed out.

"Yes, it is," I agreed. "About the height of a tall man and a tossed apprentice, wouldn't you say?"

Theo glanced up and down the street, then casually leaned back against the wall under the window and locked his hands at waist level.

Helga handed me Portia, then took a running start and jumped, landing with her knees bent and her right foot in the center of his linked hands. With a grunt, he heaved her up. She kicked out at the last possible moment for extra height and just barely grabbed the window ledge. She took a breath, then pulled herself up and scrambled inside. We saw her hand reach out and close the shutters after her.

"Thoughtful of her," said Theo.

A minute later, we heard a bolt slide and the door open. A composed and dignified young lady looked at us disdainfully.

"What ruffians are you?" she said, sniffing and wrinkling her nose. "Welcome to the Landrieux house. I am afraid that the master is not at home."

We pushed by her quickly and shut the door. She bolted it behind us.

"Congratulations, Apprentice," I whispered. "You just earned the right to swing on the gibbet alongside the rest of us."

"Stick together, weapons out," said Theo softly.

We crept through the dark hallways, feeling our way through to where Grelho thought the smoke had originated. Then we saw a faint glow from a doorway ahead. Theo and Grelho pressed themselves against the wall by it, while I peered cautiously from the opposite wall.

A single taper sat on a small stool, directly in front of the doorway, providing enough light to illumine anyone coming through. The candle's glare kept me from seeing past it into the recesses of the room. I came back to Theo's side.

"Looks like a trap," I whispered.

"One way to find out," said Grelho.

He edged up to the door frame and called softy, "Rocco?"

"First person through that door gets a bolt through his chest," said a hoarse voice. "Second gets the same."

"There's five of us," said Grelho. "You don't have enough crossbows. We're not here to harm you, Rocco. We might be able to help."

"I don't need help," said the voice. "Who are you? You sound familiar."

"It's Grelho the Fool, Rocco. And I've got some other fools with me."

"Fools?" said Rocco. "What are fools doing here?"

"Looking to find you," said Grelho. "And I'm glad we found you before that other fellow."

"Which fellow?"

"The one who killed Berenguer," said Grelho. "And he killed that big bald man the other night. He's after you, isn't he?"

"How do you know about him?" demanded Rocco. "What does this have to do with you?"

"We think he's after the same thing we are," said Theo.

"What's that?"

"Something now known only to you," I said.

"There's a woman with you?" he exclaimed.

"We are two men, one woman, one girl, and a baby," said Grelho. "All fools. Will you talk to us? It may save your life."

There was silence for a while.

"Let the woman fool stand in the doorway where I can see her," he said finally. "No weapons. If I see steel, I shoot. No one else comes into it."

I sheathed my daggers and started toward the doorway.

Theo put his hands on my shoulders, stopping me. "I don't like this," he murmured.

"We've come this far," I said.

He withdrew his hands, and I stepped into the doorway.

"Close enough," said Rocco, and I looked in the direction of his voice. There was an indistinct form just past the edge of the candlelight. A small bit of steel reflected the flame. It looked sharp, and it was pointed in my direction. I raised my hands.

"What do you want from me?" he said.

"The truth about Lady Mathilde," I said.

"She's dead and buried," he said. "Fell down the steps in '87. I could show you where we found her."

"You and Berenguer buried an empty coffin," I said. "Lowered it into a grave while your master watched. And because she did not die that day, people are dying now."

"How do you know all this?" he shouted. "Are you some kind of a witch?"

"Was it because Landrieux learned that she was unfaithful to him that he punished her so?" I asked.

"The whore deserved it," he said. "Everything that happened, she had coming to her. You can't leave these things to God to sort out. That's what the master used to say. God's got a lot on His mind, so we have to take care of His business here."

"Who was her lover?" I asked.

"It was that pretty boy troubadour," said Rocco, snickering in a high-pitched voice. "Used to come over, give her singing lessons, worm his way in until the master trusted him enough. Then the master would go off hunting, and the lessons were for something else, something nasty. But the master found out. You couldn't fool him, not the master. He pretended to go hunting, had someone dress up in his clothes and ride his horse out to the country, and all the while he was hiding here, watching her. Watching them. Oh, he smelled them out good, did the master."

"What did he do?"

"He hauls the troubadour in, makes him pay, beats him but good, and in front of the lady," said Rocco. "I didn't even have to lay a hand on him; the master does it all himself. Then he gives him two days to clear out, and pretty boy is gone in one."

"And the Lady Mathilde?" I asked, my heart pounding in my chest.

"There's a dungeon here no one knew about," said Rocco. "No one but the master, and Berenguer, and me. He puts her in there, chained to the wall, and keeps her there in the dark. She screamed and screamed, but no one could hear her. Sometimes the master would go down and have his way with her, but he was her husband, so he was in the right, wasn't he? And me and Berenguer would bring her food, muck out the cell, and throw a bucket of water on her every now and then."

"What about Rafael de la Tour?" asked Theo from behind me.

"Berenguer heard him singing once," said Rocco. "Singing about master and her. He told the master, and the master told us to bring him here. You don't disrespect the master like that and get away with it. So we waited for him, conked him, put a sack over his head and tied it good. We brought him to the master. He made him sing the song to her. Sing it over and over. It was supposed to be sung over her corpse, but she was alive, and hearing her death song over and over and screaming. Just the song and the screams. Then, at the end, she was singing it with him. Christ, she had a voice like an angel. A fallen angel, chained forever, singing her own funeral lament. And we took Rafael back and told him to get out of Montpellier, and if we ever heard him singing again, we'd cut out his tongue and feed it to him. You don't disrespect the master like that and get away with it. He was lucky."

"How long did your master keep her there?" I asked.

"Until he died," he answered.

"Eight years," breathed Helga in horror.

"And then what?"

"And then Berenguer was the steward for the boy, and he kept her there after," said Rocco.

"He kept her there?"

"He was told to by the master," said Rocco. "The master would say, 'If I die before her, boys, you keep her there until she's ready to join me.' So Berenguer did."

"Did the boy," began Grelho, and I could hear that he was weeping. "Did Philippe know about this?"

"Not while it was going on," said Rocco. "He grew up thinking she was dead all along."

"Did she die finally?" I asked, hoping that she was truly at rest somewhere.

"Don't know," he said. "The Countess kicked everyone out. I don't know what happened to her. I took a look down there when I sneaked back in here, but it was empty."

"Why did you panic?" asked Theo. "What caused you to hide?"

"A couple of days ago, Berenguer looks me up at the warehouse," he said. "Says there's people poking about, asking about her. Says a big man's offering money to find out what happened to her, and someone else is offering even more. Then I hear the big man's been killed, so I go to Berenguer to find out what's what, and someone did him, too. So, I ran."

"Who was the other man?" I said.

"Ask Berenguer," he said. "I never seen him. But if I do, I'll stick him before he sticks me first. You can count on that. And you'd best do the same, lady."

"Sound advice, thank you," I said.

"Who killed Rafael?" asked Theo. "Who killed the priest who performed the rites at the burial?"

"He hung himself is what I heard," said Rocco, and I could sense the smirk even if I couldn't see it. "And the master heard that the boy was still singing that song. He was lucky the first time he disrespected the master. Not so lucky the second, is what I heard."

"There's bad luck for everybody in this," I said. "Who knows you're here?"

"Didn't think anyone did," he said. "What tipped you?"

"You made a fire, Rocco," said Grelho wearily. "We saw the smoke."

"I was cold," he whined.

"It's colder in the grave," said Theo. "You may want to consider getting out of town entirely."

"I'm safe here," said Rocco. "I'll wait until it blows over."

"It's your funeral," said Theo. "Nice chatting with you. We're leaving."

"Wait," said Rocco. "Lady, pick up the candle from the table and hold it in front of you."

"Why?" I asked.

"Because I got a crossbow pointing at you," he explained.

I picked up the candle and held it in front of me.

"Back up slowly into the hallway and stand there," he directed. "Good. Now, two steps toward your friends and stop. I'm coming to the door. Anything funny happens from any of you, I kill her."

I prayed that he had a steady hand. The candle wax was dripping onto my fingers, but I held on for dear life.

"Tell them to put their weapons away," he said.

"Please do it," I said, and the knives vanished.

"Hold the candle over your head and turn away," he said. "If I don't see all of you when I step through, she dies."

I complied, then gasped as I felt the bolt poke me in the small of my back.

"Now, we're going to walk together to the rear door," he said. "She's last the whole time. Stay bunched so I can see all of you."

We walked carefully together to the servants' door. Helga unbolted it and opened it a crack, peering outside.

"It's clear," she said.

"Step outside, one by one," he said.

Helga stepped outside, followed by Grelho and Theo. Before I could follow them, Rocco clamped a hand on my shoulder and put his mouth by my ear.

"Maybe I should keep you here as a hostage," he whispered. I could feel the flecks of spittle hitting my cheek. "Wouldn't mind having a pretty lady like you spending the night."

Through the door I could see Theo staring at us intently. I knew he was judging whether he could throw his knife past my head into Rocco's throat without having the crossbow do any damage.

"Don't you have enough people wanting to kill you?" I asked.

He chuckled deep in his throat. "Drop the candle," he said.

I dropped it. As I did, he shoved me hard into the street and slammed the door behind me, ramming the bolts into place.

I still hadn't seen his face.

"All this time, trapped in that dungeon," moaned Grelho as we walked back to his place. "No light, no air, no hope. How could she have survived?"

"She must have been tremendously strong," said Theo.

"How old would she—? How old is she now?" I asked.

"She was twenty-four when she died," said Grelho. "I mean, when she was buried . . . when she was put in that dungeon. She'd be forty-one now."

"But where did she go when she was freed?" asked Theo. "Was there nothing about an imprisoned woman being released when the Landrieux clan was turned out of the house?"

"I heard nothing," said Grelho. "The evictions were carried out by Léon, Marie's seneschal. He would have needed only a few men he could trust. We'll never get anything out of them."

"Then we will have to go over his head," I said firmly.

It was Friday, and I had a job to do.

About two dozen women filed into the great hall, where a large table had been set up. The younger women wore gowns that looked new and showed off their figures to the fullest advantage, although there were no men about except for the servants. Of course, women have been known to compete with each other even when the prize is in another room.

It was the older women who interested me. These were the survivors, I guessed, the ones who had not incurred the displeasure of the Countess and her new king. Not yet, anyway. Each of them as she entered looked uncertainly about the hall, both to see who was there and, of more concern, who wasn't. While the younger women chattered enthusiastically, the older ones were cautious and quiet. No doubt they had chattered when they were younger. Now, they were wondering if they had said too much.

I strummed my lute and sang, choosing my songs at random, letting my eye wander across the table. Marie was in her element. I noticed that in company, she drank much less, the better to make her own observations. When she spoke, she said little but still managed to turn the topics of conversation to those that intrigued her, and she was quite content to listen, filing away the information she gleaned for later use.

At one point, she turned to me and said, "Domna Gile, sing for us that song you sang the other day, the one by that troubadour from Marseille."

"As you command, Domna," I replied.

Love was falling, Love was sinning
When it moved into my heart.
Lacking Mercy from the start,
Soon, my sorrows were beginning. . . .

As I sang, I noticed that the younger women were puzzled, but the expressions on the older women ranged from apprehension to genuine shock. A few whispered explanations to the younger ones, and they in turn whispered to each other.

Marie presided serenely over the table as if nothing at all unusual had occurred. When I finished, she applauded, and the other ladies followed her lead.

Ah, the joys of a captive audience! I bowed, then played something that was purely instrumental.

At the end of the meal, which is to say at the end of the gossiping, the ladies left and the servants cleared the table. One placed a plate of food by me. I was ravenous and dug in.

"An excellent performance, Domna Fool," said the Countess as she returned to the room.

I stood hastily and bowed. "Thank you, Domna," I said. "And if I may be so bold, your performance was excellent as well."

She nodded at the compliment, a slight smile on her lips. She sat at the head of the table and bade me take a place on the bench to her left. I did so, bringing my plate with me. Léon came into the room and whispered something to her. She nodded.

"I would like to speak with you about a matter," she said. "I have just been informed that my guards have taken your two daughters into custody."

I started, and she held a hand up in warning.

"They are unharmed," she said. "You need not worry on their account."

"Have they misbehaved in some way?" I asked. "Whatever offense they gave, I shall take it upon myself to punish them severely, milady."

"The offense is yours," she said.

"Then let the punishment be mine as well. Please, the children are innocent."

"Their fate depends upon your cooperation," she said.

"I swear, milady, if anything happens to them—"

"You'll do what?" she snapped. "Amuse me to death?"

I took a deep breath and tried to calm myself.

"Your offense is that you have mistaken our relative positions and thought me the fool," she continued. "You forget that I have Byzantine blood in me."

"Not in the least, milady."

"Report," she said to Léon.

He cleared his throat. "You and your colleagues have been observed near the scenes of three murders," he began.

"Three?" I exclaimed.

"Tuesday night, a stranger was killed," he said. "The blood came as far as the house belonging to the fool Grelho, where you and your family are residing."

"Yes, I told you about that, milady," I said.

"Be silent," commanded Léon. "Yesterday, a man named Berenguer, a clerk with the Lambert clan, was killed in his house. You and your band of fools were seen asking about it."

"We passed by, saw the crowd, and asked what happened," I said. "It was mere curiosity."

"If you interrupt again, I will tell my men to cut off your elder daughter's hands," said Marie placidly.

"Yesterday afternoon, you were seen looking at the château once belonging to the Landrieux clan," continued Léon. "This morning, a group from the Viguerie saw that the padlock had been opened. They went inside to investigate and found the body of a man named Rocco, a guard at a warehouse belonging to the Conque clan. That makes three."

The two of them looked at me. I looked back at them as defiantly as I could.

"Your appearance in this city is not by chance," said Marie. "You have found your way to my inner circle quickly and deliberately, which shows your wit and resourcefulness. Your advice has been thoughtful, for which I thank you, but it has not escaped my notice that you have been seeking information about me. It is clear that you and your husband are spies. I want to know why, and for whom."

"We have not been spying on you, milady," I said. "Although I agree that would be a seeming explanation for our conduct. But in truth, we seek something else, something we thought long in the past."

"Go on," said Marie.

"What do you know of the Lady Lark?" I asked.

The two of them glanced at each other.

"Who was the Lady Lark?" she asked.

"Mathilde, wife to Antoine Landrieux."

"She died long ago," said Marie. "What does she have to do with anything?"

"We are here because of her, and because of Folquet," I said. "A threat was made to him. My husband is an old friend of his, so he asked us to help him. These deaths came about because we are searching for the truth about the Lady Lark, and someone wants to stop us and keep the story from coming out."

"Who was the dead stranger?" asked Léon.

"A monk of Folquet's order," I said.

"He was working with you?" asked Marie.

"Not with us, not against us," I said. "But looking for the same information."

"And what did you learn about her?"

"That she did not die when Antoine Landrieux said she did. That an empty coffin was buried. That she was instead held in a dungeon for years by Landrieux."

I would have thought these tidbits would bring about a more sensational reaction, but they merely nodded.

"Berenguer and Rocco were Landrieux's men," said Léon to Marie.

"I am aware of that," she said. She looked at me, considering. "If I tell you what I know, what will you do with the information?"

"Stop the murderer," I said.

"And when you do, you will leave Montpellier," she said.

It wasn't a question. I nodded.

"I am not sure that I want this murderer stopped," she said, smiling cruelly.

"What is he to you, milady?" I asked.

"Someone with justice," she replied. "The men who imprisoned and tortured this poor woman deserved death, don't you think?"

"Yes," I said. "But Brother Antime did not. Nor does Folquet."

"That's debatable," she said. "He has been the bane of my existence, and who knows how many others? But truly, the only stories I know are my own, and that of poor Lady Mathilde."

"I beg that you tell me," I said.

"I will tell you, and then I will decide whether or not to let you leave this palais alive," she said. "Or you could leave now, take your family, and no harm will come to you."

"Without the knowledge we seek, harm will hunt us down no matter what," I said. "I will listen to your tale, and I accept your conditions."

"Brave woman," commented Léon, and I saw respect in his eyes for the first time since I had met him.

Marie held out her cup, and he filled it. She took a healthy swallow, then sighed.

"My father adored me," she began. "And I loved him above all things. I was his only child, his heir, his little princess. Then, one day, I saw him speaking to the Hawk. I crept into the room to listen, hiding behind a curtain. They were talking about Folquet, and his attentions to Lady Mathilde, and to my mother. 'I'll put her away,' my father was saying. 'Somewhere where she'll never know the sight or touch of a man again. You could do the same with yours.' 'Oh, I have a better plan than that,' said Landrieux, and he bent over and whispered something in my father's ear. I couldn't hear what it was, but my father laughed, and it was a laugh that I never heard come out of him before. It frightened me, and I started crying. He heard me, and hauled me out of my hiding place. He looked at me, and I didn't see my father anywhere in him. 'Go,' he said. 'Kiss your mother while you can.' I fled."

"How horrible," I said.

"He put my mother in a convent," she said. "A wretched, bone-chilling, rat-infested place. Then I heard that Lady Mathilde was dead. I said nothing. My father remarried, and once my brother was born, I became an exile in my own home. I saw no one, never was allowed to the court, to the dinners, to the parties. I didn't know why, only that Folquet was somehow the cause of it. It was a relief when my father finally sent me off to marry Barral. But look who was in Marseille. Folquet."

"And when Barral died . . ."

"Folquet made sure that my child would not inherit Marseille. Once again, dispossessed of a throne by this greasy songbird. It took me a long time to crawl out of that particular grave."

"Yet you did," I said.

"I did," she said. "And since I came to power here, every family that spread its poisonous gossip about my mother has been paid back, the Landrieux clan most of all."

"But Antoine Landrieux was dead," I said. "Why take your revenge on his son?"

"Why should the son profit from the father's sins?" she asked. "Yes, he was innocent. So was I."

"Did your father know of Lady Mathilde's imprisonment?"

"I don't doubt it," she said. "He was Philippe Landrieux's guardian. I assume it's why he kept Berenguer there as the steward."

"What happened to her when the Landrieux clan was evicted?"

She looked at Léon.

"When we cleared them out, we searched the place thoroughly," he said. "We thought there might be hidden storerooms with money somewhere. We found a cell, deep underground. A wraith of a woman was chained inside, pale like a bone, completely insane. She kept singing some song about a lark, over and over."

"Lady Mathilde," I said.

"Lady Mathilde was dead," he said sharply. "We didn't know who or what this woman was. We turned her over to Philippe. His house, his prisoner as far as we were concerned."

"Where did they go?" I asked.

"They were last seen leaving for Marseille," said Léon.

"Four days, five rivers," I muttered.

"What was that?" asked Marie.

"I was thinking how long the journey back would take," I said.

"Is that what you intend to do now?" she asked.

"By your leave, milady, it is," I replied.

"What will you do when you find them?" she asked.

"I will learn the next part of the story," I said. "See if there's an end to it."

"And if it turns out that this is Lady Mathilde, that she took her revenge upon Berenguer and Rocco and is now going after my old friend Folquet, what will you do with her?"

"I honestly do not know, milady," I said. "But I suggest you have the Viguerie look for her here as well. Let your own sense of justice decide what is best if you find her."

"Justice and I have never been on close terms," she said bitterly. "Very well, go. Your children are in the courtyard. Guilhema is going to miss her playmate."

"I am sorry for it, milady," I said. "And I am sorry that I was not completely honest with you."

"Nobody is completely honest with anyone," she said. "You have been more honest than most."

"It's because I am a fool," I said. "We seek the truth."

"That is a fool's quest," she said.

I stood and bowed to the two of them, then walked to the door. Then I turned back. "Milady?" I asked.

"Yes?"

"Do you believe that Lady Mathilde is seeking her revenge?"

She smiled. "I would, under the circumstances," she said. "Wouldn't you?"

"Yes, milady," I said. "I would."

TWELVE

It's a new joke now and I'm your grinning jester.

—GRAND THEFT AUDIO, "STOOPID ASS"

"Marseille?" I said in disbelief. "Did you just say Marseille?"

"I did say Marseille," said Claudia.

"You say, I say, we all say Marseille," chanted Helga.

"Stop that, Helga," I said. "It's very irritating."

"Did a group of smelly guards grab you while you were peacefully playing with dolls today?" asked Helga.

"No, but—"

"Have you recently been tied up and threatened with rape and dismemberment if you didn't tell them everything?" she continued, her lower lip trembling slightly.

"No," I said.

"And I told them nothing!" she shouted.

"I am sorry, Apprentice."

She stuck her tongue out at me. "You say, I say, we all say Marseille," she chanted again.

"I am starting to feel sorry for those smelly guards," remarked Grelho. "Well, I guess you'll be leaving in the morning. Unless you feel it is a matter of sufficient urgency for you to leave immediately. I'll help you pack."

"Do you really think Lady Mathilde is behind all of this?" I asked Claudia.

"It would certainly explain everything," she said. "She had the motive and, more importantly, she knew the song. Don't forget that the song is what started all of this."

"Peire Vidal knew it," I said. "Pantalan knew the first line. De la Tour's sister. Others may have heard it."

"But of them, who knew to connect it to Folc? Or that it would cause him that amount of distress?"

"But that would mean that she would have to go to Le Thoronet, leave that cryptic message, then come all the way back here just to kill Berenguer and Rocco," I said. "That doesn't make any sense to me. Besides, it's been a man following us in town."

"Says who? Brother Antime?" she replied. "He could have been mistaken. She could have been in disguise. Women have been known to disguise themselves as men quite successfully, as you may recall."

"True enough," I said.

"Or it could have been a man working for her," added Grelho. "Or, to raise the obvious possibility, Philippe Landrieux, avenging his mother. It would be a matter of honor for him once he learned who she was and what had been done to her."

"Unless he thought she had betrayed his father," I said. "In which case, honor would go the other way."

"Fine," said my wife in exasperation. "The point is that there is nothing more to be learned in Montpellier. Marie will have the Viguerie looking for Lady Mathilde and Philippe. There is no reason for us to duplicate their efforts. If they catch her, we will hear about it from Grelho sooner or later. But if there are no more guilty parties here to satisfy her vengeance, then she's likely to be heading back to Marseille to join her son."

"Or to Le Thoronet, if she wants to properly finish the job," said Grelho. "Maybe you should be going straight there."

"If it is her, and if that's where she's going, then she has a day's lead on us," I said. "I warned Folc to keep guard until I returned. He's smart enough to guard himself."

"Rocco had advance warning," pointed out Grelho. "Look what happened to him."

"Rocco was alone, and an idiot," I said. "Folc, at least, has his Guild training and a company of monks under his command."

"Then let us go to Marseille," said Claudia. "That's where the next piece of this story will be found, I warrant."

"Your instincts have been good so far," I said. "I'll follow your lead."

"As well you should," she said, inordinately pleased with herself, in my opinion.

We spent the evening packing our gear. Grelho disappeared with Helga while we did; then the two returned bearing a covey of roasted capons and more of that good Syrah.

"We should leave more often," I said as we plowed through the best meal we had had since we left the Guildhall.

"You really should," said Grelho. "But the cause of this celebration is twofold. Your departure, and the arrival of a new jester in Montpellier."

"And who might that be?" asked Claudia.

"Me," he said. "Grelho the Fool has been born anew, and I have all of you to thank for it. I crawled into my cave to bewail my fate when I was kicked out of the palais, and I would have stayed there until Doomsday if you hadn't shown up. You have rescued me from the depths of mopery, my friends, and you have my eternal thanks for it."

"And now, there is nothing that you cannot do," said my wife, lifting her cup in salute.

"On the contrary, there are many things that I cannot do," said Grelho. "But that won't stop me from trying to do them."

"Spoken like a true fool," I said. "To Grelho!"

"To Grelho!" chorused Claudia and Helga.

"To the Guild," he replied, and we drank.

We turned in after dinner, hoping to get an unjesterlike early morning start on our journey. Portia, after emitting a belch that rattled the shutters, fell asleep quickly, and Helga, who wasn't used to that much wine, followed soon after.

My wife cuddled into me, resting her head upon my chest. I watched her face as it rose and fell with each breath I took. In repose, with the whiteface scrubbed off, she was still as beautiful as when I first saw her. First saw her as a woman, I mean, although she had been disturbingly attractive as well as completely convincing disguised as a man.

Could Lady Mathilde have pulled a similar impersonation off that successfully? Could she have done it after so many years of imprisonment and torment? She was no actress, no fool with Guild training. As strong as she must have been, she still had to have been a broken woman on her release. And to travel all that distance . . .

An idea bobbed to the surface of my swirling thoughts, a tiny thing, but it wouldn't go away. Finally, I eased my wife off my chest and quietly got up from the pallet. Then I crept softly up the stairs to Grelho's room, taking care to knock so that he wouldn't wake straight into a knife-throwing stance.

"What is it?" he asked groggily.

"It's Theo," I said. "I have a question for you."

"This had better be worth interrupting the dream I was having," he groaned, but he sat up. "What's the question?"

"If you were coming to Montpellier from Le Thoronet, would you go through Marseille?" I asked.

"Let me think," he said. "If I were coming here directly? No, I don't think I would. I'd take the road that goes through Aix and Arles. Marseille would take me miles out of the way to the south."

"That's what I thought. Thank you."

"That's it?"

"That's it."

"Stupid question," he muttered, curling up under his blanket.

"What was the dream?" I asked.

"The Countess Marie needed a new consort," he said sleepily. "Needed him real bad. Guess who it was?"

"Go back to sleep, Grelho," I said. "I hope you pick up where you left off."

"That never works," he said, drifting off.

I went back to where Claudia lay sleeping. Or so I thought, but then I saw the dagger in her hand.

"It's me," I whispered, and she relaxed and slid it back into her sleeve.

"What is troubling you?" she asked softly.

"A new theory," I said. "One we will have to put to the test."

"When?" she asked.

"Soon," I said. "Until then, let's get some sleep."

She had her eyes closed, already ahead of me. But she usually is.

Grelho walked with me down to the stables to collect Zeus and our wain. The horse reared several times as we wrestled him into harness.

"I do not envy you, traveling with this monster," said Grelho.

"He's meant to be galloping with a single captive rider," I said. "It's not fair to put him in harness like this, but nobody else in the Guild wants him."

"I can't understand why," said Grelho. "What will you do with him when you finally reach Toulouse?"

"We'll keep him," I said. "I've had to leave places in a hurry before. He's good at that."

"You do tend to stir up trouble," noted Grelho.

"I am trying to settle down," I said. "It doesn't come easy."

"It did for me," said Grelho. "Maybe too easily. Well, you have inspired me, Brother Theophilos. Tonight, I perform at the barracks, and I will kill."

"Convey our regrets," I said.

"I shall make them forget you ever existed," he said. "Competition is good for sharpening a fool's skills."

"They didn't need to be sharpened," I said. "Merely awoken. How long do you think it will take to worm your way back into the palais?"

"Not long, now that Marie knows I'm more than a fool," he said. "She'll want me back just for the intrigue."

We reached his door, where the others awaited us, our gear packed. We loaded the wain quickly.

"Give my regards to Pantalan," said Grelho. "Tell him to visit sometime."

"Will do," I promised. "Be careful. You won't have us watching your back anymore."

"Or your chest," added Claudia.

"I am a fool," said Grelho. "I know how to protect myself."

"We don't," said Claudia. "Tell us your secret."

"If things look dangerous, I run and hide," he said.

She laughed and hugged him hard. Helga followed suit; then he lifted Portia up and brought her to his face to nuzzle gently.

He turned to me and thumbed his nose. I returned the gesture.

"Take good care of these three," he said.

"I was counting on them to take care of me," I said.

We embraced.

"That cave you were in is one I know well," I whispered to him. "Try and stay out of it."

"I'll do my best," he whispered back.

Grelho helped the ladies onto the wain while I held Portia. Once Claudia was settled, I handed our daughter up and vaulted onto the seat by them.

"See you someday," I said to Grelho.

"I hope so," he said.

I flicked the reins, and Zeus hauled us up to the main road. When we got to the gate where we had entered, we paused to see if Reynaud was on duty. He was not. The baker manning the gates waved us around them. A short time later, we crossed the bridge over the river Lez, and Montpellier became a memory.

There is always something dispiriting about a return journey, and there was little chatter among us. Even Zeus lacked his usual orneriness, pulling us down the center of the road with no attempts to take us over its worst ruts and bumps. We did not make the best time, and toward the end of the day we found ourselves in a deserted stretch of forest, with no prospects of a roof in sight.

"Looks like we'll be camping tonight," I said. "That clearing over there looks promising."

"Suits me," said Claudia. "I just want to get off this damned wooden seat."

The clearing was about forty feet wide, more than enough to allow us to hobble Zeus at one end and set up our tent at the other. A loose ring of stones on a blackened bare patch of ground let us know that we were not the first to camp here. While Claudia and Helga erected the tent, I ranged around to collect firewood, finding enough to keep the wolves away all night. I dumped it into the ring of stones and got the fire going.

"What's for dinner?" called Claudia from the tent.

"I have sausages from town," I said. "I thought I would fry them up and save the beans for tomorrow."

Helga came up to Claudia, looking pale and serious. She whispered something in my wife's ear. Claudia whispered back, and Helga nodded.

"Theo," called my wife. "Helga's not well. I'm going to take her inside for a while."

"Anything serious?" I asked.

"A woman's affliction," said Claudia, smiling ruefully. "I thought that might happen to her on our journey."

"I leave her in your hands," I said hastily. "I will call when the sausage is done."

They disappeared inside the tent, bringing Portia with them. The fire was soaring, almost to my height. I put the sausages into a pan and rested them on the edge of the flames. As they began to sizzle, I picked up an ax and started hacking at some fallen tree limbs I had dragged over for feeding the fire later.

A branch cracked somewhere behind me. Without turning, I called, "Good evening, Sieur Julien. Come warm yourself by the fire, if you like. It must be cold crouching in the woods."

Footsteps came toward me, then stopped about ten feet away. "Good evening, Tan Pierre," he said. "Or is it Theo? Your wife called you that."

"Tan Pierre is the name under which I perform," I said, turning to face him. "Theo to my friends. But I have a feeling that you are not one of them."

He stood at the edge of the firelight, his eyes dark, set back in his doughy face. Julien Guiraud, Folc's brother-in-law, smiled at me, but there was no warmth in that smile.

"Not your friend? What makes you say that?" he asked.

"The sword in your hand, for one thing," I said. "Are you any good with it?"

"Good enough to kill a fool," he said, holding it up. "Would you mind tossing that ax away? I think it's making my men nervous."

"As you like," I said, flipping it behind me. It landed on the other side of the fire, the ax-head embedding itself in the ground with a thud.

"Thank you," he said.

"Will you and your men be joining us for dinner?" I asked. "I could put on some more sausages."

"Very kind of you, I'm sure," he said. "But there is no need to put any extra on."

"Well, if you will excuse me, I think they need turning," I said, and I stooped and turned them with a stick so they would cook evenly. When I turned back, Julien was flanked by four men. The two directly next to him had crossbows pointed at me. The outer pair had drawn swords.

"Good evening, gentlemen," I said to them. "Are you here for the food or the entertainment?"

"The entertainment," said Julien. "And you will be providing it. How did you know it was me?"

"Ah, storytelling," I said. "One of my best talents. But before I perform, we must negotiate my fee."

"You are hardly in a position to make demands," he said, laughing.

"Sieur, as a merchant, you must surely understand that value must be exchanged for value," I said.

"Your answer to my question is of little value," he said. "I merely wanted to satisfy my curiosity."

"But that is all I want as well," I said cheerfully. "If I answer this, will you answer an inquiry of mine?"

"Very well," he said.

"Then we have a bargain, Sieur," I said, clapping my hands together. "Well, it all became a matter of my faith in myself. I did not think that anyone could possibly follow me from Marseille to Montpellier without my knowing about it. It's a matter of pride, you see."

"I'm afraid I don't understand," said Julien.

"Now, right there is the difference between a jester and a merchant," I said. "I would have said in response, 'I'm afraid I don't follow you.' You see the clever play on words there?"

"Get to the point," he said.

"As you wish," I said. "So, if no one followed us immediately from Marseille to Montpellier, then it meant that whoever was in Montpellier killing people had either come there before us or after us. My wife thought that our suspect had traveled there from Le Thoronet, but if that was the case, then that person should have taken the direct route through Aix and arrived a few days before us. But the killings began a few days after we arrived, which meant that the killer must have arrived after we did. So, I thought, what if someone in Marseille knew we were coming here? He wouldn't have to follow us to see where we were going; he would just have to show up later. After that, it wouldn't be so hard to pick up our trail. We are blindingly obvious in our choice of garment and makeup."

"You certainly are," said Julien. "But again, how did you know it was me?"

"Because only three men knew we were coming here," I said. "Pantalan, but I trust him. Laurent, the Viscount's seneschal, but he wanted me to come here so I could deliver a letter from him to the Countess. Then there was you. You learned on the morning that we left that we were going to Montpellier. And what occurred to me last night is that you tried to send us in the opposite direction to Toulon to find that ruined merchant. I have a feeling that that would have been a completely futile pursuit. Montpellier was exactly where we needed to go to get to the beginning of this puzzle, yet you tried to keep us from coming here."

"It would have been better for you if you hadn't," he said.

"So it would seem," I said ruefully. "It was you who killed that poor monk and used his blood to paint the line from Folc's song, wasn't it?"

"It was," he said. "I would have happily used a bucket of whitewash for the purpose, but he ran into me and I had to kill him before he raised the alarum. And then I thought, why not put him to use? And that is answer for answer."

"Hardly," I said. "Mine was much longer. Besides, I knew yours, so I haven't gained equal value yet."

"The successful merchant always comes out ahead in an exchange," he said.

"There you are," I sighed. "Another reason why you're a merchant and I am only a fool. I am left to guess at why you did all this. Avenging your sister, I suppose, for Folc's tawdry little habit of deceiving her. But to follow it up by killing, just to keep me from finding out the truth? That seems excessive, to say the least."

"Saying the least is not one of your talents."

"Now, that's something a fool would say," I applauded. "There's hope for you yet. I think that you somehow found out that Lady Mathilde still lived, and that you've been looking for her to kill her for her part in destroying your sister's happiness. And each man you killed was to keep us from following your path to her."

He smiled again. "No more," he said.

"You never married, did you?" I said.

"What?"

"This devotion to your twin sister," I continued. "There's something unnatural about it. Folc took her away from you, didn't he? Twice, now that I think of it—once when he married her, and a second time when he put her in orders. That must have killed you."

"Enough!" he barked. "No more tales. Tell your wife and that girl to come out."

"Why should I?" I asked. "You have come to kill all of us."

"Tell them to come out, and I will make a quick death for them," he said. "Resist, and I will give them to my men first."

"That is your best offer?" I asked quietly.

"This is not a seller's market," he said. "Tell them to come out, and without weapons. Do it now, or we will put a few bolts into that tent and see what we hit."

"Very well, Sieur, we have a bargain," I said.

I turned toward the tent. The crossbowmen were aiming at the entrance.

"Come on out, ladies," I called. "Everything is all right."

A pair of arrows whistled out of the woods behind me. The crossbowman on the left went down, clutching his thigh and screaming. The one on the right fell with an arrow through his throat. He didn't scream.

That left Julien and the other two swordsmen. They came at me quickly, leaving me nowhere to go but the fire.

So, I jumped through the fire.

Julien skidded to a halt just short of the ring of stones. I grabbed the ax that I had thrown to this side and hurled it with all my might back through the flames. Distracted by the fire, he didn't see it coming until it buried itself between his eyes.

Claudia charged screaming out of the woods like an avenging angel, her sword reflecting the fire, her face a white mask of fury. The ruffian on the right might as well have been facing Saint Michael for all the good his sword did him. She took his head off with one swing.

The fifth man turned and took to his heels, an arrow barely missing him. He vanished into the darkness. Then we heard galloping hoofbeats receding into the night.

The only sounds for a moment were the moaning of the man Helga shot and the crackling of the sausages in the pan. Then the moaning ceased. I walked over and pulled the sausages away from the fire.

"I am afraid they're burnt," I said.

"That's all right," said Claudia, sinking to her knees. "I'm not hungry."

Helga emerged from the woods, holding Portia in her arms. Her bow was slung behind her. "The other one got away," she said.

"Let him," I said wearily.

She looked at the man she had shot. "Theo?" she said.

I picked up Julien's sword and went over to the crossbowman. He stared unblinking up at the night sky. I kicked the crossbow away and felt his neck for a pulse.

"He's dead," I said.

"But I shot him in the thigh!" she shouted. "I did what I was told! He wasn't supposed to die!"

"He bled out," I said. "It happens. It was a good shot, Helga."

"Oh, God, I've killed someone," she moaned.

"Apprentice!" I said sharply.

She looked up at me as if I had slapped her.

"Apprentice," I said again.

"Yes, Master," she said, standing straight and wiping her nose with her sleeve.

"You heard what they intended to do with us," I said.

"Yes, Master."

"Specifically, what they intended to do with you," I continued.

"Yes, Master."

"No doubt they would have added Portia to the tally of the dead," I said. "Do you have any doubts that you acted to save yourself from a horrible fate? Any doubts that you saved the rest of us by doing so?"

She took a deep breath. "No, Master," she said. "No doubts."

"What would you have done if they had killed Claudia and me?" I asked.

"What?"

"What would you have done if they had killed us, Apprentice?"

She looked down at the man she had killed. "I would have avenged you, or died trying," she said.

"Wrong, Apprentice," I said.

"Completely wrong," said Claudia, coming over to hold her tight.

"If we had been lost, it would have been your responsibility to save Portia," I said. "We have to know that you would have done that."

"How?" asked Helga, burying her head in Claudia's arms.

"By running," said Claudia simply. "You have to run into the woods as fast and as far as you can, abandon all thoughts of vengeance, even of burying our bodies, but save our daughter."

"And then what?" she asked, her voice muffled.

"Then seek safety wherever you could find it," I said. "Find a sympathetic family somewhere and wait until the way is clear, then get back to Grelho or Pantalan for help. Then become the great jester that we have no doubt that you will be."

"And raise our daughter as your sister," said Claudia. "Will you do all that?"

"I hope I never have to," said Helga.

"So do we, Apprentice," I said. "But if you do . . ."

"Then I will," she said. "I promise."

I pulled her close, hugged her hard, and kissed the top of her head. "You did brilliantly, Helga," I said. "Father Gerald would be proud of you."

And so would your mother, I thought. May her soul rest in Heaven.

I started kicking dirt on the fire. "Get the tent packed," I told them. "We have to leave."

"Do you think that last man will go for help?" asked Claudia.

"I doubt it," I said. "But there's no point in hanging around here."

Helga and Claudia struck the tent quickly and tossed it onto the wain. I finished smothering the fire and went through the pockets of the dead men, taking what money and documents I could find. I left them their weapons. Claudia came over and pulled the two arrows from their targets.

"Don't forget your ax," she said.

I looked down at Julien, who looked back at me from both sides of the ax-head.

"I wonder if he was any good with that sword," I said.

"I am just as happy we didn't have to find out," said Claudia.

I had to yank at the ax hard to get it out. I took some water and rinsed the blood off it.

"If you don't mind, I'd like to leave that out of our juggling," said Claudia as I stowed it with our gear.

"I'll buy a new one," I said.

We harnessed Zeus and got on the road. There was a decent amount of moonlight to see by. We heard Helga's teeth chattering in back.

"Come up with us, dear," said Claudia. "Bring a blanket."

She clambered over the gear to join us, and we huddled together for warmth as we left our battleground. "Five of them against three of us," said Helga, still shivering. "What were they thinking?"

My wife was quiet the next morning, sitting on the ground nursing Portia. Helga had finally succumbed to exhaustion and was sprawled across the bundles in the wain, fast asleep.

I squatted by my family. "The baby slept through everything," I said.

"Lucky for her," said Claudia.

"Lucky for us," I said. "They might have noticed you sneaking out of the back of the tent if she was crying."

"I still can't believe it was Julien," she said.

"Just because a man kisses your hand," I said.

"He paid the price for that, didn't he?" she replied. "Infidelity comes dear in these parts. One thing puzzles me."

"What's that?"

"How did he know the song?" she asked.

"He must have encountered Lady Mathilde and Philippe when they came to Marseille," I said. "He must have learned something from them, enough to set him on this rampage."

"Maybe she went to Marseille looking for Folquet," she said. "That could have brought her to him. But why wouldn't he kill her there?"

"We'll find out when we get there," I said. "The last piece of the story."

We came to Marseille four days later, and soon entered that now familiar courtyard. We stood on the wain and sang.

Lord of emptiness, King without subjects,
Ruler with no rules.
All hail Pantalan, a jester's jester,
Emperor of Fools!

Pantalan opened his shutters and looked at us in disbelief. "Oh, no," he said. "Not again."

THIRTEEN

Vida e pretz qu'om vol de folla gen
on plus aut son cazon leugeiramen.
[The life and glory that one seeks from fools
easily collapses when it is at its peak.]

—FOLQUET DE MARSEILLE, "*HUEIMAIS NO·Y CONOSC RAZO*"
[TRANS. N. M. SCHULMAN]

"Julien Guiraud," said Pantalan in amazement when Theo finished a brief rendition of our adventures since leaving in Marseille. "I never would have guessed."

"Didn't seem the killing type?" I asked, shifting Portia to my other breast and wincing as she clamped on extra hard.

"Oh, he's certainly the killing type," said Pantalan. "He's been a successful merchant for years, so by definition ruthless. I just never thought he would carry such a strong hatred for Folquet all this time. I must say, I have always wondered why he never married. Your guess at the attachment to his sister must have been near the mark."

"Right in the center of it, I'd say," said Theo smugly.

Oh, the man can be irritating when he is right. Especially when it's at the expense of my being wrong.

"And you, little chick!" exclaimed Pantalan, ruffling Helga's hair affectionately. "Your first burglary, your first taste of combat. You have already done more at your tender age than some fools do in a lifetime."

"If it's always going to be like this, I might take up farming instead," said Helga.

"Nonsense," scoffed Pantalan. "You are to the motley born, my girl. You can be nothing else but a jester, doomed like the rest of us. Why, if you became a farmer, then you would find some dangerously adventurous farming mischief. I have no idea what that might be, but there would be havoc on the fields in no time. So, friends, what is your next step? You found the man who killed Folquet's drunken colleague, and exacted the appropriate penalty for that little crime. That fulfills the abbot's mandate, I should think."

"I would say so," agreed Theo. "I still want to get the end of the story. That means finding Lady Mathilde and her son and learning what happened after they were banished from Montpellier. And I want to warn them, just in case the mercenary who got away still has their deaths on his agenda."

"You should lie low and let me make the inquiries," said Pantalan. "Word hasn't reached Marseille about Julien's death yet, but if it does, the authorities might not look kindly upon your explanation."

"They rarely do," said Theo. "We will heed your advice and stay here. I could use a week's worth of sleep, to be honest."

"Then I will go look for a young man who came to Marseille this past summer, possibly in the company of a mad wraith of a woman," said Pantalan. "That shouldn't be too much of a quest. I shall return by nightfall."

He closed the door behind him. We heard the shouts of the children greeting him in the courtyard, then their laughter at some antic of his. Then it faded away.

"How shall we pass the time?" I asked, turning to my husband.

He was stretched out, fast asleep. I threw a blanket over him and kissed his brow.

"Free time for us," chirped Helga.

"Not so fast, Apprentice," I said. "We have been neglecting your studies."

"I've been busy," she said defensively.

"So have I," I said. "Let's start with your Arabic lessons."

I took a chance later, washing off my whiteface and changing into civilian garb. I left Portia and Helga to watch over my husband, and went to find dinner. There were some smaller markets in the Ville-Haute, so I replenished our supplies and bought extra for our host. On an impulse, I purchased some dried flowers that had a pleasant scent.

When I returned, Portia was crawling happily over her father, who was still lying down but awake enough to grab her at odd moments and dangle her upside down over his head while she shrieked in delight. Helga juggled clubs off in a corner.

This must be what domestic bliss is like for a jester, I thought. I suddenly found myself looking forward to the end of our journey, when we would settle down in Toulouse in our own rooms, and stay long enough to raise our child. Maybe I would have another—Theo was a good father, and you don't waste those.

I bustled about, preparing dinner. Pantalan returned just as the sun was beginning to set.

"I have news, my friends," he said. "The young—my, it smells good in here. Did Theo bathe?"

"We threw out all of your things," I said. "The air is much better as a result."

"I've needed a woman's touch in this household," he said. "You're hired. Anyway, I have found your Philippe, and just in time."

"He's in danger?" asked Theo.

"No, or at least, not immediately," said Pantalan. "He leaves for the Holy Land in two days."

"Business or Crusade?" I asked.

"He's taken the Cross, although I don't know that there is any battle currently going on there. They can always make him guard a wall somewhere."

"Do you know where he's staying?" asked Theo.

"Of course, but there's no point in going tonight," said Pantalan. "They say that he has been drinking his way through every tavern on the waterfront for the past several days, sopping up all the local wine and women he can before he embarks on his sacred journey. We will speak with him in the morning, or whenever he wakes up."

"Is it safe for us to go as jesters?" I asked.

"It is," said Pantalan. "I paid a visit to the Guiraud store. I thought a certain someone might like this."

He tossed a small bag to Helga, who opened it and dived in.

"Ank ou," she said in a garbled voice, her mouth full of rock candy.

"Demosthenes, she is not," he observed. "Anyhow, nobody there was saying anything about his death or disappearance. I heard someone asking for him, in fact, and the clerk replied that he was away on business and not expected for some weeks."

"That's a relief," I said.

"The bodies should have been discovered by now," argued Theo. "I didn't find any identifying documents when I searched them, but that doesn't mean someone might not recognize them. There is also the problem of the mercenary who escaped."

"But he didn't come here," said Pantalan. "There would be an uproar if the news had gotten out. I suspect in any case that the investigation will be carried out from the Montpellier end when they are discovered. It's in their jurisdiction. That gives you enough time to meet with the son of the Hawk and then get out of town."

I shivered suddenly. We had been chasing so many stories from the past that the idea of actually meeting someone from them was as unreal as encountering a monster out of Homer or a knight from the Round Table. What would this boy be like?

In the morning, we did our stretches in the courtyard. Pantalan joined us, to our surprise and the glee of the neighborhood children.

"I have been getting careless about my morning routine," he said, almost touching his toes. "I have been coasting along on sheer brilliance alone for years, but I have let the other skills lapse. Let's see if I still can—ah, good."

He kicked up into a handstand and walked several paces in that position before toppling over. The children clapped.

"I am not ready to marry you yet," called Helga.

"Then I shall keep exercising," replied Pantalan, rolling to his feet.

"Let's go see Philippe first," said Theo.

There were only a couple of ships in the harbor. It was late in the year for traveling, and the Ville-Basse was at half-bustle at best. Pantalan led us to an inn called the Pelican and had a whispered conversation with the barmaid. She pointed to a young man who was leaning on the plank tables, picking dispiritedly at a plate of boiled eggs. He was the right age, and had a handsome face with almost delicate features. His hair was black and tied into a greasy braid in back. He wore a sword in a shabby leather scabbard at his side, and a plain wooden cross dangling from a chain around his neck.

"Sieur Philippe?" said Theo.

The man looked up us and blinked. "No singing, for Christ's sake," he said. "I have a headache larger than my head."

"We won't sing," said Theo sympathetically. "But are you Philippe Landrieux?"

"I am," he said. "Who are you? I can see that you are jesters."

"My name is Tan Pierre," said Theo. "This is my wife, Domna Gile, and our daughters. You recognize Sieur Pantalan, no doubt."

"I have seen him perform, of course," said Philippe, nodding politely at the introductions. "What business do you have with me, Sieur Fool?"

"My family and I have lately returned from Montpellier," said Theo.

"I know the town well," said Philippe. "Knew it, anyhow. You must know Grelho."

"We do. We were visiting him. We heard about your—displacement."

"A pretty word," said Philippe bitterly. "Were you sent to taunt me in my misery?"

"We came because we know your story," said Theo.

"No one knows my story," said Philippe.

"We know about your mother," said Theo.

Philippe looked at him steadily. "My mother is dead," he said.

"Please, Sieur," I said. "We have no wish to cause you scandal. Our path intersected yours quite by accident, and we cannot tell you everything about it or why it is important. We do know that your mother survived her foul imprisonment. We also know that several people have died since her release because someone sought vengeance upon her for an old sin. We came to warn both of you."

"I don't know how you learned that," he said. "But she is beyond your help and anyone's vengeance but God's."

"She has died, then?" asked Theo.

"Oc, she has," replied Philippe.

"We are sorry for your loss," I said gently. "We know how she suffered in life. At least she was reunited with you at the end, if only for a short time. That must have been a great ease to her."

"You are kind to say so," he said.

"I hope that her death was a peaceful one," I continued.

"Peaceful," he spat. "She deserved a soft bed, angelic music playing, and me by her side holding her hand. No, Domna, she was killed. A stupid tawdry accident, and it was my fault."

"How so, Sieur?" I asked.

"I had so little when we were exiled," he said. "I wanted to find a place where she would be taken care of, where there would be no walls, where she could feel the sun and the fresh air. A place where she could spend her remaining life peacefully while I went to the Holy Land to atone for my sins and earn my fortune so that I could provide for her in her old age. A place where she would not be persecuted by men."

"Oh, God!" I said as a sudden sickening realization hit me. "Gémenos. You put her in Gémenos, didn't you?"

"I thought she would be safe there."

"A stampede," I whispered. "She was crushed to death by a herd of cattle, wasn't she?"

He leapt back from the table in horror. "What witchcraft is this?" he cried. "How did you know?"

"We were there recently," explained Theo hastily. "My wife heard the story, but we did not know it was your mother. Again, our condolences, Sieur. May Our Savior watch over your pilgrimage and keep you safe."

He grabbed my arm and dragged me out of there, the others following in confusion. My last sight of Philippe was of him holding up his cross in front of himself to ward me off.

"He put her in a death trap," I cried as they escorted me back. "He put her with Folc's wife, this poor mad woman. And Hélène found out who she was. Lady Mathilde was murdered, don't you see? Hélène killed her, and got her brother to leave that message for Folc. This wasn't about his vengeance. It was about hers. All along it was her."

"She must have panicked when she heard we were investigating it," said Theo. "She sent us to her brother so that he would know to go after us if we continued on to Montpellier."

"We have to go to Gémenos, Theo," I said. "We have to see her. She's the last piece of the story."

"Poor woman," said Pantalan.

"Which one?" asked Theo.

"Both of them," said Pantalan. "By the way, it's been a long time, but don't you think young Philippe bears a striking resemblance to his father at that age?"

"You knew the Hawk?" asked Theo.

"No, but I knew Folquet," he said. "I wonder if the boy knows."

"I doubt it," said Theo. "It is not our place to tell him. There's enough woe in his life. Let him vanish beyond the sea."

"I wonder if he sings," said Helga.

We loaded up our wain immediately upon our return.

"I am not going to say good-bye this time," said Pantalan. "If I do, you'll only show up again. Tell Folquet that his prick has gotten us in much too much trouble, and that I sincerely hope it has fallen off."

"If it hasn't, we might arrange something," I said.

"You must let me know what you learn," said Pantalan. "I am beside myself with curiosity."

"We will," said Theo. "Until then."

We could not make Gémenos by nightfall, so we made camp. Helga took the first watch without being told. We rose at dawn, none of us having had much rest.

We reached the Valley of the Eagles by midmorning. In the distance, we could see members of Hélène's order on the hillside with their herd.

"How do you think she did it?" asked Theo. "How do you stampede cattle?"

"With dogs," I said. "A pair of dogs so obedient that they become an extension of your own will. She had such a pair with her when I met her. God, she sat and told me all about Lady Mathilde's death, and she smiled as she did it. It was a joke to her, and we only just got it."

"It's how you tell it," he said grimly. "How do you want to handle this? She may be dangerous."

"So are we," I said. "Let us all go. Watch out for cows."

The women watched as we approached. One detached herself from the group and walked up to us. "What would you here?" she demanded curtly.

"We seek Hélène of Marseille," I said.

"You are the ones who saw her before," she said.

"Oc, Domna."

"She is not here," she said, and turned to leave.

"Please, Domna, we must see her," I begged. "There may be lives at risk."

"I told you she is not here," she said.

"Where is she?" asked Theo.

"She left," said the woman. "Two days ago, a man rode into Gémenos and sought her out. They spoke, and she started screaming and tearing at her face and clothes. Something about her brother's death, and then the most vile imprecations against her husband. Is it true that Sieur Julien is dead? He was a great patron to us, thanks to his sister."

"We heard nothing about it in Marseille," I said. "Tell us, Domna, when did she leave?"

"We had to subdue her to keep her from doing further harm to herself," she said. "I gave her something to help her sleep, but when we woke the next morning, she was gone."

"Let me ask you this, Domna," I said. "There was a death here, maybe two months ago. A new member of your order."

"That is none of your business," she said.

"I am afraid that it is," I said. "Her name was Mathilde, was it not?"

She was silent, then nodded briefly. "She was new to our ways," she said. "As a novitiate, she had to learn how to tend to the herd."

"Who was tending the cattle with her when it happened?" I asked.

"What does that have to do with anything?" she asked. "It was an accident, a horrible stupid accident."

"Who was with her?" I shouted. "Was it Hélène?"

"Oc, but you cannot—"

"Was she on foot or on horseback?" asked Theo.

"We have only the two horses for the wagons," she said. "She left them."

"Alone and on foot," said Theo, thinking.

"She's not alone," said the woman. "She took her dogs with her."

"She has a day and a half lead," Theo said to me. "But she has to go through the massif to get to Le Thoronet, and she's on foot. I can catch up to her if I leave you here."

"Go. We'll be all right," I said.

"What are you talking about?" demanded the woman.

"There will be time for explanations later," I said. "Theo, take us to the farmhouse we stayed at."

He turned us away from the hillside as the woman stared after us dumbfounded. We reached the farmhouse in short order. He jumped down from the wain and unhitched Zeus. Helga tossed him his saddle, and he threw it on the horse's back.

We came down to join him. He gave Helga a quick hug, kissed the baby, then kissed me much harder.

"You be careful," I said. "A woman out of her mind can be more dangerous than you know."

"I learned that lesson a long time ago," he said, smiling at me.

He kissed me one more time, then vaulted onto Zeus's back.

"If I am not back within a week, go back to Marseille," he said. "I will find you at Pantalan's. Oh, and you had better take these."

He reached into his pouch and pulled out a pair of scrolls, which he tossed to me. Then he waved and kicked his heels into Zeus's flanks. The horse shot off like an arrow.

I looked at the scrolls in my hand, then opened them carefully.

"What are they?" asked Helga, looking at them over my shoulder.

"This one frees me if he ever joins holy orders," I said. "This one is his will."

"Sealed by a notary," she said, impressed.

I watched the pair of them galloping up the road through the forest.

"You son of a bitch!" I screamed after him. "Don't you dare make me use these!"

Then I collapsed to the ground, weeping until Portia crawled into my lap and demanded to be nursed again.

FOURTEEN

Farai o doncs aissi co·l joglars fai,
aissi com muoc mon lais lo fenirai . . .
[I will do as a joglar does / and end my verse as I began it . . .]

—FOLQUET DE MARSEILLE, *"S'AL COR PLAGUES, BEN FOR'OIMAIS SAZOS"*
[TRANS. N. M. SCHULMAN]

There are two ways up a mountain. One is to take the easy road, trotting safely back and forth using the switchbacks, laboriously repeating yourself, getting a little farther up each time until you reach the top and have to come back down the other side the same way.

The other is to go straight up the slope in reckless disregard of all hazards and sense.

I looked at the road, then at the steep ascent.

"She didn't take the road," I said to Zeus. "The climb is easier for a two-legged beast than a four-legged one."

He snorted and pulled at the reins.

"Fine," I said, yanking him to the left. "But if you break your leg, I leave you."

We reached the chapel at the Eagle's Pass in no time, and I was breathing harder than he was.

"The corollary is that if I break my neck, you leave me," I gasped. "All right, we have proved that we are sufficiently brave, stupid, and masculine. Let's see how fast we can get across the massif without a wain and family dragging us down."

The trip had taken three days coming from the other direction, but that was at a wain's pace. Still, this was not the place to let Zeus go all out. At his top speed, we would have plunged off the first cliff we came to. I spent the day reining him in from a full gallop until my hands bled from the effort. By the time night fell and forced us to stop, I was so exhausted that I barely had the strength to gather wood for a fire. I poured Zeus a pile of oats, then shared my water skin. In my haste, I had brought only food, no blankets or bedding. The remains of an old shepherd's lean-to gave me some shelter, but no amount of dead leaves could compensate for the cold of a November night in the mountains. I wrapped my cloak around me as tightly as I could and missed my wife intensely. Not just for the warmth, either, although I confess that became the predominant desire after a while.

I awoke early and rolled out of the lean-to. I didn't bother with a fire, but I did do my stretches. No amount of urgency would make me forgo that routine, especially with another day of riding facing me. Zeus looked at me blearily.

"Cheer up, old friend," I said, putting his saddle on. "We should be off the massif by noon. Then you can stretch your legs."

I winced as I gripped the reins. The early morning mists were clinging to the mountain, and even Zeus saw the wisdom of a relatively cautious pace. I huddled into his neck on the straightaways, hoping to draw some warmth from the animal, but we were high up and the chill refused to leave.

Then I heard a wolf howl, somewhere off to my right. It seemed far away, but it echoed through the mists and crags. I hoped that we were not its prey. A second answered it, much nearer, and that was all Zeus needed to hear. He bolted, with me screaming at him and hauling back on the reins to no avail. The road twisted and writhed like a pinioned serpent ahead of us, and with each turn I was thrown to one side or the other. Finally, I just wrapped the reins around my wrist and clung to his neck, hoping and praying that we would emerge unharmed.

After an eternity, we burst through the last pass on the massif and

I managed to bring him down to a trot, then a walk. Finally, he stopped, his sides heaving, his eyes rolling wildly.

There was the sound of a stream somewhere ahead of us. I slid down into an untidy heap, my right wrist still tangled in the reins. I had to pry my fingers from them. My hand looked like it had been whipped repeatedly.

"Well done," I croaked. "Come on. I'll buy you a drink."

I led him to the stream, and he plunged his muzzle in, sucking in the water greedily. I plunged my blood-caked hand in quickly, hoping that the cold would numb the pain, but I only ended up with a hand that was frozen as well as in agony. I washed the blood off and clumsily wrapped my kerchief around it, tying the knot with my teeth. Then I drank. The water was as cold, crisp, and clean as any I have ever tasted, and I would have gladly traded the entire stream for one cup of wine right then and there.

It was near noon, but the clouds still covered the sun. After a couple of false starts, I succeeded in heaving myself back onto the saddle, taking the reins in my left hand.

"Maybe this is all for naught," I said to Zeus as he walked down the road. "Maybe the wolves took her, or the cold. Maybe she despaired and threw herself into one of those ravines you kept barely missing, thank you very much."

But she had her dogs with her, I thought. They wouldn't have left her on that massif. They would have stayed by where she fell and howled in mourning.

Was it the dogs and not wolves doing just that as we plunged madly through the massif? Were they what had panicked Zeus? The howling sounded like wolves to me, and I have done enough hunting in my youth to know the difference. Still, I could have passed her on the massif.

I looked out at the plain stretching ahead of us. I saw some farms, and a small village. I did not see a woman with two dogs.

We reached the base of the descent an hour later. There was nothing but even terrain ahead.

There was no point in searching for her. Either I was right about where she was going, or I wasn't. Either I would get to the abbey at Le Thoronet before her, or I would be too late. Whatever the possibilities were, my course of action was the same. My only goal now was to stay on my horse for the rest of the journey.

"No more mountains," I said to Zeus. "Shall we?"

I took a deep breath, then nudged Zeus's flanks lightly with my heels. He took off like a stone from a catapult. We scattered a flock of chickens as we passed by the nearest farm; then we were on the road heading east, my cloak flapping in the breeze. The sun finally broke through the clouds and warmed my back. As it began to set, I sighted the hill with Le Cannet to the south, and I knew the road to Le Thoronet must be near. Either I could ride through the woods in the darkness to reach it, or I could stop and find shelter for one more night.

But I still hadn't seen her on the journey. I stopped at the edge of the forest so that we could have one more meal, then found a dry tree limb that could serve me as a crude torch. I lit it from the small fire I had made, then pulled myself up onto the horse.

Every muscle I owned ached. Zeus was looking much the worse for the journey himself, and was clearly disinclined to leave the safety of the fire for the gloom of the forest.

"One more push," I urged him. "Only a few miles, and I promise that I'll let you rest for two days. Three if I get killed. Come on."

Reluctantly, he trotted ahead.

The torch did not light our path very well, but I was hoping that it would keep any wolves at bay. Of course, it would also alert any human predators that we were coming, but that was a chance I had to take. There was little moon to help us tonight, so I had to trust to my sense of direction and my memory of the previous time I had come this way.

Then I sensed the randomness of the forest changing into the regular spacing of the groves by the abbey, and I thanked God, who watches over those too foolish to care for themselves.

I got down from Zeus and slapped him approvingly on the rump.

My torch was out. I tossed it into the stream running by the abbey, then led the horse to the entry door and started pounding on it.

"Open up!" I yelled. "Open up in the name of God!"

I did this for a long time, but eventually I heard soft footsteps approach and a bar slide back. The door creaked open, and a very sleepy and irritable-looking monk stood before me with a torch.

"What do you seek?" he asked grumpily.

"God's mercy," I replied.

"Find it somewhere else tonight," he said, and I saw for the first time that he had a sword in his other hand.

"I need to talk to the abbot," I said. "It's a matter of life and death."

"My orders are to admit no one after sunset," said the monk. "Come back in the morning."

He started to close the door. I shoved it into him, sending him staggering backwards.

"Help!" he screamed. "Intruders! Bandits!"

"Stop it," I said wearily.

Other shouts came from beyond him, and I could see a group of robed men pour into the end of the entry hall, staves and knives at the ready.

"I bring news of Brother Antime's death!" I shouted.

There were gasps and murmurs, but no attack.

"I was here to speak with your abbot some weeks ago," I continued. "Many of you saw me. Some of you may have been in the group that so graciously escorted me."

"He was that fool who was here when Brother Pelfort was killed," said one of them.

"That's me," I said. "The mad fool who runs errands for the abbot. I must speak with him immediately."

"What happened to Brother Antime?" one of them asked.

"I will first speak with Abbot Folc about that," I said. "Will you let me pass?"

"Throw down your weapons," said the monk who had first opened the door.

My dagger and knife clanked onto the stone floor by his feet.

"Will you consent to be bound?" he asked.

"I will not," I said. "I will consent to your taking my horse to your stables and treating him better than you have treated me. He is a heroic beast, and I have run him nearly to death in your abbot's service. Let me pass."

I strode forward, tossing Zeus's reins to the startled monk. The others fell back, then surrounded me as I emerged into the gallery by the cloister. There was a frightened yelp behind me.

"Mind his teeth," I called over my shoulder.

I looked around at the circle of staves and blades pointed at me.

"I'm in a generous mood, so I won't take you on," I said to the group. "This way."

I set off down the gallery to the steps to the church, my escort shuffling quickly around me to maintain the circle. Then I stopped.

"This is the right way, isn't it?" I asked.

"It is, if it's salvation that you seek," said Folc from the top of the steps leading to the church. The torches held by the monks around me cast their light unevenly on his face from below, putting his eyes into shadow.

"The salvation that I seek may not be my own," I said. "I am the bearer of sad tidings. Brother Antime is dead."

"How did he die?" asked Folc.

"For your sins," I said. "Care to discuss them?"

He looked at me impassively, then turned abruptly, beckoning me to follow. The monks in front of me separated. I started up the steps. They did not follow.

Folc was waiting for me inside the church, holding a lit candle. "My office is this way," he said, indicating a small flight of steps to my left.

"No bodyguard?" I asked.

"Some things must be done in private," he said.

We walked up the steps and through a door. We were facing the dormitorium, which was above the librarium and chapter house. Folc's office was a cell to the left, not more than eight paces by six, with a tiny writing desk below a small rectangular slit of a window. He put the candle on the desk and turned to me, his face in shadow.

"Close the door behind you," he said.

I did.

"You wished to discuss my sins," he said.

"Here is a turnabout, when the fool confesses the abbot," I said. "I do not know if we have time enough to discuss them all. Let me begin with the one that cost so many lives."

"Lives?" he said. "More than just Brother Antime?"

"Since I was last here, seven men have gone to their doom," I said. "I would say to their graves, but some may still be lying where they fell. All because you are a coward and a liar."

"In what way?" he asked calmly.

"You knew that message was from a song," I said. "One that you had composed to mourn the death of your lover, Mathilde. The Lady Lark. Had you owned up to it immediately, we could have gone straight to Montpellier to learn the truth. Instead, you left us in ignorance, and our investigation set off a chain of violence and revenge that has yet to reach its conclusion."

"I don't know what you're talking about," said Folc.

"We started by speaking to your wife," I said. "Then to her brother, Julien. He's the one who painted the bloody words, by the way."

"Julien?" he exclaimed. "Why would he do that?"

"He was merely the brush," I said. "Hélène was the artist. It was a love note from her to you, Sieur Folquet. A little message to tell you that she had triumphed over her greatest rival. She had finally killed Lady Mathilde, the supreme love of your petty life."

"This is pure fantasy," said Folc. "This Lady Mathilde you speak of—I remember her vaguely, but she died years ago."

"That's what everyone was meant to think," I said. "The truth was something uglier, something profoundly evil. Her husband faked her death, but kept her alive and imprisoned. He tortured her every day for her dalliance with you. She remained in darkness for seventeen years, Folquet. Then, when she finally regained the sun, cruel Fate sent her to Gémenos for the final act of vengeance. Your wife killed your lover."

"This cannot be!" he screamed. "It is some vicious trick of yours. Have you come all this way merely to throw this in my face?"

"No, I came here to save your life," I said. "Although I am beginning to have second thoughts about that."

"Save my life? Who seeks it?" he demanded.

"Vengeance," I said. "Vengeance is coming, Folquet, trudging through the mountains, crawling through the forest, on bloodied feet by now, but coming nonetheless. A long time ago, you betrayed your wife. A short time ago, you lied to me. Had you told me the meaning of the song, then Julien and Hélène would never have known why we were searching, and would never have killed to prevent us from finding the answer."

"Julien is coming to kill me," he said.

"Julien is dead," I said.

"What? How?"

"Because he tried to kill me!" I shouted. "Because he tried to kill my wife and child, not to mention this extremely promising apprentice of ours. Because you lied, my family was put in danger, Folquet. Because you lied, we were forced to kill. And Vengeance still comes. I wonder if she is here now."

"Hélène," he said in disbelief.

"Hearing of her brother's death was the last straw," I said. "Although I think that her reason deserted her years ago. You took everything from her. You were her husband, her only desire, but you cheated on her for years, then abandoned her for this pile of dry stones. You took her children away, her friends, her life. What did you give her in exchange?"

"God's love," he said.

"Looked like a bunch of cows to me," I said. "But I am not the expert on God's love that you are."

"You can't prove any of this," he said.

I was tired. I was sore. I lost my temper, I confess it. I simply stepped forward and struck him, knocking his thick skull against the thicker stones.

"I am not here to prove anything," I said angrily. "My mission was to get you to come to Toulouse, nothing more. Now, if you will excuse me, I have had a long journey, and am weary to the bone. I am going to sleep. I suggest you double your guards."

I opened the door and walked out. I sensed a rustling of cowls in the darkness as whichever monks were eavesdropping scurried back to their pallets. I found one that was unoccupied and collapsed on it.

I felt as if I could sleep for a month, yet my eyes would not close. Every sound, both within and without, carried with it an unseen threat. Every breath taken in that room of sleeping monks was Hélène, watching in the night, waiting to make her move.

When the cock crew, the monks rose as one and filed into the church. I followed. Folc stood in the nave, counting them, like a farmer with his chickens. A young lay brother came up and whispered something that caused him to frown. I went up to them.

"What is it?" I asked.

"Someone left a body for burial in the *enfeu,*" Folc said. "That's a niche in the outside wall for such purposes."

"Who is it?" I asked.

"I did not look," said the lay brother, shocked at the idea. "The body was shrouded."

I gave Folc a glance.

"Go look at the face," he ordered. "Take Brother Olivar with you."

"Very well," said the lay brother.

He beckoned to another, and they left the church. A minute later, we heard shouting, and they burst back into the church.

"It's Brother Calvet!" one shouted. "Someone's attacked him!"

"Is he alive?" asked Folc, moving quickly to the door.

The members of the order streamed up the two stairs to the outside of the church, stumbling over each other in their haste. Folc had gotten out ahead of the pack, and it cost me a minute to shove my way through them to the outside.

A crowd formed around the *enfeu.* One of the monks, presumably the infirmarian, knelt by the victim, who was bleeding from the head.

"He lives," said the monk. "Three of you help me carry him."

I scanned the crowd of robes until I found Folc at the center of it. As the three monks and the infirmarian gently lifted Brother Calvet from the *enfeu,* the shroud fell away. He was naked.

Someone has his robe, I thought.

I started through the crowd toward Folc. Then I heard a short shrill whistle from behind me, followed by shouts from outside the abbey wall. A sound of rumbling, growing, coming ever closer. Then the gates to the fields crashed open, and a dozen cattle surged into the abbey grounds, rushing in a blind frenzy in all directions, bowling men over right and left. A lean pair of dogs raced about, nipping at the animals' heels, scattering them. Another whistle, and the dogs turned their attentions to the monks, attacking them.

Men in white and brown robes were everywhere, running for cover, dragging injured brothers from the paths of the stampeding brutes, or simply screaming in panic.

Folc stood twenty feet from me in total disregard of the danger of his position, barking directions, trying to bring some order to the chaos swirling around him. I leapt up onto the shelf of the *enfeu* and looked toward where I first heard the whistling, but all I could see were identical robes and cowls running back and forth.

Except for one who walked calmly through the midst of it all, striding purposefully toward Folc, hands concealed in the sleeves of the robe.

Her feet bloody.

I reached for my knife, but that had been surrendered at the door. Shouting, I launched myself toward Folc. An onrushing cow clipped me and spun me around, but I kept moving. Folc looked at me, then turned in her direction and froze in shock as he saw a knife coming from inside her sleeve. I summoned all my strength and launched myself at her, tackling her midbody and bringing her to the ground. She slashed at me, slicing across my left arm before I could stop her. Folc seized her wrist, twisted hard, and wrenched the knife from her.

One of the dogs charged us. Folc instinctively threw the knife, hitting the beast square in the chest. It thudded to the ground, limbs splayed, then lay still. The other was in a bloody heap nearby, trampled to death by one of the berserk cattle. Hélène craned her head to see them. Then an unearthly scream erupted from her.

With the dogs dead, the fury of the cattle subsided. They slowed to a walk, seeming astonished to be inside the abbey walls for the first time in their lives. There was grass on the ground. They started to graze.

Hélène continued to scream. A few of the lay brothers came over, confused to see a woman there.

"Find some rope," Folc commanded them. "Bind her fast."

They looked at him stupidly.

"Rope! Now!" he shouted, and they ran.

He sat down next to us and looked sorrowfully at his wife's face. "I am so sorry, Hélène," he whispered.

Her face contorted in rage, and the screams changed to a stream of profanity. He bowed his head and accepted it. The lay brothers returned with a coil of rope. Folc and I held her as they bound her wrists behind her back, then wrapped the rope several times around her, securing her arms to her sides.

"Put her in the storage room," said Folc. "Both of you stay with her. Give her food, water, whatever she needs, but under no circumstances untie her."

They nodded and took her away, while she continued to curse her husband.

He looked at me. "You're bleeding," he said.

"It's not too bad," I said.

"Come with me," he said.

He led me through the cloister to the lavabo, a small octagonal building where they washed their hands. He carefully peeled off my tunic, then poured water from a ewer over the cut. It was long, but not deep.

"Stay here," he said.

He left, then returned with a needle, thread, a piece of cloth, and a wineskin.

"We keep this for special occasions," he said, handing the last to me.

"To your health and fast work with a needle," I said, drinking it.

It wasn't great wine. I didn't care.

He handed me the cloth, which I put between my teeth; then he sewed up my wound, adding a bandage when he was done.

"Nice job," I said.

"I hope it didn't hurt much," he said.

"It stung like the Devil, but it was over quickly," I said. "The real pain is yours. Shall we go see her?"

He washed the blood from his hands and wiped them on his robe. "Let's get it over with," he said.

She sat with her back against the wall, gazing unblinking as we entered. The two lay brothers stood before her, staves at the ready.

"Leave us," said Folc.

They glanced at him, then each other. One of them held his staff out to me. I took it. They left.

Folc knelt before her. "Forgive me, Hélène," he said.

"You apologized before," she said hoarsely. "That's all you do, apologize and apologize. You apologized when you told me about her the first time. You wept and begged for my forgiveness, and dragged me off to church to pray with you. You put your head in my lap and cried like a baby, and swore to me by all that was holy that it was over, that she was dead, and that you would always love me, only me, and I cried and stroked your hair and forgave you. Do you remember that?"

"I remember," he said.

"Then you drove me from Marseille," she said. "And you apologized, but you wouldn't tell me what you were sorry for that time.

You left me in Gémenos and took my boys away forever. You never told me why."

"I'm sorry," he said.

"Stop that!" she shouted. "Stop being sorry! It does nothing. It's just another lie. She wasn't dead. She came to Gémenos, just when the pain was finally beginning to ease. I didn't know who she was, just another lost woman come to join the community. So quiet in the beginning, but one day, she started to sing. And I knew the song. The words were new, but the music—"

She started to weep.

"It was my song, the one you wrote for me, the one you sang to me and me alone," she sobbed. "And it was coming out of that filthy whore's mouth. You gave her my song, you heartless bastard. She had such a beautiful voice, and I have this ugly croak, no wonder you loved her. 'Cold is the hand that crushes the lark.' That's how it goes, isn't that right, husband? There she was, the woman who destroyed my happiness, brought to me by God for punishment. I stopped that lovely voice, stopped it forever."

"No more, Hélène," whispered Folc.

"Only it didn't stop," she shrieked. "She's still singing that damned song. I can't make her stop singing, no matter what I do. Make her stop!"

And the screams came again. Folc put his hands over his ears and ran from the storeroom. The lay brothers came back in. I handed back the staff and followed the abbot.

He staggered like a drunken man toward the church as monks and lay brothers watched him without moving. He pushed the door open and vanished inside. I was the only one to follow.

He was kneeling before the altar when I came in. The church was otherwise deserted. I thought he was praying, and quietly sat on a bench to let him do it undisturbed. But I was wrong. Suddenly, his voice came pouring forth.

Cold is the hand that crushes the lark.
Cold is despair unending.

Cold is the rain that douses the spark,
And cold is the grave uncomprehending.
Sweet Lady Lark, why will you not fly?
Fie on a fate so unsparing.
Where lies the voice that made lovers sigh?
And where lies the grace beyond comparing?

High flew the arrow, missing its mark.
High was the tree unbending.
High was the branch and smooth was the bark
That kept this poor creature from ascending.
Sweet Lady Lark, why flew you so high,
Tempting the Hawk with your daring?
Ta'en in his claws and pluck'd from the sky
While all passed below and watched uncaring.

Gone is the sun, slipped down from its arc.
Gone is the love offending.
Gone is the hand that struck in the dark,
And ended a life well worth commending.
Sweet Lady Lark, my love was no lie.
Know that my heart was unerring.
Yet, in the end, e'en true love must die,
And vows lovers all will be forswearing.

The last note echoed through the space and died out. I cleared my throat, and he stood quickly and faced me.

"Good acoustics in here," I said.

"Is that all you can say?" he asked.

"Well, I thought of two things," I admitted. "The other was that you once committed an act of adultery with a woman whose husband found out, beat you, and drove you out of town, then imprisoned and tortured his own wife until she went mad, and that pretty little song won't make up for that, no matter how well you sing it. That was the other thing I was going to say, but it was awfully long, so I thought I would just keep it to the comment about the acoustics."

He was silent.

"I didn't know the third verse, by the way," I continued. "Quite lovely. It is your work, isn't it?"

"I never knew she was alive," he said. "I heard she had died in a fall, and thought that Landrieux had murdered her. I watched from the woods as they buried her, and I wept. Then I found a singer—"

"Rafael de la Tour."

"Yes. Rafael. I paid him to sing the lament. I told him never to sing it again."

"He was a simpleton. You couldn't expect him to remember anything that wasn't a lyric. He sang it in a tavern, and the Hawk got wind of it. He made him sing it to Lady Mathilde in her cell. Rafael was killed later, probably at Landrieux's orders, but we'll never know for certain. Tell me, why did you flee to the Cistercians?"

"You've guessed so much," he said. "You tell me."

"You joined the order in '95," I said. "That was the year the Hawk died. Did you try to go back to Montpellier when you heard he was no longer there to threaten you?"

"Yes," he said. "I wanted to see her son. Our son."

"But the Hawk wasn't your only enemy in Montpellier," I said. "Guilhem still had it in for you because of your dalliance with Eudoxie. I take it he threatened you?"

"He told me that if I didn't abandon the world, my life would be forfeit," he said. "Mine, and Hélène's, and our sons. I was terrified. I came here. I have been atoning for my sins and praying for forgiveness ever since then."

"How's that working out for you?" I asked harshly.

"I thought that God had absolved me," he said. "I thought I had been punished enough. I was arrogant to presume that."

"Hélène was right. You do apologize too much."

"She has gone mad," he said.

"That's what you want to call it," I said. "So be it. What will you do with her?"

"There is a place I know where people who are so afflicted may live," he said. "Where holy people will watch over her and pray for her."

"Good, another cell for a woman who loved you," I said.

"Would you rather I handed her to the authorities for punishment?" he asked.

I took a deep breath. "No," I said. "I'm sorry. Forgive me."

He sat on the bench next to me. We were silent for a long time.

"The world is a dangerous and evil place, Theophilos," he said finally.

"Not all of it," I said. "Not all the time."

"This is what you fight against, isn't it?"

"On my good days," I said.

"Maybe it's time for me to take part in it again," he said. "Toulouse, you said."

"Yes."

"They already have a bishop, and Count Raimon hates me," he said. "Do you really think that you can pull this off?"

"I won't know until I try," I said.

"When you succeed, send for me," he said, standing up. "I will be ready."

He walked up the steps to the dormitorium. The door closed behind him.

I was alone in the church. I stood, snapped my fingers one time, and listened to the reverberations. Then I left.

I had promised Zeus two days of rest. I decided to leave the abbey and find somewhere else to do that. An accommodating farmer let us rest and heal in his stables in exchange for some help with the haying and a dozen songs and stories. On the morning of the third day, we followed the road back over the massif.

I had a pair of blankets this time, a gift from the abbey. One for me, one for Zeus. I kept the fires going at night, and kept our pace reasonable by day.

Two days later, we came to the Eagle's Pass. I stopped to offer a brief prayer of thanks at the old chapel, then rode Zeus carefully down the switchbacks and through the forest, stopping to drink at the same stream where we stopped when we first came this way, eons ago.

Then we rode to the farm. As I tied Zeus to the fence, I heard a welcoming shout. Seconds latter, I was being embraced by all my foolish women. I closed my eyes and basked in the attention.

"Papa!" said a tiny voice.

I opened my eyes and looked at Portia in astonishment.

"Papapapapapa," she said.

"How long has she been doing that?" I asked.

"Ever since you left," said Claudia. "She says 'Mama,' too. Helga is working on her."

I held her up and kissed her on the nose. "Kiss Papa on the nose?" I asked.

She did. Then she pointed at Zeus. "Papa!" she called to him.

"So there is still some learning to do," laughed Claudia.

I spent the day resting and recounting what had happened to the others.

When I was done, Claudia shook her head sadly. "Poor Mathilde, poor Hélène," she said. "Poor women everywhere."

In the morning, we embraced our hosts, loaded up the wain, and drove to where Hélène's order tended their herds. I spoke briefly to the woman who led them, telling her only that Hélène would not be returning to them. She did not press me for more information.

We left and passed by the tiny church in the village.

"Stop for a moment," said Claudia.

I pulled up Zeus, and my wife jumped down and motioned for us to join her.

To the rear of the church was a small graveyard. One of the graves was recent, the grass having yet to take root on it. There was no marker. Claudia produced a bunch of flowers and placed them on the bare patch of ground.

"Mary forgives you, Mathilde," she whispered. "Rest now."

We stood quietly for a moment.

There was a sudden burst of song to our right. A tiny brightly colored bird with a splotch of red on its face was hopping around in a bunch of thistles, unperturbed by the thorns around it.

"A chardonneret," said Claudia, brightening. "And no hawks in sight."

"They call it God's bird; did you know that?" I said.

"Why?" asked Helga.

"The story is that when Our Savior suffered on the cross, a chardonneret took pity on Him and tried to pull the crown of thorns from His head. It failed, but the mark left by Christ's blood on its face has stayed with it. And God rewarded its attempt by giving it protection from thorns ever since."

"So God will reward us even if we fail?" asked Helga.

"As long as we keep on trying, Apprentice," I said.

We returned to Zeus, and took the road out of Gémenos to the west.

"Where to?" asked Claudia.

"Back to Marseille to bring Pantalan up to date," I said. "I'll need a few days to write a report to send to Father Gerald at the Guildhall. I think we had better bypass Montpellier. It may be too hot for us now."

"So after Marseille, straight to Toulouse to displace a sitting bishop?"

"That's the plan," I said.

She laughed softly. "It won't be easy," she said.

"It never is," I agreed.

HISTORICAL NOTE

Folco mis disse quella gente a cui
Fu noto il nome mio;
[Those people to whom my name was known called me Folc;]

—DANTE, *PARADISO* IX, 96–7 [TRANS. N. M. SCHULMAN]

I. *Troubadours and the Fools' Guild*[1]

In January 2004, an earthquake measuring 4.1 on the Richter scale shook the southern reaches of the Dolomites in Italy. What was first believed to be a natural cave formation was revealed. However, closer inspection turned up unmistakable evidence of a man-made structure. An archeologist who was supervising the excavation of the ruins of a nearby monastery was called in. With trepidation, for the soundness of the surrounding hillside was suspect after the recent seismological shock, she examined it, first thinking that it was no more than an ancient mine. Then she found a group of tightly sealed casks and amphorae.

In a creditable display of patience, she did not open them right then and there, but brought in a team to carefully remove them to a clean room at a nearby university. There, they were opened, and were found to contain manuscript after manuscript of records, both in Latin and in Tuscan dialect. Each had at the top the seal and motto of the Fools' Guild.

---

[1] Portions of this note have been adapted from a paper presented at the First International Symposium on Medieval Foolery, at the University of Chelm, April 1, 2006.

My translations of the handful of known copies of the chronicles of Theophilos held in Ireland were known in Italy, ironically in Italian translations of my English translation of his Tuscan. I was asked to join the team of scholars in making an assessment of these records. While many of them were of accounts and records of daily life at the Guildhall, many others were histories ostensibly written by various fools. Carbon-dating and close examination of the inks used suggest that the last of them date from the fifteenth century, but the oldest may hail from as far back as the tenth century, perhaps from the time the Guildhall was first constructed at that location.

The Irish papers were all later copies, so you can imagine my excitement at discovering what purported to be manuscripts in Theophilos's own hand. Would that his handwriting were better, but these were no doubt written in haste or on the run. We should be grateful that they were written at all.

With the accounts of everyday life in the Guild, we now know with more clarity its organizational structure. Its leadership was drawn from a small band of friars from an order unaffiliated with any other, but with a history stretching back to the early Middle Ages. Its relationship with Rome was problematic, as we have seen—more of an uneasy coexistence than an outright allegiance.

The decennial lists, the ten-year count of the Guild members, divide them into four categories: the aforementioned religious, the jesters, the troubadours, and the novitiates. The usage of Guildnames without their real world *noms des bouffons* prevents an accurate tally of the membership, but it does give us a better understanding of the relative roles of the jesters and the troubadours.

It is likely and logical that the vast majority of jesters in the Christian and Muslim world of this period were affiliated with the Fools' Guild.[2] The variety of skills required for the successful jester, described by Theophilos as the seven foolish arts,[3] would preclude the profession from all but a talented few.

However, the same cannot be said of troubadours. While the Fools'

---

[2] A. Gordon, "The Fools' Guild: A Prosopography, Part 1. A Comparison of Decennial Lists with Accounts of Known Jesters and Jongleurs," *Stultorum* 3 (March 2005): 168–204.

[3] *The Chronicles of the Fools' Guild* (Gordon, A., *trans.*): *Thirteenth Night* (1999).

Guild was able to corner the market on foolery, music was beyond their control. The decennial lists contain the names of many of the most noteworthy troubadours of the day, as well as some who have been lost to history, but history itself records many troubadours who never passed through the Guild's doors.[4]

The reasons for this should be obvious. Music was part of a basic medieval education, one of the seven liberal arts, and a part of every household rich and poor. The liturgy of the time was sung, the histories of the time were sung, and the cheapest and most accessible form of entertainment of the time was, well, beer, but with music a close second and a frequent companion.

With the proliferation of music came the troubadour movement, particularly in educated and noble households. Scholars and tradition award the honor of being the first troubadour to Guilhem IX, Duke of Aquitaine, Count of Poitiers (1071–1126).[5] The Fools' Guild, on the other hand, differs on their origins, naming several from the previous century, and it hardly seems likely that the ballad was suddenly invented in Aquitaine.[6]

Other so-called scholars have disagreed on this point.[7] But they have not had the benefit, as I have, of reading the actual Guild records.[8] In any case,[9] it is clear that the Guild defines the word, "troubadour," in a different sense than the popular one.[10]

In an unpublished paper, unaccountably held back due to the shortsighted editorial policy of a certain formerly respectable journal,[11] I have ar-

---

[4] A. Gordon, "The Fools' Guild: A Prosopography, Part 2. A Comparison of Decennial Lists with Accounts of Known Troubadours, Trouveres, Trobairitzes, and Minnesingers," *Stultorum* 5 (May 2005): 573–612.

[5] G. Brunel-Lobrichon, and C. Duhamel-Amado, *Au temps des troubadours* (1997): 253.

[6] A. Gordon, "Geoffroy d'Arles, the First Troubadour?" *Stultorum* 6 (June 2005): 719–723.

[7] S. Marcolf, "Why Gordon Is Wrong," *Stultorum* 8 (August 2005): 874–875.

[8] A. Gordon, "No, I'm Right, and Marcolf, S., Is Stupid. In Fact, That's Probably What the 'S' Stands For: Stupid Marcolf," *Stultorum* 9 (September 2005): 923.

[9] S. Marcolf, "It Stands for Solomon, and Speaking of Stupid, Gordon Is So Dumb, He Thinks Langue d'Oc Means Quacking: A Reply," *Stultorum* 10 (October 2005): 1002.

[10] A. Gordon, "I Know You Are, But What Am I? A Response to a Reply," *Stultorum* 11 (November 2005): 1137.

[11] Editors, "A Restatement of Scholarly Principles: Why Gordon, A., and Marcolf, S., Will No Longer Be Permitted to Publish in *Stultorum*," *Stultorum* 12 (December 2005): 1204.

gued that the role of the troubadour in the Fools' Guild, in addition to his traditional function as composer at the Courts of Love, was to act as a circuit-rider or courier. A successful troubadour was accustomed to riding from town to town and court to court, carrying with him his ballads, the news reports of the day.

The only requirements were a talent for composing and a horse, and Guild troubadours ended up coming from a variety of backgrounds. Some were noble, such as Gui de Cavalhon, a seigneur and knight from Provence. Some came from the merchant classes, like Folquet de Marseille or Peire Vidal, who was the son of a Toulousan furrier. There were even some who doubled as jongleurs, such as Peire Raimon de Tolosa and Guilhem Adémar, and that their contemporaries distinguished the two professions shows both their proximity and their difference.

However, anyone with a little training and a lute could start banging out ballads and call himself a troubadour, and the lists include such notables as Richard I, the Lion-Hearted, who not only was not a member of the Fools' Guild, but stood for everything that the Guild opposed. These musical amateurs with money and connections filled the world with bad songs, the medieval equivalents of garage bands. It is not a surprise that the movement eventually died out, although not without leaving its mark on future poets such as Dante and Petrarch. It was Dante, writing a century later, who would help Folquet to a small slice of immortality.

II. *Folquet and Folc*

Readers who wish to learn more about Folquet/Folc are invited to read Nicole M. Schulman's *Where Troubadours Were Bishops: The Occitania of Folc of Marseille (1150–1231),* (New York and London: Routledge, 2001). Ms. Schulman acknowledges that the birthdate is an estimate, averaging a likely range of 1145 to 1155 given the known circumstances of his early years.

Some nineteen to twenty-one songs attributed to Folquet have survived, several with music. Most come from his time as a troubadour, but the last three, a pair of calls to Crusade and a song of penitence, date from his time as a Cistercian monk. Of the songs sung or heard by Theophilos and Claudia in this manuscript, only the fragment sung by the latter in chapter 11 can safely said to be his, being a Tuscan translation of *Mout i fetz gran pechat Amors,* Song 8 in the Stronski numeration (making my English translation twice removed from the original).

The song in chapter 1 attributed by Theophilos to Folquet bears none of the latter's style or characteristics. It is too merry and ribald to have been written by this generally melancholy and lovelorn troubadour, and I suspect that the true composer was Theophilos himself, based upon other songs I have encountered in his manuscripts.

"The Lark's Lament," however, could very well be a lost composition by Folquet. Grelho's comment about the common theme of the high branch is well said. Folquet himself may have been aware of that criticism—Song 14 commences with *"Ja no·is cug hom qu'ieu camje mas chansos, pos no·s camja mos cor ni ma razos;"* [No one ever thinks that I change my songs, since neither my feelings nor my themes change.][12] Unfortunately, we are once again dealing with a Tuscan translation of a lost song written originally in langue d'oc, so it is impossible to comfortably assert its provenance. Until further information is found, we will leave the Stronski numeration untouched.

There are two medieval portraits said to be of Folquet. One shows him as a young man, smiling and possessed of a healthy head of hair. The other shows him as a monk, tonsured and with a stern and somewhat sour expression. I like to think that the first was of Folquet, and the latter as just plain Folc, but there is no authority for this supposition.

Those who would walk where Folc once did are directed to the restored abbey of Le Thoronet. Its construction began in 1161, part of the vast growth of the Cistercian order in what might be thought of as a Middle Age spread. Le Thoronet was unusual both for its design elements and its use of the irregular landscape, creating a quirky but unforced layout of extraordinary beauty. It can be seen on a day trip from Marseille, traffic permitting, but

[12] Translation by Nicole M. Schulman.

those who stay in the area may have the added experience of visiting the old village of Le Cannet des Maures. (Follow the sign at the traffic circle to "Vieux Cannet." Check with me about where not to stay. The motel I was at was a horror.)

Until the discovery of this manuscript, the name of Folc's wife was lost to us, along with her history. However, there is one interesting fact. In 1205, a year after the events depicted here, a Cistercian order for women was founded in Gémenos, thanks in part to the influence of Folc. It became a daughter-house to the abbey of Le Thoronet, and Folc maintained a relationship with Gémenos throughout his life. It is not known if Hélène returned there, or where and when she died. The abbey still stands, although it was deserted centuries ago.

Of Folc's further involvement with Theophilos, we shall hear more. The translation proceeds apace.

ACKNOWLEDGMENTS

For the life of Folquet, a debt is owed to Nicole M. Schulman. For additional sources on Folquet in particular and troubadours in general, the author gratefully acknowledges the work of H. J. Chaytor, Frede Jensen, Rita Le Jeune, Joseph Anglade, Margarita Egan, William Paden, Geneviève Brunel-Lobrichon, and Claudie Duhamel-Amado.

For the history of Marseille: Paul Armorgier, Roger Duchêsne, Raoul Busquet.

For the history of Montpellier: Kathryn L. Reyerson, Jean Combes, Ghislaine Fabre, Thierry Lochard, Elizabeth Haluska-Rausch.

Other historians: T. M. Bisson, Damien Smith, Brian Catlos, Jean Guyou, Fernand Pouillon, Laure Dailliez.

Special thanks to lyricists and friends Alison Loeb and Jim McNicholas, for their comments on my own meager attempts, and to Bill Eggers, neighbor, friend, and fan, for directing me to a source for names from the time and place.

Finally, to my wife, Judy, and son, Robert, for letting me wander around southern France on my own, and letting me grow a beard while I did it.

THE JESTER RETURNS, AND TIME IS RUNNING OUT...

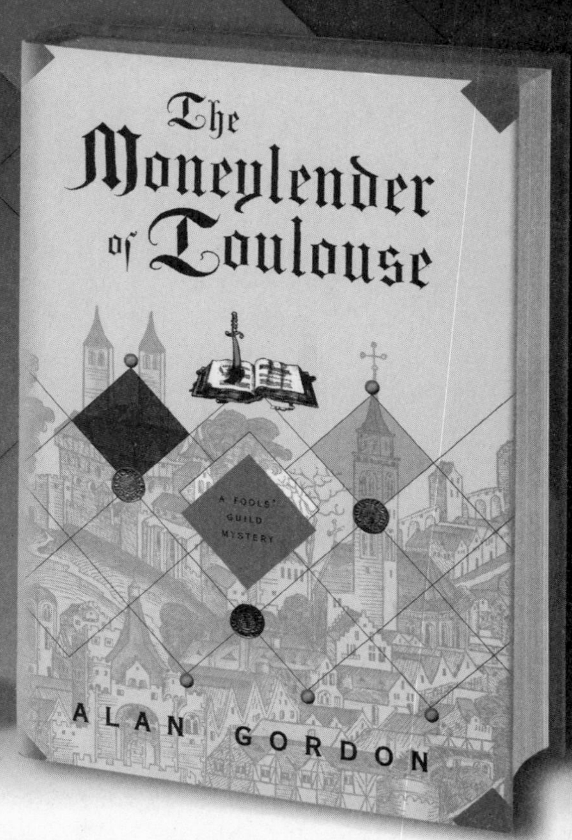

ıen Theophilos arrives in
ılouse with his family in
). 1204, he has one simple
ssion—force the current
hop to resign. Theophilos
covers that the Bishop is in
: water with the local money-
der, a man who, a day after
ssing the Bishop particularly
d, is found floating facedown
ı tanner's vat. With time run-
g out, Theophilos has but one
ion: find out what actually
pened the night that the
neylender of Toulouse ended
spectacularly dead.

"Gorgeous historical details . . . a fool who is also a family man, banter that makes a reader grin while at the same time serious issues move in the depths, and a puzzle that smacks sweetly into path. Only a fool would pass it up."
—Laurie R. King, author of *Locked Room,* on *The Lark's Lament*

AVAILABLE WHEREVER BOOKS ARE SOLD